RUBY'S
Secret

HEATHER B. MOORE

A NEWPORT LADIES BOOK CLUB NOVEL

RUBY'S
Secret

Covenant Communications, Inc.

To Josi, Annette, and Julie—
This has been a priceless and incomparable journey.
I hope it continues into forever.

Cover image: *Wooden Chair on the Beach* © Steve Cole Images; Getty Images.

Cover design copyright © 2013 by Covenant Communications, Inc.

Published by Covenant Communications, Inc.
American Fork, Utah

Printed in the United States of America
First Printing: October 2013

19 18 17 16 15 14 13   10 9 8 7 6 5 4 3 2 1

ISBN-13: 978-1-62108-460-0

Acknowledgments

WRITING THE NEWPORT LADIES BOOK Club series with three other authors has been one of the most creative endeavors I've ever undertaken—creative in scheduling, plotting, writing, revising, and promoting the series. It all began in 2009 with an early-morning breakfast meeting with Josi Kilpack and Julie Wright presenting an idea to Annette Lyon and me. Of course, it was impossible to say no, and the early brainstorming eventually blossomed into what would become the Newport Ladies Book Club series.

My three coauthors are amazing to work with. They are dedicated to their craft of writing and graciously accepted feedback and revisions in order to make the series cohesive. As the characters went through their own journeys of coming together in friendship and offering support, their progression often mirrored our journeys as coauthors. We've loved hearing back from our readers, and when they tell us how it's made them more willing to reach out to others in love and friendship, we feel blessed.

Other "staff supporters" include my effervescent critique group, where there is never a dull moment—Sarah M. Eden, J. Scott Savage, LuAnn Staheli, Michele Holmes, Robison Wells, and Annette. Many thanks to my publisher, Covenant Communications, as well as Deseret Book, who have been willing to copublish this series unlike any project they have undertaken. Their faith in us has made a world of difference.

Managing editor, Kathy Gordon, and editor, Samantha Millburn, have been supportive from the first-pitch meeting and have been wonderful to work with. Many thanks to cover designer, Christina Marcano, and publicist, Grant Pillar, as well as many others who have moved this project through final production.

And most of all, I'm deeply grateful for the support of my family and friends. I hope you'll love Ruby's story.

BOOKS IN THE NEWPORT LADIES BOOK CLUB SERIES

Set #1
Olivia—Julie Wright
Daisy—Josi S. Kilpack
Paige—Annette Lyon
Athena—Heather B. Moore

Set #2
Shannon's Hope—Josi S. Kilpack
Ruby's Secret—Heather B. Moore
Victoria's Promise—Julie Wright
Ilana's Wish—Annette Lyon

For ideas on hosting your own book club, suggestions for books and recipes, or information on how you can guest-write about your book club on our blog, please visit us at http://thenewportladiesbookclub.blogspot.com.

Chapter 1

I TAPPED A LONG CORAL-PINK nail against the book-club list on my counter as I listened to my daughter-in-law, Kara, reprimand me over the phone.

"Ruby, you've got to stop doing everything for everyone." Kara's voice was a bit shrill today. "You should join the senior center—I hear they have wonderful activities. You'll love getting to know women your own age."

My own age? I scoffed. Although my birth certificate claimed I was sixty-two, I felt I could be forty—if it weren't for my aching knees—or thirty . . . Well, maybe not thirty. That was the year I discovered my husband's first affair. I'd never wish to be thirty again—at least not thirty and married to Phillip.

I actually gasped at my horrible thought and said out loud, "God rest my husband's soul," as if that would erase the poison running through my mind.

"Amen," Kara said automatically, then she plowed on, and I continued to tap. I loved my daughter-in-law, but she could also be quite irritating. Not that I wasn't grateful she lived in Illinois with my only son, Tony, but she wasn't exactly what I'd imagined having a daughter would be. Shouldn't we be like bosom buddies and support each other in everything?

Finally, just to stop the stream of words, I said, "I'll think about it, sweetie. Now I should really let you go. Love you."

Any thought of the senior center immediately fled as I hung up. I refocused on the book-club list. Seven names graced the list now—seven women who were quickly becoming nonirritating daughters to me. The Newport Ladies Book Club had turned out to be a success after all. A few fliers and several phone calls later, we had started out strongly and had already met four times.

I read through each name slowly so I could forget my tortuous thoughts. There was a reason I had a locked box upstairs . . . and it did its job well by keeping certain things locked away—literally. But it was harder to lock up feelings. I attempted to focus on my friends.

Every couple of weeks, I did something special for one of the women on the book-club list. I knew Kara would really chide me about it, so it was something I kept to myself. Like pretty much everything in my life— kept to myself. I glanced at the calendar to mentally map out who was doing what today. Tuesday . . . February 1. My heart stilled.

Today was the second anniversary of Phillip's death. No wonder I felt off. It hadn't even taken much to practically argue with my daughter-in-law. I took a deep, cleansing breath, determined to not let myself get rattled.

I mulled over the names on my list with a new fervor. Paige, Daisy, Athena, Ilana, Olivia, Victoria, and my niece, Shannon. It had taken some convincing to get Shannon to join, but maybe she'd felt bad that she was my only relative in California and hadn't wanted to turn me down.

Each of the women at book club was so different, yet we'd bonded over our love for books and fabulous characters and twisty plots, not to mention delicious refreshments. Food was always the great equalizer. I bypassed Athena's name on the list since I'd taken her to the spa recently—I'd hoped to give her a bit of relief from the cares of her ailing father. I was plainly having a hard time deciding which lady to focus on this week. Usually, my intuition was keener, intuition I'd learned to trust at thirty for reasons I refused to think about now.

I settled on Ilana with no specific, clear reason, except I just felt I should call her. So Ilana it would be. I called her before I wasted another second. After all, this was the time I'd set aside to make the phone call. The rest of my day was scheduled down to the minute, as usual.

When she answered, she sounded quite harried, so I got right to the point. "I know you're probably working right now, but I wondered if you would like to meet for lunch today or tomorrow." I felt I'd have more of a chance if I gave her more choices.

Ilana sighed, small but unmistakable. I gripped the phone a bit tighter, waiting for her answer.

"I usually only have a short time for lunch—"

"That's all right," I said. "I can meet you anywhere—someplace quick will work for me too."

A pause, then she said in a more cheery tone, "Maybe in a couple of days. Let me call you if I think something will work out."

Trying not to feel completely deflated because I didn't want to doubt my intuition, I said, "All right, dear, that would be wonderful."

Her good-bye was equally pleasant, but I knew better. She wouldn't be calling me.

Disappointment pulsed through me as I ended the call. A lunch would have been wonderful with just Ilana. She was the one lady I felt I knew the least in the group. She'd been married for three or four years, didn't have children, but seemed completely wrapped up in her career. Although, when the other ladies at book club discussed their kids, I saw the wistful look in her eyes. I thought if she needed someone to confide in, I could be that person.

I circled her name on the list and wrote, "Call back on Thursday." I didn't want to be a pest, but I hoped she'd know the door of friendship was wide open.

What are you doing? I mouthed to myself. I was being obsessive, I knew, yet I couldn't help it. Ilana wasn't a stain in the carpet that needed scrubbing. She was a grown woman who knew her schedule and who didn't want to hang out with a senior citizen—well, *barely* a senior citizen.

Maybe my daughter-in-law was right. Her words rang through my mind—*You'll love getting to know women your own age.* Just because Kara's voice wouldn't leave my head and today of all days I needed a distraction, I grabbed the phone book and looked up the Oasis Senior Center. Maybe I'd pay a visit, glance over the activities, and then I could tell Kara I'd done at least that.

A phone call wouldn't tell me about the atmosphere of the place— first impressions were so important. I read the address listed in the phone book and realized it was closer to me than I'd thought and in the same vicinity as Athena's father's rest home. "Rest home" left a bad taste in my mouth, and without thinking about it, I moved to the refrigerator and poured myself a glass of lemon-fresh filtered water.

Washing and drying the glass so it wouldn't be alone in the dishwasher, gathering bacteria, I set it back in the cupboard, rim down. Not everyone kept their cupboard shelves clean enough to store glasses in the proper fashion, but I didn't mind adding the cupboard shelves to my weekly cleaning routine.

Since I was at the cupboard, I organized the glasses into straighter lines. When satisfied, I moved to the next item on my day's agenda—watering the huge hibiscuses along the front walkway. They did best if watered before the heat of the day set in.

Stepping outside, I noticed the cloudy sky looked oppressive and grayer than usual. The California sun wouldn't be out today, and I worried that my hair would wilt before I had a chance to visit the senior center. I turned on the hose to low pressure and watered the base of the flowers, watching the soil darken and swell. It was a small pleasure I'd indulged in a few weeks after Phillip's funeral. We'd been traveling so much for the last ten years that I'd never been able to tend any sort of garden or flower bed, not even a row of flowers, always having to rely on the landscapers.

Besides, Phillip didn't care for hibiscuses, so it was with a bit of guilty delight that I brought home three dozen from the nursery right after his death and learned everything I could about them.

The wind pushed through my cropped hair, and raindrops started to fall—I'd definitely have to redo the styling now. But perhaps I'd delay it for a while; I hated running errands in the rain. I hadn't expected the day to be overcast, and my favorite thing to do on rainy days was read something deliciously amusing. And today of all days, I needed an escape.

I had no idea what the book-club ladies would think of my devouring regency romances. Perhaps I'd suggest a specific one—a notable one—at the next meeting to gauge their reaction. Jane Austen always seemed to be well respected, but there was so much more out there than just Jane . . .

I would be the first to admit there was not much value in reading them—unless I counted sheer contentment, the ultimate relaxation in delving into a world of the past where people were concerned with frivolous nonsense, notions, and ideas that had no consequence in today's world . . . unless one wanted to study human nature. Why someone did what they did. Why a *man* did what he did.

Perhaps there was more value than I thought besides a historical study.

The rain no longer fell in innocent drops but made great splashes on the pavement. It seemed the sky would water the flowers for me today. Turning off the hose, I went into the house. Passing by the kitchen, I paused and looked at the calendar again. February 1 . . . It had been a horrible day. Even with the passage of two years, it was still fresh in my mind.

But I didn't want it in my mind. I'd given most of my life to that man, and now I wanted to put everything in our relationship behind me. So . . . I decided to forget my schedule and do something different.

I left the kitchen and headed upstairs. I had several bookcases stationed throughout my home, but I kept the nearest and dearest in my bedroom, which was no longer the master bedroom—that room I had converted into a guest suite. When my son had questioned me about it, I didn't know how I could tell him I no longer wanted to sleep in a room I'd shared with my husband.

I converted Tony's old bedroom into my sanctuary, with a queen-sized bed, two elegant bookcases containing my favorite books, and long, flowing, gauzy curtains. I had the next book-club book, *The Help*, on the coffee table downstairs, but that could wait. I needed something light . . . something that could take me completely away from Newport and memories of my husband's last day alive. Running my fingers along the spines, I stopped at my Georgette Heyer collection. I bought all of her books in a single, crazy afternoon browsing on Amazon, but I'd read only about half so far.

The next in line was *Bath Tangle*.

Ah . . . Bath . . . the place of healing and relaxation. The perfect respite in winter to get away from cold London.

I smiled to myself, already feeling the magic of the era seep into my skin as I turned the first page. If I closed my eyes, I could very well imagine that I was in drizzly England, if even for a short time.

* * *

A barking dog woke me, or was it hunting hounds sprinting through the forest of a grand estate? I shook off half thoughts of ballrooms connected to endless hallways and sat up. Falling asleep hadn't been on my agenda, and the barking dog could mean only one thing.

Lance was home.

Not Lance in the *knight* sense—or any sort of hero—he's the furthest thing from it. Of course, he might argue with you, one of his better talents, that he's just the man for me. Who else but a financial planner was in a better position to take care of a lonely widow with a healthy inheritance left by her late husband?

The only thing even Lancelot-like about Lance was his purebred hunting dog. It was supposedly trained at some prestigious farm to catch the finest pheasants, but I'd never known it to be gone from the neighborhood. However, its training had at least taught it to bark only when it saw Lance coming home.

I parted one gauzy curtain and watched the thinning head of hair make its way to the door of the next house. Sunlight peeked through the clouds, making Lance's gray hair look golden in the late afternoon. One thing about financial planners on the West Coast—they started early and closed up early. Predictably, when Lance opened his front door, his ivory Labrador bounded out, putting its narrow paws into Lance's waiting hands, and Lance promptly leaned down for the mutual nuzzle.

I drew back with a shudder, remembering the single attempt Lance had made at kissing me. It reminded me of that nuzzle, although it had probably been much shorter than what he just gave his dog, since I'd promptly screeched, nearly causing Lance to lose his balance. The timing hadn't been good, since it had been only a couple of months after Phillip's death, but even if it had been a couple of years, I would have still been surprised at the move. Especially since a second marriage, or any sort of relationship with a man, was the furthest thing from my mind.

Besides, Lance and Phillip had been friends—at least they'd chatted about the economy and stock market on occasion.

Turning away from the window and realizing Lance was the only person I really saw, apart from the book-club ladies, I decided that perhaps Kara was right. Perhaps I did need to meet a few more people—ones my age and ones who didn't live next door to me.

Chapter 2

I ADJUSTED THE TURQUOISE STUDDED purse over my shoulder, a dirt-cheap bag I'd picked up in Mexico. I hesitated outside the senior center, eyeing the pretty green-and-white striped awning.

A man stepped out from the main doors, his head mostly bald, with scruffs of white hair making a semicircle just above his ears. He grinned when he saw me and held the door open wide. "Hello there. Coming in?"

"Yes," I said, passing his tall, lanky figure. "I suppose I am."

He chuckled, a merry sound, his eyes squinting slightly as he watched me walk toward him. "I was a bit hesitant the first time I came too. But you'll see we're all harmless."

I flashed him a smile and murmured a thank you as I stepped into the warm interior. It was February, and even in Newport, we had to turn on the furnace in the "winter" months, but this place was too hot. I immediately felt overdressed in my long turquoise jacket and merino wool turtleneck. I had chosen my outfit carefully, knowing it complemented the coloring of my hair.

A woman at the front desk greeted me with a dark-red-lipstick smile. Her bright lips pulled across her row of tight teeth—dentures, definitely. A name tag on her pale-blue blouse proudly announced her name as Debbie.

"Welcome to our humble adobe," she sang out a little loudly, as if she'd intended the gentleman who'd just held the door open to hear her.

Adobe? I think she meant *abode*, but I didn't want to correct her. I glanced behind me; the door had already swung shut. I turned to face Debbie again, catching the tail end of her question. ". . . are *you* from?"

"I live in the area," I said in an easy tone, deliberately vague. I wasn't sure how much I wanted to tell . . . Debbie.

"Oh?" Her penciled eyebrow rose. "Have you been to the center before?"

"First time," I said. *Most likely the last time.* "I looked it up in the phone book, and when I realized how close I was, I decided to drop in."

Debbie was already shuffling through a stack of what looked like brochures. Was this a travel and tourism office?

"What's your name?" she asked.

"Ruby," I said.

"Ruby . . ."

"Crenshaw, but Ruby is just fine."

She scrawled it in elongated cursive letters on a name tag.

I took the sticky tag from her, a bit reluctant to put it on my jacket in case it pulled the threads when it came off, but her blue eyes were appraising me, so I stuck it to my lapel.

Her smile was triumphant. "You'll love it here. Each Monday we have a guest speaker." She paused, glancing at the silver watch on her bony wrist. "Lark is speaking today. He just stepped out to grab his pictures. We'll be starting in about five minutes." She handed over a collection of brochures she seemed to have selected just for me. "Here are some activities you'll be interested in. I'm here until six thirty if you have any questions."

"Thank you," I said, glancing at the top brochure—Movie Night— 4:00 p.m., Tuesdays. Probably so everyone could drive home before it grew dark. That was just fine with me.

The door whooshed open behind me.

"Oh, here's Lark now. You can just follow him into the garden room. I'll peek in soon, if I'm not too busy." Another smile. Debbie seemed very comfortable at her desk job. I was impressed.

"You're still here?" Lark said, glancing at the scrawled name tag. "Rudy?"

"Ruby," I corrected. "Yes, I didn't make it far though."

"I see Debbie took good care of you."

If possible, Debbie smiled even wider. And suddenly, I felt I was in the middle of something—of what, I wasn't entirely sure—and I looked from Debbie to Lark, then back to Debbie.

I swallowed back a laugh. She was absolutely beaming like a twelve-year-old girl with a crush. Lark tilted his head toward her, and her pale skin pinked.

This might be a lot more fun than I expected. Who would have thought? A budding romance in the foyer of the Oasis Senior Citizen Center? It was rather sweet.

I followed Lark into a long rectangular room that had several rows of chairs set up. About a dozen men and women were already seated. If I had entered with a clap of thunder, I wouldn't have had more attention on me. All heads turned and watched me. I kept a half smile on my face, glancing at everyone, giving out slight nods, but not really seeing any specific face, just a collection of colors and various hairstyles.

I sat near the back but not too far back to be conspicuously separate. I tried to act casual, as if I were anticipating the "lecture"—whatever it was about. Several people nodded and smiled as I settled in. One lady was already snoozing with her head slumped forward, and no one seemed to mind. I exhaled carefully so it didn't sound like a sigh. First hurdle jumped.

"Thanks for waiting," Lark said, his baritone voice carrying easily across the room. "I thought it would be more interesting to see the places I'm telling you about." A few people chuckled, and I smiled encouragingly as he looked in my direction. Although I wasn't exactly sure what I was encouraging him for.

"Paris was the most crowded but also the most interesting," he continued. "So I thought I'd discuss our trip there."

I leaned back in my chair, my attention raised a notch. It had been about three years since I'd been to Paris, and I was interested in hearing about his impressions. The first picture he'd started passing around reached me. I glanced at the familiar skyline that included the Eiffel Tower and then paused. The smiling man in the picture was definitely Lark but a much younger version. Perhaps twenty years younger.

I passed the picture on, slightly confused. The man in front of me handed over the next picture. Again, Lark smiling, clearly with his wife and children, but the children were teenagers, Lark perhaps forty-five or fifty years old. Was this trip he was talking about taken that long ago? I wondered why he was speaking on it.

He continued for another twenty or thirty minutes, and I tried not to check the clock too often since I didn't want to appear rude. Some of the details he offered were very outdated. I wasn't about to speak up and discredit him though.

Debbie slipped in beside me, her smile gracing everyone who glanced at her. She patted my hand as she sat down next to me. But I was quickly forgotten in her supreme focus on Lark. I hid a smile and spent a moment straightening the large diamond on my finger. I hadn't worn my wedding ring very consistently around the house, but I always made a point to wear it out in public.

At this moment, I was grateful for the glittering message it sent. I wasn't ready for the more-than-friendly glances passed among some of the men and women in the room.

Debbie leaned toward me, her skinny arm brushing against mine. "Wouldn't you just love to go to Paris? It's the city of life, you know."

"You mean the city of love?" I whispered, trying not to get caught in a conversation while Lark was still talking.

"Yes, that too," she whispered back, although a bit more loudly than I had.

I sensed her looking at me, and I could no longer avoid her gaze. I turned my head slightly and saw her staring at my ring. I stopped fidgeting with it. It had been a while since someone had gawked at my jewelry. That was one thing Phillip never neglected. Bedecking his wife with jewels—for better or worse.

"That's stunning," Debbie said, her voice not even close to a whisper.

Several heads turned, obviously not the ones with hearing aids. Heat flushed my neck in the already too-warm room. "Is your husband . . . ?"

"He passed two years ago," I said. *Exactly.*

Debbie patted my hand, then let it linger. "It's been three years for my Ron."

I assumed Ron was her husband. I nodded with understanding yet hoped the conversation would end. A few people kept glancing at us, and I didn't want to take away from Lark's travelogue. I pointedly looked at Lark as he described driving through the Alps and how his son had suffered from motion sickness on the windy roads.

As he spoke, I almost felt the breeze tugging at my hair as my own Phillip steered our rented convertible around the bends. Our first trip to Paris was with our son, Tony. He was about six, and after that, I vowed not to take him on such an extended trip again. I often wondered, if I had continued traveling with Phillip during those early years . . . if perhaps he wouldn't have had so much time to himself in the evenings . . . maybe he wouldn't have—

"Oh, look at this one," Debbie said, handing me a picture of Lark and his family standing in front of a cathedral.

"The Chartres Cathedral," I said without thinking.

Debbie cocked her head. "Oh, you know it? You've been to France?"

I couldn't deny it now. "Yes, a few times," I said in a quiet voice.

"A *few times?*"

Heads certainly turned at that.

Now all I needed was . . . "Ruby?" Lark's voice. Great. "When did you visit France?" he asked.

The entire room focused on me. "Uh, three years ago in the fall." I couldn't help myself and blurted, "France is gorgeous in the fall. Most definitely a significant rival to the eastern states." I practically had to bite my lip to say nothing more, but Lark leaned against the table in the front of the room and crossed his arms, a smile on his face. "I was there in June. Of course that was nearly twenty years ago."

I nodded. "June is a beautiful time as well."

"Ruby's been there *several* times," Debbie pitched in. Murmurs rose in the room, eyes widened, and heads nodded. "By the way, everyone, this is Ruby . . ."

"Crenshaw," I supplied for her.

"Ruby Crenshaw. She's new here," Debbie finished.

As if everyone in the room didn't already realize that.

"Ruby, you *must* be one of our guest speakers," she gushed. "We just love hearing about France."

Lark joined in. "Everyone has heard about my trip so many times, I'm surprised not more of them are asleep." Laughter resounded, waking up a couple of ladies on the front row—ones who were actually sleeping.

"You must say yes," Debbie said, her smile so wide I wondered if it hurt.

My reply came automatically. "Of course." My heart dropped an inch or two. It was impossible for me to say no to such a direct request. I had been doomed the moment Lark had held the front door open for me.

Chapter 3

"You did what?" Kara asked over the phone. My son never seemed to be available when I called, and I pushed aside the nagging worry that he was becoming more and more like his father.

"The center calls it a lecture series," I said in the most nonchalant tone possible, "but it's really just sharing some experiences from various trips I've taken."

I imagined Kara's stunned expression through the phone. "So now you're a weekly guest speaker?" Her couple seconds of silence told me she was about to lecture me. "Ruby, can't you just go there and enjoy something another person has put together?"

"Oh, there are plenty of activities I'm not involved in," I said.

Kara didn't seem to be listening. She kept talking about my age and the things I should be doing, like resting and enjoying something or other. I listened patiently, as usual, then hung up as soon as it was polite to do so.

Kara was such a fusser—and she was the same way with my son. He didn't seem to mind, but then again, I had fussed over him when he was a child. It was Phillip who didn't want to be bothered with my questions and concerns. I replaced the phone on the receiver in my bedroom, then made my way down the hall to the bathroom. I used the one in the hall and left the master bathroom as a guest bath. Opposite, I knew, but going into the master bedroom was like facing the past—which was locked away in a box in the master closet, which I wouldn't think about now. It bothered me greatly that things having to do with Phillip were on my mind so much right now. I'd admit that the first year after his death was tough, but the past year had been great. Why ruin that now?

Once my nightly routine was completed, I climbed into bed and opened *The Help*. I'd finished *Bath Tangle*—too soon—and I tried not to be daunted by the size of *The Help*. If Daisy loved it, as picky as she was, I could certainly read it.

Two hours later, I was startled to see how late it was. I'd been completely caught up in Skeeter's world and her network of very interesting friends. The era of 1960s Jackson, Mississippi, was certainly a volatile one. The book was not what I had expected, and I even sympathized with Hilly—who was a product of her unfortunate narrow-minded world.

If I'd learned one thing in all my travels to different countries and states, it was that fear controlled a lot of people's behavior. Fear of change, fear of the unknown, and fear of being alone.

Even here, in beautiful, mild-weathered California, fear had controlled my behavior.

* * *

For a rather large book, I was surprised at how fast I read *The Help* in preparation for the February meeting. I even let the phone ring a few times— two calls were from the senior center. I'd already "lectured" on my trips to France, and Debbie had me scheduled for the next week to lecture on Scandinavia.

Book club would start in less than an hour, and I still had to freshen up. I'd had the landscapers trim the outside bushes—although I'd refused to let them touch my hibiscuses—and I'd had the oriental rugs on the main floor cleaned the day before. Now I was regretting not having the white couches in the great room steam cleaned but then remembered that dessert was red velvet cake, so perhaps it was better to wait after all. With book club a regular occurrence, I was starting to notice a few specks that hadn't been there before.

It was, of course, nothing like the days when Phillip was alive and we entertained in our home frequently. The young ladies who came to book club weren't much like Phil's friends, who carefully picked and even more carefully ate the catered desserts. I never knew exactly what to expect from my new friends. Once, Paige brought a green Jell-O cheesecake dish. Green! And Jell-O! I was grateful we'd met at Daisy's apartment that time.

Thinking of Daisy, my heart sank. The poor woman was bedridden with a high-risk pregnancy and wouldn't be coming to book club tonight. We'd offered to hold it at her place again—she had a new apartment, but she said her place was quite small. Besides, she wasn't feeling up to it, and that deadbeat husband of hers was no help at all.

I planned to call her later tonight to fill her in on all the details. I was sure she was already looking forward to being included, even if in a small way. After all, Daisy had chosen *The Help* to read. It was quite a shame, really.

At 6:45 p.m., I turned off the oven and left the red velvet bread pudding inside so it would stay warm until I could serve it. Since red velvet cake was such a popular item now, I wanted to serve it but also make it Southern, like *The Help*. I had a small chocolate pie in the refrigerator to remind us of Minnie's practical joke in the book. I didn't know if anyone would dare eat it—even though it really was chocolate—so I bought that one from the store.

My kitchen smelled heavenly, and I set the timer on the stove so I'd pull out the vanilla ice cream in time for it to soften a little. I figured about twenty minutes into book club, we'd be ready for dessert.

I glanced out the front window just in time to see Olivia pull up. I opened the door as she climbed out of her car. As she walked toward me, my heart soared. There was a spring in her step, and she smiled when she saw me waiting for her. True to her nature, she carried a plate of something—even when I'd repeatedly told her she didn't need to bring anything to book club.

Her recent new hairstyle fell softly against her shoulders, and she exuded peace and warmth. I thought back briefly to the first time I'd met her. She had seemed so nervous, her hair a frizzed mess, but even then she'd brought a plate of delicious cookies.

"Olivia, you didn't have to bring anything."

"I know," she said, grinning. She hugged me, and I laughed.

When I asked her how she was doing, she said, "It's a beautiful day."

And it was. Not much more needed to be said. I shut the front door, and we walked to the kitchen. "Daisy won't make it today, but Shannon is bringing her stepdaughter." Olivia was probably the most compassionate stepmom I'd ever seen. She had four children of her own as well as two grown stepkids. And she seemed to volunteer for everything under the sun. I was secretly hoping Shannon and Olivia would strike up a friendship.

Olivia cracked open the oven and inhaled. "Divine."

"Just set them in the kitchen, then make yourself comfortable," I said, noticing two more cars pulling up. "I'll be there in a minute."

Athena and Victoria had arrived at the same time. Athena looked gorgeous, her short dark hair newly highlighted with red tones, and she wore black jeans with a rose-colored top. Ever since she started dating seriously, her edges had softened.

"How's that man of yours?" I asked as I pulled her into a hug.

"Grey?" she said, her voice muffled by my embrace.

"Of course I mean Grey," I said. He was the only man who had been able to completely capture her heart. I pulled back, satisfied to see a faint blush on her cheeks.

"He's . . . really great." She laughed. It was good to hear her laugh.

"And your father?" I asked. I'd helped Athena clean out her father's home when she'd moved him into a full-time-care Alzheimer's home.

"No changes, but that's good news," Athena said in a quiet voice.

I pressed her hand. Then Victoria stepped in behind Athena, and I hugged her too. Victoria squeezed back, hard. I loved a good hugger.

"So when are you going to tell us about your boyfriends, Tori?" I asked, using the nickname everyone called her.

Tori laughed out loud. "You'll be the first to know."

She released me and stepped back. Her dark hair was pulled into a loose ponytail-bun sort of thing. She'd probably come straight from the set, but she looked radiant. Her deep-brown skin offset the white blouse she wore, and I wondered what her secret was in keeping her shirt spotless all day. She worked as an assistant director on the wedding reality TV series *Vows*. I didn't usually watch such shows, but since getting to know Tori and having her tell us all of the stuff that happened behind the scenes, it had become quite fascinating to me.

"Your home smells like heaven. Where's the kitchen?" Tori asked.

"If you're hungry right now, I can bring out some hors d'oeuvres."

"Oh, don't trouble yourself," Tori said. "I'm saving myself for whatever it is you're baking."

I shooed them in the direction of the living room just as Ilana arrived. I waited with the front door open as she stepped out of a new Taurus. She seemed to have a frown line between her brows, which must have been due to her boring trade-show job, but as she rounded her car, I saw she had a sling on her arm. I wondered what on earth had happened and decided that was why she'd never called me back about lunch. I decided not to ask her about lunch again—she probably had enough on her mind.

Then I wondered if they'd had to use a child-size sling. Her petite frame, curly black hair, and olive skin only added to her appeal. I hugged her carefully. "My goodness. What ever happened?"

She shook her head, her curls bouncing. "I broke my elbow at work. I might be facing surgery. They won't know until the swelling goes down."

Maybe her job wasn't so boring after all. "I'm so glad you could make it," I said.

"Me too," Ilana said, and I sensed a bit of extra meaning behind her words.

She didn't have any children, so there was only Ilana and her husband—who was some sort of big-deal doctor, so who knew how much he was home to help out his wife.

"I certainly hope it doesn't result in surgery," I said. "How awful that you have to wait. Has the pain been terrible?"

"Nothing that a few pills can't manage," she said with a small smile.

"Olivia, Tori, and Athena are already here," I said, following Ilana to the living room.

Just then the doorbell rang. I turned back down the hall and opened the door to greet my niece, Shannon, and her stepdaughter, Keisha. I hugged Shannon, then turned to Keisha, who stood on the porch steps, examining the hibiscuses. I sure enjoyed someone with an appreciation for the flowers in life. "Welcome, my dear," I said. She turned, looking remarkably better than anytime I'd seen her before.

Her brown eyes lit up as a smile spread across her face. I couldn't help but find her adorable despite her thick eye make-up. It was a far cry from her druggie days. I'd welcome anyone into my home that Shannon and her husband, John, did, and, of course, how could I turn away John's daughter? He'd always been a dear and checked on little things throughout the house when I asked him to. Shannon was lucky to have such a thoughtful husband.

Another glance at Keisha had me thinking that maybe she felt obligated to wear heavy make-up since she was attending cosmetology school, where there was so much focus on appearance. I hugged her, showing her she was absolutely welcome in my home. "You've grown into a beautiful young woman." She had to be about twenty by now, although she looked younger. Well, everyone seemed to look young these days.

"I love your flowers," Keisha said, smoothing her long hair back.

I straightened, pride coursing through me. "I grow them myself and leave the lawn and bushes to the gardeners. Come in."

Shannon passed by me, and I shut the door, linking my arm through Keisha's. Shannon looked relieved that Keisha and I were so chummy.

Shannon's back seemed to stiffen as she entered the living room. She was way underdressed, not that anyone wore anything fancy, but Shannon was in her work scrubs. They were definitely well worn and definitely not spotless like Tori's blouse. But I'd never say so to Shannon. The fact that she was here, giving my book club a chance, meant a lot to me. I knew she didn't love the idea of the book club, but I hoped she'd change her mind.

Since Phillip's passing and my brother's move and my son's relocation to halfway across the country, I'd realized my family members were sparse, and I wanted to stay close to them. Keisha's bright eyes seemed to soak everything in, but Shannon looked decidedly uncomfortable. Maybe I would mention the pharmacy scrubs later in a private conversation, not because anyone cared but because Shannon might feel more comfortable if she dressed up a little more for book club.

I'd carefully chosen my silver earrings to go with my silver and peach blouse. Fortunately, my nails were already a peach color, and I didn't have to make any change there.

I escaped to the kitchen for a couple of seconds while Olivia and Ilana started talking to Shannon. I overheard Ilana asking Shannon's name again—they'd only been at one book club together.

Olivia's cookies were sitting on the counter, still covered, and the bread pudding still looked soft and moist in the oven. The doorbell rang, and I hurried past the living room just as Keisha was talking to the ladies about getting a medical assistant certificate. Everyone seemed interested in what she was saying. I smiled to myself. Maybe Keisha would become a regular part of the club too. She seemed to be an intelligent young woman.

Paige was at the door, and I pulled her into a quick hug. She had circles under her eyes. She always worked too hard—between her job at the dental office and being a single mom to two small boys, book club was probably the only night she got out each month. "Come in, come in. You're going to love dessert."

Paige smiled. "Ruby, you're the best."

We entered the living room together. "I guess we're all here," I said, clapping my hands together, getting everyone's attention.

"Is Daisy still on bed rest?" Athena asked.

My heart did a little twist. "She is," I said. "I offered to have us go to her place like we did last month, but she said she'd moved and her new place was too small." I looked at Paige—Daisy and Paige were very close. "I didn't want to pry by asking too many questions."

Paige gave me a sympathetic glance and told the rest. "She got her own place a couple of weeks ago, close to where her first ex-husband and daughter live. She's still on partial bed rest, but the baby's doing well. She's able to work from home half-time now."

"Did her life turn a 180 or what?" Tori said. "But she's okay?"

"Yeah," Paige said, smiling. "I think she's doing really well. She said to thank everyone for the phone calls and prayers—she says she's felt every one."

I made a mental note to call Daisy after book club—maybe if this bed rest thing continued, I'd insist we meet at her place in March. I sat down in a chair I'd brought from the kitchen. Our group was quite large now, even with Daisy gone. It couldn't have made me any happier. The ladies asked a couple of questions about Daisy, then I said, "Well, Daisy chose the book, but since she isn't here, I guess I'll lead the discussion. What did everyone think?"

I didn't really intend to look right at Tori, but she had been on my mind. Because she was a black woman, I wondered what her insights were about the book. She wasn't African American but was actually from Barbados.

Thankfully, Athena jumped in and started discussing the lack of opportunity for black women during that era. The other ladies agreed and talked about how they related to the characters. As they talked, I became more and more curious to know what Tori thought about it all. When there was a slight break in the conversation, I asked Tori, "Have you ever felt persecuted?"

She met my gaze. "For me personally, I haven't experienced racial prejudice in the US. Maybe because I'm in the entertainment industry, it just hasn't been an issue for me. I find it much harder to be a woman than to be black."

"You've experienced prejudice for being a woman?" I asked.

"Oh yes," Tori said, raising her eyebrows. I admired the sculpted look; maybe I'd ask her where she had them done. "There's still a lot of opportunity for me within my industry, but most of the top spots are filled with men, and most of the decisions on who *fills* the open positions are *made* by men. And a lot of women fall victim to unprofessional ways of furthering their career, if you know what I mean."

Everyone nodded in agreement. I knew all about women who did unprofessional, unethical, and immoral things. It seemed my husband had been surrounded by them. I was suddenly glad I was in a room full of ladies who didn't know anything about my husband.

"It wasn't until junior high that I really understood what racism meant," Athena said. "There was a group of kids in my school who decided to make me their target."

I stared at Athena—she was simply beautiful in a natural way. It just proved to me how cruel and misguided some people could be. I wasn't too surprised that Ilana had had some similar experiences. It seemed that the Jewish culture was a never-ending brunt of bad jokes and criticism. I guessed World War II hadn't really solved much.

My memory didn't exactly go back as far as I would have liked, but I hadn't felt discriminated against, unless I counted the couple of times I took the car into the mechanic after Phillip's death and had received an inflated bill.

Ilana and Paige both said they had experienced prejudice due to their religious beliefs—though Ilana pointed out that she wasn't a practicing Jew.

After Ilana finished her comments, I turned to my niece. "Shannon, what did you think?"

She seemed startled that I'd addressed her. I knew she'd read the book, so I hoped she'd contribute just a little.

"Uh, I liked it."

I smiled, sensing her nervousness. She'd be comfortable in no time. The ladies in the club were nothing but great.

Shannon cleared her throat and continued. "It's been a really long time since I've read a novel; I don't like much fiction." She seemed a little embarrassed to admit it, but I had no problem with diversity in our group. It could only make it more interesting. "I really liked this one though."

"Great to hear," I said. Everyone was smiling at Shannon, but she still looked nervous. She glanced down at her hands.

Before I could redirect the conversation, Paige chimed in. For a young thing, she seemed to have a wealth of knowledge. The ladies talked comfortably, and at one point, Keisha even chimed in, saying, "I thought it was totally sweet that Johnny still loved his wife, even though she couldn't have kids."

I grinned at Keisha, proud that she'd contributed. The conversation started to wrap up, and I excused myself to get the dessert. A couple of ladies started to rise, but I said, "It will only take a second. You stay and visit."

While they continued chatting, I went into the kitchen and pulled the chocolate pie out of the refrigerator, then walked back into the living room.

"The chocolate pie was the best part," Keisha was saying, and all the women laughed with her.

I smiled and held out my pie. "Speaking of chocolate pie, would anyone like a slice?"

"Oooh!" Everyone squealed, a mixture of horror and delight on their faces. I chuckled at their reaction and set it on the coffee table. Several visibly scooted away.

"Don't worry, I have a *real* dessert prepared."

The conversation overlapped as the women all made comments about Minnie and her trick on Hilly.

I left for the kitchen again and sensed someone behind me. Shannon had followed. "I hope I didn't sound uneducated in there," she said, her voice a bit breathless.

At least I knew she cared—I hoped that meant she'd continue to come, despite her protesting. "You could never sound uneducated, my dear. You have more degrees than anyone in the room."

Shannon's laugh was a bit hollow. I pulled out the bread pudding from the oven and set it on the counter. Then I grabbed the ice-cream scooper.

"Why don't I serve this up since you're leading the discussion tonight?" Shannon said.

"It won't take long," I started to say, but Shannon took the scooper from my hand with a smile just as laughter came from the living room.

"Go on. You don't want to miss anything."

She was right. I wanted to know what they were laughing about. And since I was leading the official discussion, it might be nice to not miss part of it. I joined the ladies, and a few minutes later, Shannon bustled out of the kitchen, several plates of dessert on a tray. Everyone exclaimed over the red velvet bread pudding.

"I wanted to fix something a bit Southern to go along with the book." I smiled as they took the first indulgent bites.

After Shannon delivered cups of chilled water to everyone, she disappeared back into the kitchen. She hadn't brought out her own plate yet, so I expected her to join us any second. Several minutes passed, and still, Shannon hadn't reappeared. Perhaps she'd taken a phone call, but I couldn't hear any conversation coming from the kitchen. I was about to get up and check on her when she came in, and at the same time, Paige asked me, "Will our next meeting be March 5?"

"Yes." I'd already checked the date beforehand. "Does that still work for most of us?" Heads nodded.

Shannon sat by Keisha, no dessert plate in hand. I threw her a questioning glance, but she wasn't looking at me. I hoped she'd feel a part of the group by now, though so far, she hadn't joined in unless I'd specifically asked her to. After her comment about not caring much for fiction, I thought I'd see if she wanted to choose the next book.

"Why don't you choose one, Shannon?" I said.

"Oh, that's okay." Her smile was wan. "I'm not nearly as well-read as you guys are."

That resistance again! "Oh, baloney." I waved my hand. I wanted these ladies to know exactly how smart my niece was—she just needed some time to warm up. "You have a PhD; surely you're as well-read as anyone here. Just choose a book for us to read, something you'd like to share with us."

"Really?" Shannon looked at the others as if she were about to pass the torch. "I don't know. I don't read much fiction."

"It doesn't have to be fiction," Athena said. "Do you read nonfiction?"

Thank you, Athena!

"Mostly only for work." Shannon glanced at me with a look of *why me?* But I offered her no mercy. She looked at down at her copy of *The Help*. "Well, there is one that might be interesting."

"Oh, good," I said, clasping my hands, eager to hear her suggestion. "What is it?"

"Well, *The Help* kind of reminded me of it since it also involves a black woman in the 1950s. It's called *The Immortal Life of Henrietta Lacks*."

I hadn't heard of it myself, and I looked at the other ladies, hoping someone had.

"I read a review about it," Paige said. "I tried to check it out at the library once, but it had a few holds on it—that was almost a year ago though. I heard it was really well done."

"It *was* really well done," Shannon said. "It's about a woman who had cervical cancer. The doctors biopsied the tumor and discovered that her cells reproduced continually, which opened the floodgates of medical research."

I breathed a sigh of relief. Shannon looked quite animated as she talked, and all the women were caught up in what she was saying. Maybe she'd agree to stay in the club after all. Nothing would make me happier.

She talked about how the woman's immortal cells were why we had a vaccine for polio as well as advances in cancer treatment.

At the end of it all, Keisha laughed. "You're such a nerd, Shannon."

Shannon's face reddened, and I was about to say something to deflect Keisha's comment when Tori laughed too. "We love nerds." She smiled at Shannon as if they shared some great joke.

"I think it sounds great," Athena said. "What was the title again? I want to order it from Amazon right now before I forget."

Shannon was busy picking at a spot on her pants. I hoped the nerd comment hadn't offended her.

Paige came to the rescue. "*The Immortal Life of Henrietta Lacks.* The author had a weird name though. I can't remember what it was."

"Skloot," Shannon said. "Rebecca Skloot—*s-k-l-o-o-t.*"

I exhaled in relief. Keisha's "nerd" comment seemed to have been forgotten.

"I'd have never remembered that," Paige said.

Everyone started tapping the information into their cell phones or other devices. It was official. Shannon had picked the next book. I looked over at her with a smile, but she was standing up, reaching for the plates to clear.

She gave me a nod—one that said, "Let me do this, okay?"

I nodded back and stood as the others prepared to leave, all caught up in various side conversations. Tori and Paige headed for the door, and I followed them, hugging them good-bye. Returning to the living room, I saw Keisha slouched on the couch, texting while waiting for Shannon.

I couldn't very well ask Shannon if she was okay with Ilana, Athena, and Olivia still visiting in the living room.

But before I could go find Shannon in the kitchen, she came in with a smile plastered on her face.

"You ready?" she asked Keisha.

Keisha stood and gave a polite good-bye to the rest of us. I hugged her, then hugged Shannon as well. I'd have to call her later.

"I hope you'll come next month," Olivia said to Keisha, then smiled at Shannon.

"Me too," Keisha said. "This was really fun."

Shannon mumbled something, then they were gone. Well, at least she'd chosen the book.

I crossed over to the other ladies. "Ilana, do you need help with anything this week? With your arm, I'm sure regular chores are almost impossible."

"I think I'll manage. My husband is pretty much spoiling me."

I laughed as if I knew exactly what she was talking about, as if I'd ever had a spoiling-type husband. "If anything comes up, will you let me know?" I pressed. No husband could do that much, I was sure. "Day or night."

"Thanks for the offer, Ruby," Ilana said. "But I think it's covered."

The other ladies offered their help as well, but Ilana put us all off. She was polite about it, though maybe she was just uncomfortable.

When the house was empty, I went into the kitchen to clean up. Shannon had left it spotless—no wonder she'd been in there for so long. Still, I rearranged some things before going up to my room, wondering how long I should wait before calling Shannon.

Chapter 4

PURCHASING *THE IMMORTAL LIFE OF Henrietta Lacks* was the 10:00 a.m. item on my list Monday morning. I had also set aside some time, starting at lunch, to read it, knowing my schedule was becoming busier since I'd started participating at the senior center.

Before I started lunch, I had to call Ilana. She'd been friendly at book club, but with her broken elbow, I knew she'd need help. Even if her husband was Mr. Wonderful. I dialed her number purposely at 12:15 p.m., hoping she'd be on a lunch break.

The phone rang twice, and Ilana picked it up. Her tone sounded more cheerful than usual, and I took that as a good sign.

"It's Ruby. How are you, dear?"

"Just fine, considering I go into surgery tomorrow." She sort of half giggled.

I didn't find surgery funny at all. I wondered if she was just nervous. "Oh, wow. It's that serious?"

"It's a rather minor surgery but necessary. I probably won't even have to stay overnight." Her tone sounded more hopeful than sure. I hoped it would be minor.

"That doesn't sound too invasive," I said.

"Yeah, all those robotic machines make everything so easy now."

Even though her voice sounded upbeat, I couldn't imagine she felt settled inside. After all, it *was* surgery. "Can I drive you to the hospital?"

"My husband will be taking me and staying the whole time."

"That will be wonderful for you," I said, thinking of how else I could help. "What if I bring dinner to the both of you tonight so you can just relax and not worry about anything?" I knew I didn't imagine the hesitation in her voice, but she probably realized I didn't give up easily.

"All right. That will be fine." Ilana said something else that sounded muffled, probably to her husband.

"Do either of you have any allergies?" I asked. As she was saying no, I suddenly realized. What about kosher food? "Do you eat only kosher?"

"As far as my mother is concerned, I do." Her tone was definitely lighter again. "You don't need to worry about cooking kosher for us. Ethan and I will eat anything you bring."

I laughed, mostly with relief. "Super," I said. "I'll be there around six."

Hanging up, I felt better. Not about Ilana having to go through surgery but that I was finally able to do something for her. Once I knew exactly how long she'd be laid up, I'd enlist rotating visits from the book-club ladies as she recovered.

I added "shop for Ilana's dinner" to my to-do list, then I prepared my lunch and sat down with a grilled panini and small salad. On to the book-club choice of *Henrietta Lacks.*

I read the prologue with great interest in how a cancer cell could continue dividing indefinitely if it had a supply of nutrients. Very strange and quite scary to think of it. Henrietta Lacks's cancer cells had been reproducing since 1951. I shuddered, thinking of cancer cells multiplying over and over—their poison never dying. The author, Rebecca Skloot, did a nice job of explaining why she wrote the story, but I also wondered how she planned to make an entire book out of it.

Halfway through chapter one, I'd lost my appetite and pushed away my half-eaten panini. Henrietta's husband, David, had slept with multiple women, bringing home plenty of diseases to share. I had undergone a few STD tests myself, until it no longer became necessary when I refused to let Phillip come near me. Here I was dwelling on Phillip again. *Heaven help me.*

Henrietta, as a "colored" woman, could be treated only at the John Hopkins hospital because of her race and had a list of untreated medical conditions that made my skin crawl. Because of her poor financial status and her ignorance, she didn't follow through when a physician recommended specific medical care. Then she ended up with cervical cancer. I shook my head. Poor woman—it seemed she didn't have much of a chance to start with.

I looked down at my practically gourmet meal and thought of my regular health checkups. And my designer-decorated and immaculate house stood around me, shielding me from the ugliness that was much of the world . . . even in today's age.

Henrietta and I had little in common, unless you counted our husbands' penchant for other women. I set the book down and left the kitchen.

Walking into my front yard, I breathed in the sunny, flower-fragrant air. Decades ago, a young woman with five children went through an awful lot of suffering. It was hard to imagine it on such a beautiful day.

I thought of the life story that sat on my kitchen table, waiting to be read. I took a deep breath and went back inside.

By five, I'd rinsed off the spinach leaves and cut up strawberries to go with the spinach salad for Ilana and her husband. I cheated on the rolls and had popped Rhodes into the oven, but they smelled just as delicious as homemade rolls. Now I turned my attention to the cooling lasagna. It was nice not to have to worry about any dietary restrictions and make a good, old-fashioned hearty meal.

I presliced the lasagna and made a mental note to tell Ilana I'd pick up the dishes later in the week so she wouldn't have to worry about it. The snickerdoodles I made for her had cooled and were sitting on a pretty paper plate. I'd cover them right before I headed out the door. I still couldn't believe Ilana had never tried snickerdoodles. While the rolls baked, I sent an e-mail to the book-club ladies letting them know I was taking dinner to Ilana tonight and that it would be great if we could set up a rotating schedule of either phone calls or visits. Having one person a day making contact with Ilana would mean a lot to her.

With ten more minutes on the oven timer, I decided to fit in a few more chapters of *The Immortal Life of Henrietta Lacks*. The chapters went back in time to when she grew up—with her cousin Day—as in David Lacks. They were first cousins? This story was getting even more complicated. I laughed at the antics of "Crazy Joe" as he tried to woo Henrietta but shook my head in disgust when he stabbed himself after finding out Henrietta and Day were getting married. Not in disgust that Joe stabbed himself but that Henrietta could marry her first cousin.

I breathed out, realizing that wasn't what really bothered me. It was still legal to marry first cousins in some parts of the world, and people had done it all the time the Bible . . . What really bothered me was that Henrietta picked Day/David, whatever his name was, when Joe so clearly loved her and would do anything for her. Yet Henrietta picked a man who would abuse and cheat on her.

Didn't she see the signs? Had *I* seen the signs with Phillip? Looking back, I could pick out a few things—but I hadn't seen them as red flags at the time. And if I had, I would have just thought they were prewedding jitters.

So Phillip was a ladies' man. Plenty of men were like that. Plenty of them got along great with women and always seemed to be surrounded by them but didn't seem to have affairs. I continued to read and marvel at Henrietta and all she put up with. And to learn that she loved to sneak out of the house to go dancing with her sister. She always pressed her clothes nicely and wore pretty little shoes. I liked her more and more by the minute.

The oven timer went off, and I set the book down to pull out the rolls. The aroma filled the room, and I realized I was a little hungry myself. But it was after five and the drive to Long Beach would be about thirty minutes. Luckily, I would be driving in the opposite direction of rush-hour traffic.

The drive went smoothly, and I found Ilana's apartment without a problem. The food had managed to stay in one place with the trays I'd brought. I debated whether to make one or two trips carrying the stuff. Ilana wouldn't be able to help me at all.

I made two trips, and on the first, I set the salad and the main dish by her door, then went back to get the dessert and rolls. Then I rang the doorbell and hoped Ilana and her husband would enjoy the meal.

A moment later, the door swung open, and Ilana stood there, wearing a matching lavender leisure outfit. Her hair was pulled back from her face, and she looked a bit pale. The pain must have been taking its toll, poor thing.

I bustled in, telling her to take a seat and that I'd take care of everything.

"Thank you so much for this, Ruby."

Ilana sat at the kitchen table, and as I uncovered the salad, I took a quick look around at the apartment. The taupe walls were a nice contrast to the chestnut leather couches. Several plants decorated the place as well as an antique-looking menorah.

"My husband should be here within the hour," Ilana said. "He was just delayed with a multicar accident."

"Oh, goodness," I said with a shake of my head. I was certainly grateful for doctors, but I could never be one. I uncovered only half of the lasagna, keeping it as warm as possible while I scooped out a slice and put it on a plate for Ilana.

"You don't have to do all that," she said, but I saw the appreciation in her eyes.

I smiled at her. "What would you like to drink?"

"Water is fine."

I found a glass in a cupboard and filled it with ice and water from the refrigerator. When I set it on the table, I said, "Is there anything I can do for you while I'm here? Fold any laundry?"

Ilana waved a hand. "No. Ethan is good about all of that. He's quite a fuss-pot actually."

I chuckled. Ethan sounded a bit like me. Of course, Phillip wouldn't have touched the laundry, even when I had the flu or something else unpleasant. He'd just buy a new pack of socks if he became desperate enough.

"All right, then," I said, scanning the kitchen and living room, looking for something to help her with anyway. Everything looked in order. There weren't even dirty dishes in the sink. I couldn't very well stand and watch her eat. "Don't worry about returning the dishes. I'll stop by later in the week to check on you and grab them then."

"Thanks again, Ruby," Ilana said with a smile. She picked up a fork. She must have been quite hungry, which made it time for me to go.

I headed to the door and paused as I opened it. On the wall over one of the couches was a framed picture of Ilana and her husband in Jerusalem. "Did you take a tour to Israel?"

"We've been a few times," she said.

I was about to question why so many times, then realized that was probably pretty normal for her culture. "It's a lovely place. I went there in 2005." I turned to face her. "I'll never forget the heat and the fact that we had to wear long pants or skirts at the holy sites."

"Oh yes, they're pretty strict about that," Ilana said.

"Well, I'll keep you in my thoughts tomorrow. Please let us know how everything goes—or maybe you can delegate that to Ethan." I looked back at the man in the picture. His sandy-blond hair gleamed in the sun, and he was a very nice-looking man. Ilana looked happy next to him.

"I will, Ruby," Ilana said with an appreciative smile. "Or Ethan will."

I opened the door and waved, then stepped outside and let out a breath. Ilana had been friendly and polite, but I still worried about her—going into surgery. I decided to make a few follow-up phone calls to the book-club ladies. I wouldn't bother Shannon too much, since she had such a heavy work schedule, but I knew Athena and Tori had more flexible schedules, with Tori often working at odd hours.

Chapter 5

LEAFING THROUGH THE PICTURES OF Greece I'd brought, each with its own 4 x 6 sheet protector to ward off any potential smudges with all of the hands touching it, I found the ones I'd begin with. I handed the first three pictures to Debbie, who had become my official assistant. She beamed as she started the pictures down the row after looking carefully at each one, of course.

Scanning the group, I was sure the crowd was bigger than the week before. It seemed that my "travel" class had become quite popular. Even the predictably sagging heads were upright.

"Today, I'll share my travels through Greece."

Several ahh's sounded and eyes brightened.

"I don't exactly feel qualified, since the trip was over twenty years ago." I glanced at Debbie. "But it was too hard to say no."

Debbie beamed as if it were the most wonderful thing in the world.

As I explained the sites in the pictures being sent around, I thought back to my one and only trip to Greece. It was soon after returning home, so many years ago, that I'd discovered Phillip's first affair.

Lark had his hand raised.

Grateful for the distraction from my thoughts, I said, "Yes?"

"Did your son travel with you on all of your trips?" The picture he held was obviously missing what most of my traveling pictures had—a picture of Tony with either Phillip or me.

"At that time, Tony stayed home—he was about eight. Just old enough to leave with grandma and grandpa for a week."

Perhaps I had sensed then that Phillip was pulling away from me—that there was a disconnect between us. And that's why I'd made the bold effort of having Tony stay home for the trip to Greece. But traveling through the foreign country with just my husband was not the bonding experience I'd hoped for. I'd spent nearly every evening alone while Phillip had met with associates. It was far from the romantic venture I had envisioned. And I was left with little more than jet lag and missing my young son.

I passed out several more pictures, relating the basics of each area we'd visited. But as I spoke, the lump in my throat grew, expanding to my chest. I tried to take deep yet imperceptible breaths to steady the flood of emotions. It was so unexpected. I hadn't thought about Greece in such a long time.

When I finished my spiel and the pictures had made it around to the front again, I felt anxious to leave as soon as possible. My eyes were starting to sting, and I looked forward to a long, very hot bath. Anything to ward off the trembling I felt building deep inside of me.

"That would be wonderful. What do you think, Ruby?" Debbie was smiling at me.

When I blinked and focused on her, I realized the entire room had gone quiet—everyone staring. Obviously, they were all waiting for my answer.

"I don't know," I stumbled out, putting on a half smile, hoping I could figure out what they were asking.

Debbie grasped my arm. "We'd go with one of those tour agencies, of course, but we'd love to have you there because you're one of us now and you already know so much."

"Tour agencies?"

"We'd see Greece, of course, maybe Italy . . . Lark and I have a friend who runs a travel agency just down the road." She paused, everyone watching both of us eagerly. "You've probably been to Italy as well." She laughed.

I nodded. Tour . . . They wanted to tour Greece and Italy. *Greece.*

"I don't know," I said in a careful voice. Truth was, my throat was on fire, and I was seconds away from the tears spilling over. "There are a lot of other places to see—if you're thinking of a tour."

"Of course we're thinking of a tour," Debbie said. "The senior center will help support it. We do something big every two years." She lowered her voice. "For those of us who can still travel."

My mouth was absolutely dry. I couldn't. Not to Greece. "I—I'll think about it."

The buzzing voices continued again, and I quickly gathered my pictures. I made my way to the door, saying as little as possible to make a faster exit.

Once in my car, I closed my eyes before starting the engine. I'd overdone it. By agreeing to help out, to share my travels, I'd allowed the pain to enter all over again.

You're better than that, Ruby, I told myself. *Hold yourself together. You can't change the past.*

Deep inside, I knew I wasn't better than that. I had failed at being a wife. Completely.

Was there a special hell set aside for women who were lousy wives?

Despite all the churches I'd been inside, all the services I'd witnessed all over the world, I didn't know if I believed in an afterlife—a heaven or a hell. I didn't know if I could imagine heaven. Although I could certainly imagine hell.

Opening my eyes, I started the car and drove away from the senior center. I didn't want anyone coming out to wonder why I was sitting in my car with my eyes closed.

I arrived home just at the sun was setting. Lance stood in the opening of his garage, fussing with something. I raised my hand in greeting but hurried to the front door so he'd know I was in a rush.

Once inside, the quiet of my house contrasted with the noise of the senior center. I could now let out my breath and let the burning tears fall.

"You are past this," I whispered.

I tucked the Greece pictures into the photo box I'd left out on the kitchen table. I'd put them away later. Meanwhile, I was drawn to my former bedroom. I walked upstairs, my heart resolute. I hoped that by opening the box, I'd realize the things Phillip had done could no longer hurt me. And all of the obsessing I'd done lately would end once and for all.

I switched on the light since the curtains and shades were drawn in the master room. In *his* side of the walk-in closet, Phillip had installed a safe. I typed in the combination and opened the door. Inside, along with a couple of jewelry boxes containing my nicer jewelry, was a wood box about the size of a bread box. It was actually an antique wine box. I'd filled it with the things I'd collected over the years to remind me . . . to give me courage to leave him.

But I waited too long. Phillip left me first.

My fingers shook as I inserted the key into the lock and turned it. There was no loud sound or dramatic music, just a small click. A slight scent of mustiness rose in the air as I lifted the lid, as if I'd opened a book in a used bookstore.

For a moment, I gazed at the contents—everything from a concierge business card of a hotel Phil had shared with another woman—Pamela— to a piece of red gravel I'd found in his shoe from a night out with Gina.

Each item was placed in order from the first to the last—at least of the ones I'd known about. I'd been pretty thorough and was pretty sure I knew each woman and almost every rendezvous.

My gaze rested on a dried starfish with its missing arm. Janelle. She'd been the first. When we'd returned from Greece, Phillip had been hit hard by jet lag, so I'd opened the phone bill. Normally, Phillip took care of such things, and I was more than grateful. Finances made me crazy, especially taxes.

The nearly $700 long-distance total had sent my heart racing. I'd rushed upstairs to the master room, not caring that Phillip was sleeping, intent on showing him the bill right away. But something had made me pause before opening the door.

What if this was normal? What if Phillip's phone charges were just a part of his business dealings? Maybe he expensed the phone calls.

Feeling silly for panicking, I walked downstairs, wondering why I'd been worrying at all. And then I knew.

The calls were all made in the evening—times when he was with clients—and I wasn't with him. Was he really making all of those calls when he was at a business dinner? This was before cell phones, so if he had been making calls, they should have been made from our hotel room.

The hotel listed was not where we'd stayed. And it was not a place I'd remembered him telling me he had a meeting.

With Phillip sleeping upstairs, I called our phone company. Fortunately, my name was listed on the bill as well, and I was able to make a request for a list of the destinations of the phone calls.

All I had to do was wait a week to receive the list.

I always made it a point to be home when the mail arrived. And to sort through the mail to look for the letter from the phone company.

When it finally came, I locked myself in the bathroom with our phone, my heart pounding as I scanned the numbers Phillip had called while I was in a hotel by myself in Greece. One number. Over and over. Hour upon hour.

Before I could second-guess myself, I called the number. When a woman answered, I launched into a spiel about a free carpet-cleaning offer. By the time I'd hung up with Janelle, I had her address and full name.

The next afternoon, I drove by her condo in Dana Point and wrote down the license plate number of her Mercedes. I walked the shore of the nearby marina, trying to catch my breath and decide if I should confront Phillip. It was then that I found the starfish in the sand. I picked it up, determined to take it home with me and keep it as a reminder until I decided what to do.

I did nothing. I put the starfish in a box. I drove past her condo a few more times. I even followed Phillip down there once.

Putting my focus into Tony became my life. I headed up anything and everything from school fundraisers to neighborhood barbecues. I was the host of all hostesses. When the Internet became wildly popular, I took a couple of computer classes and became quite the sleuth. What used to take me days of careful investigating and false phone calls now took me about twenty minutes on the Internet.

I picked up the starfish and turned it over. It hadn't changed in thirty years. I didn't even know if Janelle was still alive. I'd decided that once Phillip stopped seeing a woman, so would I—I stopped tracking her.

She's probably gone. Phillip's dead. Just like this starfish. Let it go.

Debbie's bright smile popped into my thoughts. Why was I letting this dead starfish and old box of my husband's indiscretions stop me from traveling someplace with friends?

I put the starfish back in its place and shut the lid, locking the box before I could spend any more time on the dusty memories. That's all they were. Dusty and decaying. I needed to let them completely decay.

Taking a deep breath, I decided I'd go.

I'd go to Greece with Debbie, Lark, and whoever else could "travel."

I'd go with people who weren't related to me and whose secrets couldn't hurt me.

* * *

I picked up Debbie and Lark on the way to the travel agency. They stood waiting together beneath the awning of the senior center. Lark towered over Miss Petite, but when she looked up at him, it was like she grew a foot. I wondered what was taking Lark so long in acknowledging her attention—maybe he was blind to her adoring smiles. Maybe he needed someone to fill him in.

Debbie settled into the front seat, excitement nearly bursting from her. Lark pulled his knees up to fit into the backseat.

We parked in front of a small building that announced itself as the "International Traveling Company."

"Is this the right place?" I asked, peering at the faded sign. I guess I'd been expecting something nicer.

"This is where we always go," Debbie gushed. "You'll love Maria and her brother, Gabriel. They're Greek, so I'm sure they'll be tickled that we want to go to their home country."

I turned off the car, and we entered the single door. A heavyset woman who looked to be in her midfifties smiled up at us from a long desk in the lobby. I slowly realized this wasn't a lobby but the actual office.

"Debbie!" the woman said, rising to greet her with a hug. "I was very excited when you called. I've already pulled up several tours."

Debbie squeezed her in return, then pivoted to introduce me.

I reached out a hand toward Maria, but she enveloped me in a crushing hug. I couldn't help smiling. I would, indeed, love Maria. She pulled away and kissed my cheek. "Ruby Crenshaw, I'm Maria Alexakis. So pleased to meet you."

After embracing Lark, she bustled us into the chairs across from her desk. "Have a seat, my friends. I'll pull up the schedules, and you can see which dates you prefer." A large monitor was perched on her otherwise cluttered desk. She reached for the mouse and clicked a few times, squinting her eyes, even though she wore thick-lensed, mauve-colored glasses.

Maria wore several rings on her fingers, all large and glittery. I might have met someone who could outdo me in the jewelry department. She pursed her lips as her hand paused in its clicking. "Oh, one is already filled. At least, there wouldn't be enough for a whole group . . ." She looked up at Debbie. "How many are going?"

"Fourteen, maybe fifteen," Debbie said, throwing me an excited glance. "Two are married couples, then there will be five other men and the rest women."

More clicking, then Maria said, "There are still some good options here. A nice ten-day tour should be perfect. Not too long and tiring but enough time to see the best sights."

"Is Gabriel here today?" Debbie asked.

Maria looked up again, her eyebrows arched in surprise. "No, no. Gabriel has gone back to Greece for the rest of the year." She shook her head. "He says he needs a change—after the divorce, you see."

"Divorce? From Rhea?" Debbie said. "But that was . . . a year ago."

"Still hard on him, it seems," Maria said, her mouth pulling into a frown. "But not nearly as hard as it's been on Rhea. She's been sick, calling me at the office lately, trying to get ahold of him. Gabriel is off in beautiful Greece while his sick ex-wife is here feeling miserable."

"What's wrong with her?" Debbie asked.

Maria shrugged. "She's always had a poor constitution. If it's not one thing, it's another. Gabriel was always able to make her feel better."

I looked from Maria to Debbie. The woman was Gabriel's ex-wife. Did Maria think he still had the responsibility of caring for her? I guess stranger things had happened . . . like my marriage.

"I worry about him over there by himself," Maria continued. "What if he rebounds and gets caught up in a relationship with another woman? Someone I don't even know? He might even have a girlfriend I don't know about. He should be here, with family, where I can look after him."

"Well," Debbie said and left it at that. It seemed we felt the same way about Maria's overconcern for her brother.

"I'm just grateful they didn't ever have children—can you imagine Rhea as a mother?" Maria said. "Her health has never been good enough to chase after a baby."

Debbie folded her hands together. "No, I suppose not. That would have added injury to insult."

I was about to correct her but stopped myself. How much did Debbie know about this Rhea, or how much did she know about the personal lives of her travel agents? Lark shifted in his chair, his face a bit flushed. He obviously wasn't comfortable with so much free-flowing information.

"I must confess that I have to laugh at Gabriel's stories," Maria said. "He's a tour guide himself, you see. I never thought I'd see the day."

"Then we must go on Gabriel's tour," Debbie burst out.

Surprise crossed Maria's face, then a smile. "He might just enjoy that very much. Seeing some familiar faces from home."

I wondered if he really would—or would reminders of "home" make the memories resurface?

Maria was madly clicking again. "Oh." Her expression fell. "The only room I can see on one of his tours is . . . in March." She looked up again. "Starts in three weeks. The other months are much more in demand."

Lark cleared his throat and leaned forward. "Three weeks? That's pretty soon to make so many arrangements. Is there nothing later? Or we could travel with another guide?"

Debbie patted Lark's arm. "I don't think we want to miss out on Gabriel's expertise." She glanced over at me. "I think even Ruby would be impressed."

Maria was back to the computer screen. "He only has a handful of openings for the upcoming tours the rest of the year, it looks like. He must have turned quite popular over there."

"I don't mean to state the obvious," Debbie said. "But we all know Gabriel has always been popular with the ladies."

Maria drew her brows together and peered over at Debbie. "Gabriel is just a gentleman, nothing more."

It seemed that only Maria could speculate on Gabriel's relationships, not anyone else.

"Of course," Debbie said, but her eyes sparkled. Not like they sparkled for Lark, but they sparkled nonetheless.

More clicking, and Maria said, "Yes, March is the only month I can sign a large group up. It's the month right before the heavy tourist season starts—that's the only place I can fit you all in. Unless you want another guide at a later time."

Lark started clearing his throat again, but Debbie jumped in. "Can you pen our group in? We'll go back to the senior center and discuss it with everyone." She turned her wrist over and looked at her watch. "We'll have an answer for you tomorrow."

"All right," Maria said, typing on the keyboard. Then she pushed away from her desk. Smiling at me, she said, "You'll just love Gabriel. Wait until you meet him."

I smiled back and was soon enveloped in another huge hug.

On the ride back to the center, Debbie kept up a constant chatter. Lark added some half sentences here and there, but neither of us was a match for the excitement Debbie could hardly contain. Gabriel this, Gabriel that. I glanced in the rearview mirror a few times and saw the disconcerted expression on Lark's face.

Maybe he was noticing Debbie after all.

I stopped in front of the senior center, planning to drop them both off. Debbie insisted that I come in, but I insisted right back that I had another appointment.

As soon as Debbie was out of the car, she hurried to the front doors, not even waiting for her Prince Charming to open them for her. Lark climbed out more slowly, unfolding his long legs from my midsize car.

"Well," he said, leaning down and looking at me inside the car.

I smiled, and he closed his mouth and turned away to follow the long-disappeared Debbie.

I drove to the far side of the lot and parked. Then I pulled out my cell phone and called Athena. I had some misgivings about going to Greece in March, and I was hoping she could enlighten me.

I was preparing to leave a brief but urgent message when Athena picked up the phone. Surprised, I quickly recovered and told her about the trip.

"Who told you March wasn't a good month?" Athena asked.

I hesitated. "I'm not sure now whether it came from Maria or Debbie. Do you happen to know Maria Alexakis?"

"Why, because I'm Greek?"

"No," I said, my stomach dropping.

Athena started laughing. "I don't know her, but I'm sure if your friends have booked through this travel agency before, it's a safe bet."

"What do you think about March though?"

There was a slight pause on Athena's end. "March is perfectly fine. There might be some rain but nothing to worry about. Tell me, Ruby, what are your real concerns?"

Real concerns? What was she talking about? "I just want to make sure I do my homework, is all." The location of Greece was my concern. I had determined to go, but at the time, it had seemed like months away—six months or even longer. Not a few weeks.

I switched the cell phone to my other ear since my right hand felt slightly sweaty. Athena was still quiet, as if she knew I wasn't telling the whole story. "I don't know these people all that well," I said. "I thought I'd have more of a chance to know them before spending two weeks with them."

"At book club, you mentioned Debbie. And who was the gentleman?"

"Lark," I supplied.

"I know you're a good judge of character. You always make the most insightful comments at book club," Athena said.

If she only knew I was a horrible judge of character. Or at least I'd judged Phillip completely wrong. She kept talking. "When are they making the final decision?"

"Tomorrow." I glanced over at the senior center as if I could see right through the walls into the minds of all of the travelers-to-be. I was sure Debbie was getting everyone excited about a March trip. I breathed out slowly.

"Things always look better in the morning," Athena said.

I'd said that more than once to myself, to my son. "Of course they will."

"Why don't you call me in the morning, and we'll see what your thoughts are?"

"All right," I said, pleased at her offer.

Athena was a known workaholic. I'd been able to drag her away a time or two to have lunch, but she always seemed in a hurry. The spa day had been a huge exception. The offer to chat again in the morning really meant a lot to me.

We hung up, and I drove home as twilight began its descent. The only problem was, morning was still fourteen hours away.

Chapter 6

BY THE TIME ATHENA CALLED me in the morning, I had made up my mind. It would seem strange if I came up with a reason overnight not to go on the trip. I could say I had a trip planned to see my brother Jason and his wife, Kodi, but I knew Debbie would be very disappointed. One of my biggest weaknesses was thinking I'd disappointed someone.

"I'm going to do it," I told Athena over the phone.

"Fantastic," she said. "I'd be tempted to go along as well, but it looks like the merger with my magazine is finally going to happen."

"Besides the fact that you'd be half everyone's age."

Athena laughed in her rich voice. "I wouldn't mind."

I laughed with her. "I know you wouldn't." Of all the ladies in the book club, I knew Athena wouldn't mind the age difference at all. In fact, she'd probably thrive in it. She'd become good friends with the book-club ladies, but from what I knew about her life, she was normally too busy for any sort of socializing.

"Ruby, I'm happy for you," Athena said.

I warmed at the genuine tone of her voice. Even though I knew I was probably a check mark on Athena's morning list, I appreciated her call.

"You're always too kind and generous with everyone, so it will be great for you to get away and just enjoy yourself," she said.

I smiled, even though she couldn't see it. We chatted a few more minutes, and I was surprised by the length of the conversation. Most of what I'd had with Athena in the past were very brief conversations. Even with her challenges last fall, she hadn't opened up too much. I felt we had just reached a turning point.

I phoned Debbie next, and she already had everyone's commitment. I wasn't surprised at all.

"You must come to the center today," Debbie said. "We're all madly trying to put together a list of essentials for the trip. We desperately need your input."

"I can come down in about an hour," I said, my pulse quickening as Debbie's enthusiasm infiltrated my thoughts over the phone.

"Perfect. Lark will be here too," she continued. "Between the two of you, we'll have a great packing list to send home with everyone."

I wondered what sort of packing list they'd come up with on their last trip. I doubted my "expertise" was really all that necessary. Besides, some of my necessities might not be someone else's. Although I did take quite a bit of pride in my packing skills.

When I arrived at the center, Debbie had everyone assembled in the garden room. I didn't know she was making everything so formal. All eyes turned to me as I entered. At the front of the room, Lark stood from his seat. I was happy enough to take a seat, but he motioned me forward. He handed over a piece of paper with some items scrawled on it.

"It's what we've brainstormed so far," Lark said. Debbie had followed me to the front and was taking her seat next to Lark's.

I read through the items quickly. Pretty much everything useful was missing. I looked up. "I think I can help."

For the next twenty minutes, we put together a good packing list. When we were finished Debbie stood up and said, "I'll take this to the travel agency to see if Maria has any more recommendations. Then I'll type this out and get it to each of you."

She turned to me. "Can you come with me to the travel agency? I think it would be better if you talked to Maria as well."

I agreed. This time Lark didn't come with us. He still seemed affable enough, but something had changed. Maybe it was all the talk about Gabriel. I hid a smile. Jealousy could be a powerful motivator. Lark hadn't seemed to notice the attention Debbie had given him until Debbie's attention was diverted.

I was pretty sure that whatever Debbie thought about Gabriel, it wasn't much compared to her feelings for Lark. No one could doubt it when they saw Debbie around Lark.

Maria met us at the door. I wasn't sure if she had just arrived herself or was about to leave. "I'm so glad you came. I just got a distressing e-mail from my brother."

Debbie gripped my arm, and I shook my head at her. Maybe the tour was about to be canceled.

A combination of relief and disappointment flooded through me.

"He says . . ." Maria took a deep breath as she settled into her chair on the other side of the desk. "He says he's extending his stay over there."

Debbie released my arm and sat down across from Maria. "So the tour will still happen?"

Confusion marked Maria's face, then her expression cleared. "Oh yes. Sorry if I misled you." The frown came back. "Gabriel said he needed a year. Now he's saying probably two, maybe longer."

Debbie didn't seem too disturbed by this news. She smiled. "He should take his time. It will be wonderful to have him as our tour guide."

Maria's eyes flicked to me.

"I'm sorry," I said. "Will you be all right running the agency without him?"

Debbie's expression sobered. Apparently, she hadn't thought too far beyond the March tour.

"It's not really that," Maria said in a quiet voice. "I have some help come in on Fridays and Saturdays—our busiest days. I just . . ." She looked away, and I worried that she might actually start crying in front of us.

I hurried to her side and draped an arm around her shoulders. "You miss him, don't you?"

Maria nodded and wiped at her eyes. I grabbed a tissue from a box on her desk. "I have a brother who moved as well. To Arizona."

I guess Maria found this hilarious. She burst out laughing. "Arizona . . . Greece. Yeah, they're *so* similar."

Soon we were all laughing so hard tears came.

When Maria dried her eyes, she said, "We've been very close, you know. Working together for so many years, and now . . . I know he's hurting, and I can't be there to help him. We've never been apart from each other like this."

I nodded, using a tissue myself as I settled in the chair across from her again.

She waved her hand at the computer. "E-mail is not good enough."

"You should come with us," I said. I wasn't sure where the idea had come from—I'd spoken it almost before I'd thought of it. "Even if you don't stay for the whole tour, you should come for part of it. You'll feel better seeing your brother."

Maria touched a photo frame facing her on the desk. I hadn't paid attention to it when I had been hugging her. It was probably of her brother.

"Is that a new picture?" Debbie asked in a soft voice. She was sufficiently subdued now.

"No, I found it among his things last night. I was cleaning out a few boxes in the garage and came across the ones he stored after the divorce." Maria turned it around, and I was captured by the two smiling faces. Maria and a man I assumed was Gabriel were standing together on a beach somewhere, their arms around each other's shoulders. Maria was positively beaming. Gabriel's smile looked like he was caught in the midst of laughter.

I couldn't help scanning the rest of his features, looking for any resemblance to his sister. They had the same dark, expressive eyes and olive skin. Other than that, Gabriel's face was chiseled and gently lined whereas Maria's was full and round with her added weight.

I leaned back in my chair, unaware of when I'd started leaning forward. I didn't want to be caught gawking. I understood now why Debbie had been all aflutter when Maria had mentioned that we could tour with Gabriel. He was a very, very nice-looking man, either about Maria's age or a couple of years older. And if a picture could really tell a thousand words, this one told plenty.

Phillip had been nice looking and charismatic too. I pulled my gaze away from Gabriel's welcoming face. I had no use for nice-looking men. One in my life had been plenty.

Debbie handed over the packing list we'd put together at the center, and Maria studied it, then added a few items of her own. "Does everyone have their passports?" she asked.

"Only two don't," Debbie said, "and they're at the post office today putting a rush order on them."

"Very good." Maria's eyes were mostly dry now. She hadn't turned the picture of her brother back toward her, and I refrained from taking another peek. "I'll think about going with you, but I really don't think I should." Her voice trembled slightly. "I have a feeling Gabriel is extending his stay because of me."

Before I could stop myself from prying, I said, "Whatever for?" The smiling brother and sister duo in the picture seemed to be in perfect harmony.

"I think I annoy him when I talk so much about Rhea. I just want him to open up and know I'm always here to listen. I read in a divorce-recovery book that it's important to have at least one person you can confide in—a safe person. But the more I talk, the more quiet he becomes." She lowered her voice. "He snapped at me when I mentioned that Rhea would be willing to get back together if he was."

I almost laughed. Of course he'd snap. And it didn't surprise me in the least that Gabriel found it easier to just not say anything when asked so many questions. Men were typically like that. Especially Phillip. I often wondered what Phillip talked about with his lovers. Or did they just silently commune, grateful for a break from the spouse?

Debbie started dishing out advice and soothing Maria's worries, so I just listened for a moment.

"That's why I'm hesitating on visiting Greece," Maria said, despite Debbie's fervent assurances. "What if my presence sets him back even more?"

I glanced at the picture of Gabriel again. He didn't look like a particularly fragile man. No, he looked quite the opposite. Healthy, sensible, happy. Confident. I wondered if the picture was taken before or after the divorce, but I didn't dare ask.

I really couldn't offer any advice, but I did anyway. I'd never met Gabriel, and I'd only spent a few minutes with Maria. "Why don't you call him and ask him?" I said.

If there was anything I'd learned from my years and years of a failed marriage, it was that tiptoeing around something wasn't really going to make anything better. Of course that was much easier advice to give out than to take.

"Call?" Maria said.

"It's just that e-mails can be so impersonal. If you call him, you'll at least benefit from hearing his tone of voice—no matter what his answer, you'll know for sure. An e-mail might leave you still doubting."

Maria clasped her hands together and gazed at me. It was as if she saw me in a new light. "I'll call him tonight." The light was back in her eyes.

Debbie smiled at me and patted my hand.

By the time we left, Maria was back to her cheerful self. She'd promised both Debbie and me that she'd call Gabriel and let us know what he said.

On the drive back to the center, I let Debbie chatter about something to do with making sure everyone received a copy of the packing list as soon as possible and wouldn't it be wonderful if Maria came with us too.

It would be wonderful. I found that I really liked Maria—even if she was interfering in her brother's life. It might be interesting to know Gabriel's side of the story. I pursed my lips tightly together. I wasn't interested in Gabriel's secrets; they could stay where they were. I'd kept enough of my own in my life, and I didn't need to share in anyone else's.

* * *

With all the busyness surrounding preparations for Greece, time flew by, and March book-club night arrived before I knew it.

Shannon had called, telling me she was bringing her stepdaughter, Keisha, again. But when they were late, I began to feel more and more nervous with each minute. Keisha had been through drug rehab twice, and although Shannon promised Keisha had made a huge turnaround and looked so different from when I'd seen her last month, I wondered if something had happened with Keisha to make them late.

All the other ladies arrived on time, but I was still waiting for Shannon. I couldn't sit in the living room with the idle chitchat, so I waited in the kitchen, looking out the window and listening to the women's voices filtering from the living room. One burst of laughter was followed by another. It warmed my heart that we were all becoming such great friends. I hoped Shannon would feel that way too.

Minutes later, Shannon's car pulled up, and Keisha was with her. I exhaled with relief. When Shannon stepped out, I immediately noticed she'd worn something other than scrubs; I could hardly believe it. It looked like she was carrying dessert—if the covered platter in her hand was any indication.

I'd never admit that I'd made brownies as a backup and had french vanilla ice cream in the freezer. It wasn't that I didn't think Shannon would come through, but I knew how busy she was with work, her son's basketball schedule, and now Keisha in her home.

I spent too much time dwelling on the dessert Shannon carried and didn't reach the door in time to open it for them. Shannon and Keisha had knocked once and let themselves in just as I came into the hall. They looked harried, as if they knew they were the last ones to arrive.

"Come in, come in," I said and hugged both of them.

Shannon smiled back—definitely a nervous smile, which I hoped would change soon. I offered to take the dessert into the kitchen so Shannon could join the ladies. I felt her hesitation, but to my surprise, she agreed and went into the living room by herself.

Keisha walked into the kitchen with me. "Your house is so great. I love it."

I smiled at her—hoping she was looking toward a future and thinking of a day when she'd get married and have her own place. "Do you like to decorate?"

"If I had the money for it," she said. "And the place."

I laughed. "Someday you'll get there—just keep working hard."

She smiled broadly and walked over to the window, peering into the side yard. She *was* really interested, although I shouldn't have been surprised. She certainly seemed to be a bright and energetic girl, and I did have a unique home. I'd made several adjustments to the house plans when we were building. I was tempted to give her the full tour, but now wasn't the time.

I heard the murmured greetings surrounding Shannon as I placed the platter on the top shelf of the refrigerator. I wasn't sure if it needed to be refrigerated, but just in case . . . I lifted a corner of the foil and peeked. Blonde brownies—and they didn't look half bad. I wondered if she'd intended to serve them without ice cream. She hadn't carried anything else in with her.

Well, well. It *was* a bit unconventional, but who was I to complain? Shannon was here, looking presentable and perhaps even a bit excited.

"Let's go in," I said to Keisha.

I walked into the living room and sat next to Tori, who'd saved me a spot on the couch. Keisha found a place next to Shannon.

"Welcome, everyone," I started. "As you know from my e-mails, Daisy is still on bed rest and won't be here today. I offered to have it at her place again, but she was very reluctant." I hoped to have time to stop in and visit Daisy before the Greece trip. "Anyway, now that Shannon is here, let's get started." I looked at her with a smile. "Why don't you lead us off, dear?"

Her face pinked, but she jumped right in as if she'd prepared for this moment. "I thought I'd ask if anyone had any questions about the medical events that took place." She gripped her hands together on her lap but kept a steady gaze on all of us.

"I think I was lost half of the time," Tori said with a laugh. "My brain can compute production schedules but not so much how the different parts of cells work. It's amazing—and terrifying—to try to comprehend how anything that small could be so destructive."

"And *constructive*," Paige added. I smiled at her with encouragement. "Even though they were cancer cells, they spearheaded many important discoveries. I found the whole thing absolutely fascinating."

Athena spoke next. "I found it so interesting to note that if any of the factors had been missing when they harvested Henrietta's cells, it might have been another failed attempt, and all the advances that have happened because of the Hela cells would perhaps never have become a reality."

Shannon nodded enthusiastically. I was pleased to see her so responsive to what the others were saying.

"It was interesting to read about the doubts that medical professionals had about the main doctor"—Tori looked down at her book—"Gey. He was revolutionizing medicine, and yet so many people discounted him."

I leaned back into the couch, relieved to hear the discussion between Tori and Shannon. I wasn't sure how Tori would react to the horrific things done in history to the "colored" people in the name of medical science.

"And this certainly isn't the only example of doctors who dealt with that type of thing," Shannon continued, sounding very excited to discuss something she had expertise in. "William Harvey was a doctor in the seventeenth century who first introduced the concept of blood circulating through the body, and the medical world considered it a ridiculous theory. Josiah Nott introduced the possibility that mosquitoes were responsible for transferring diseases like malaria and yellow fever. He was completely discounted for fifty years before his ideas were given any credence, which was one of the single largest discoveries regarding pathology and has affected billions of people. Medicine is such a transitional field, with things changing and new ideas being acknowledged all the time. Henrietta's story is one more example of the need for an open mind and skilled ability to test and prove theory."

Many of the women nodded.

"I also found it interesting that despite the eventual tragedy for Henrietta, she went to the right doctor at the right time," Tori said. "I don't know that any other hospital could have done what Johns Hopkins did back in the 1950s."

Shannon agreed, then said, "Even with all the mistakes along the way and the breakdown of ethics, Henrietta left behind an incredible legacy that has changed the world."

"But an unwilling legacy," Tori said.

I stiffened, wondering what Tori might say next. She had every right to be infuriated by the treatment of her people—even if she wasn't African American—because it still hurt to consider it.

"I think this is one of the most important books of our century," I said.

A look of surprise crossed Shannon's face.

"Really." I hurried on. "It's amazing how Henrietta's contribution has led to saving millions of lives and treating even more people. Her story should be required reading in every high school."

"I would have loved to read it in high school," Keisha said. "Of course it wasn't published until last year."

Several of us nodded.

Keisha leaned toward me and whispered, "Can I use your bathroom?"

"Of course, dear. Just down the hall." She was gone in a flash, and I turned back to the book-club conversation.

Paige was discussing how God's plan was sometimes not apparent from the beginning.

Ilana scrunched her face a bit, then said, "The development of modern medicine was a rocky road, but it had so many breakthroughs along the way." She glanced down at her arm still in a sling. "I mean, with my arm, what they've been able to fix is remarkable when you think about it." She looked over at Shannon. "Although, now they explain things a little more before surgery. It made me sick to think of how they didn't inform the women about the side effects of those surgeries. Henrietta had a real shock when she found out she'd been made infertile."

Tori broke in before Shannon could answer. "But getting rid of her cancer was more important than having another baby."

"But they *didn't* get rid of her cancer," Ilana said, her voice trembling.

"Still, I couldn't believe Henrietta said she wouldn't have done the surgery if she'd known she wouldn't be able to have any more children," Tori said. "I mean, Henrietta was a little bit crazy to even think that. Her life was more important than having more babies. She already had five."

Ilana pursed her lips together as if biting back a reply.

"Women have to make hard choices sometimes," I said, not sure why Ilana was so upset. I didn't want to rely on Shannon to steer the conversation away from this, so I patted my book and said, "It broke my heart when Henrietta's daughter talked to the author in that first phone call."

I leafed through my book until I reached the earmark. Everyone was quiet, waiting, so I decided to read a little of Deborah's reaction to the author's questions. "Here, Deborah says, 'You know what I really want? I want to know, what did my mother smell like? For all my life, I just don't know anything, not even the little common little things, like, what color did she like? Did she like to dance? Did she breastfeed me? Lord, I'd like to know that.'"

No one said anything for a moment, and when I looked up, I felt the tears burning at the back of my eyes. We all had a mother—love her or hate her—and we at least had known our own mothers.

"How old was Deborah when her mother died?" Tori asked.

Shannon answered that Deborah was the baby of the family, but she didn't know how old Deborah was when Henrietta died.

Olivia's voice was quiet when she added, "Henrietta was only thirty-one when she died, I think."

Athena started typing something on her Blackberry. "Deborah was born in 1949, two years before her mother died."

"No wonder Deborah didn't remember her," Ilana said, more subdued now. Maybe her elbow was hurting.

"How tragic," Olivia, who had been fairly quiet during the whole discussion, said. "At least with my mother, I knew her . . . Of course that means that I miss her even more. But I do have the memories and the heavenly reminders."

Athena wiped at her eyes, and the room grew quiet for a moment, everyone thinking of Athena's recent loss.

Keisha came into the room, back from the bathroom. She'd heard the end of the conversation. "Deborah sounded like a hillbilly."

I inhaled but didn't say anything. Even if Deborah had no education, it wasn't fair to call her a hillbilly. No one else seemed to be cringing though.

"She wasn't well educated, and she lived in poverty her whole life," Shannon said. "And yet, people were making millions off the tissues they biopsied from her mother while Henrietta's children couldn't get health insurance."

Still reading that tiny Blackberry screen, Athena said, "Deborah passed away in 2009. She never even saw the book in print."

"That's so sad," I said, feeling even worse now. I flipped to the copyright page of my book and stared at the 2010 date printed there.

"At least she knew about it, and she probably read a draft," Tori said. She brushed her fingers through her long dark hair. "It would have been nice for her to see the book come out and to know about its success though."

"Are any of the other children still alive?" I asked.

Athena scrolled through her phone. "It looks like two sons are."

When the conversation turned to the relationship between Henrietta and her cheating husband, my stomach dropped.

Olivia spoke up. "I wonder what would have happened if she'd lived. Would they have stayed together, do you think?"

"I bet they would have," Athena said, turning her phone over on her lap. "Times were different back then, and Henrietta knew Day was unfaithful all along. I think it was much more common in that generation for women to turn a blind eye to infidelity."

I nearly scoffed, but instead, I straightened, suddenly self-conscious of my posture—as if anyone could tell a discarded woman by the way she sat. Out the corner of my eye, I saw Shannon look at me, but I didn't meet her gaze. I was afraid my expression would give something away—which was ridiculous because Shannon knew nothing.

Yet, I was surprised to hear Shannon comment on the fact that even though Day had been with plenty of other women, he certainly loved Henrietta a lot.

Why was Shannon still looking at me? I bit back a retort. She didn't know anything about Phillip's indiscretions, but it made me crazy when she tried to make excuses for Henrietta's husband.

"I agree," Paige said in a soft voice.

Now I was surprised. Paige's ex-husband was a known creep—having an affair then divorcing her and marrying the "other woman," leaving her to raise their two small sons.

Paige cleared her throat, her face reddening as everyone looked at her. Surely she knew we were all surprised. She looked down at her book, thumbing through the pages. "Remember how he took her to the hospital every day so she could be treated for pain? And when not having her children nearby upset her too much, he kept the kids right outside, under her window, so she could at least see them? I thought that was very sweet. Maybe he just didn't know another way to live."

I looked down at my red-painted nails and picked at the edges. Maybe Paige did have a point. But did that make up for the unfaithfulness? Could anything make up for it?

Shannon said she had wondered about it too, concluding with, "Their lives were a bit dysfunctional, but Henrietta seemed to be an overall happy person."

"Because she chose to be that way," Tori broke in. I looked over at her but not before noticing Ilana's frown. Tori continued to talk about the harsh trials Henrietta had dealt with, then said, "I think she was a very strong, optimistic person. Maybe it's not so surprising that a woman like that would leave such a mark on the world—even if it took fifty years for the world to know it. Maybe the cells she left behind were the only way the world would notice this black woman from the South who was so easily discounted by the times."

Shannon complimented Tori on her point, then Shannon leaned forward and talked about how Henrietta made the best out of her trials. I was impressed when Shannon added, "She lived her life with such a great attitude and left that legacy for her children while at the same time creating opportunity for the world. She worked hard, and she loved her family. Even though they didn't know the impact she had on medicine, they knew the impact she had on them."

I breathed out, trying to steady my emotions. That was all any of us could do. To do what Henrietta had done and keep a good attitude. I looked around at the women in the book club, knowing a good deal of their challenges and thinking of what possible challenges Keisha, as a young woman, had ahead of her. Henrietta had done it, but that didn't mean it was easy. Just that it was possible.

"She changed the world," Olivia said with a smile. "How many people can say that?"

"Mothers can," Paige said with a quick nod and smile at Olivia. "Mothers have that kind of impact on the lives of their children. All of society starts with a child's mother."

I glanced over at Ilana. She was the only married woman here without a child. She was looking at the floor, and my heart went out to her. I hoped this conversation wasn't making her uncomfortable.

"I'm really glad you chose this book, Shannon," Tori said, pulling my thoughts away from Ilana. I smiled at Tori, thrilled she was complimenting Shannon. "I learned so much."

I could tell Shannon was pleased.

Everyone else chimed in their thanks, then Olivia said, "I wonder what Hela will do in the future." She glanced at me. "I mean, it's done so many great things already; I wonder where it will go from here."

The ladies chimed in with their thoughts on possible cures and advancing medical research, some of them using terms I'd never heard of. The younger generation seemed to know more than I ever did at their age.

Things were wrapping up, but before everyone started to leave, Athena said, "So, Ruby, do you have any trips planned?"

Athena was so obvious, and I bit back a smile. I guess it was time to make my big announcement. "Well, actually, yes, I do have a trip planned. I'll be going to Greece on a two-week tour"—I switched to a conspiratorial whisper—"with a group of people I met at the senior center."

Athena grinned from across the room. She was the only one who had known in advance.

"You are?" Shannon said, surprise obvious in her voice. "When are you going?"

"We leave March 10." I sent a reassuring look Shannon's way. I could tell she had a dozen questions, but Tori jumped in first.

"How lovely!" Tori said. "I've heard that Greece is *gorgeous.*"

"There's nothing like the Greek isles," Athena said. "Anytime my mother heard someone say Disneyland was the happiest place on earth, she would lean over and tell me that was only because they'd never been to Greece."

We all laughed. "I'd certainly take Greece over Disneyland," Shannon said.

I could attest to that. Shannon had no patience at all for a zoo like Disneyland. I'd taken Tony plenty of times but usually with a friend so he'd have someone to run around with.

"Not me," Keisha said, shaking her head. "There aren't any princesses in Greece to sign my Mickey Mouse autograph book. Though there are a lot of hot guys if *Mamma Mia* is true to life."

I'd heard of the movie remake of *Mamma Mia*. I made a mental note to watch it before going on the tour. Pierce Brosnan was a fine-looking gentleman. Not my type though—too much the ladies' man like Phillip.

"Yes, I went there many years ago with my husband." I clasped my hands together. "It will be a nice treat to visit it again, and I should still be able to find time to read our next book—whatever that is."

"Do you have a Kindle?" Ilana asked. "They're great for travel; you can take thousands of books with you for less than a pound."

"Oh dear, I don't want thousands," I said, but the others just chuckled. "Just one would be good, maybe two. I worry those things—are they called e-readers?—are hard to use." A regular old book was anything but complicated.

"Or you could invest in an iPad," Tori added. "It's more like a small computer. Then you can e-mail us updates and pictures and not worry about trying to find a computer. I have mine in the car if you'd like me to get it and show you how it works. It's very user-friendly."

"Oh, I'd absolutely love an iPad," Paige said. "My boys would go crazy over it."

"The Kindle is pretty easy to learn. I could show you how to work it," Ilana said, holding up her Kindle.

Tori stood. "Ilana, why don't you take my place, and you can show Ruby the Kindle."

Shannon excused herself to go get the dessert, and Olivia followed her out.

Ilana brought her Kindle over and showed me the dozens of books she already had loaded on it. I took it in my hands. "It's so light."

Ilana showed me a few more ins and outs. The hour had flown past like usual. I wondered what was taking Shannon and Olivia so long in the kitchen. Well, it wasn't their turn to choose the next book anyway. "Tori," I said. "You can choose our next book."

She looked at me in surprise. Maybe I should have let her know a little earlier. But her eyes brightened, and she said, "I have the perfect book. *The War of Art* by Steven Pressfield."

Just then Shannon and Olivia brought in the dessert. Shannon had cut up the brownies and dished up vanilla ice cream as well. It took me a second to realize the ice cream had come from my own freezer. Maybe Olivia had suggested it. I smiled at Olivia with renewed appreciation. She always thought of the extra touches.

Athena was already typing in her Blackberry.

"I read it a couple of years ago, but I'm due for another reading," Tori said.

"It's that good?" I asked.

"It's that *important*." Her complexion glowed. "It's about following your dreams and not letting anything stop you."

I smiled at Tori. How sweet. I used to have dreams . . . but they sort of faded away in marriage and managing the household. Now I just wanted to stay busy and productive so I wouldn't have to dwell on the past so much.

Tori looked over at Shannon. "And it's another nonfiction book."

Shannon said she was interested, and I was pleased that she seemed more comfortable with the group.

"*The War of Art* it is," I said.

Tori added a couple more things about why she loved the book so much. I wondered how many times she'd read it—sounded a bit hokey to me.

"And it's on Kindle," Athena added when she could get a word in. "*The War of Art: Break through the Blocks and Win Your Inner Creative Battles.*"

It didn't sound entirely interesting to me, but I didn't want to put a damper on anyone's enthusiasm. I'd had enough of self-help books; I had never found one to fix my broken marriage. "Well, it's settled, then. And I'll have a full report on Greece at our April meeting."

Chapter 7

I HOPED THE SLEEPING PILL would do wonders on the flight from New York to Athens. I was also grateful that we were somewhat spread out on the international leg. As much as I loved to chat with everyone, I was exhausted and needed my space, if only for a short time.

It was hard to believe I was on my way to Greece, but there was no turning back now.

Everything about this flight—and the trip—had been completely different so far from my last trip over with Phillip. The senior group was all booked into coach class. Phillip had always insisted on first class, and I didn't want to act superior around my new friends, so I meekly followed everyone into the coach section, even though I'd hoped for a random upgrade at the gate. Lark helped Debbie and me load our bags in the overhead compartment, then went to find his own seat.

"Would you like the window?" Debbie asked.

I had requested the window seat, but at the hope in Debbie's voice, I changed my mind. "I don't mind the middle. Why don't you take the window."

I was rewarded with a broad smile. I glanced down the aisle as Debbie settled in. Lark was a few rows back—in the "men's section," as Maria had called it. Lark nodded toward me and the man sitting next to him—Carson, I think—and smiled. I wasn't sure what Carson's last name was. Everyone just called him Carson.

He'd sat behind us on the domestic flight and had been chatty with me. He was a pleasant fellow. He seemed a few years older than me and had retained most of his gray-blond hair. But I definitely didn't want to chat now. Debbie had told me more than once that he always flirted with the new ladies. As far as I was concerned, I could enjoy talking to him but wasn't interested in any flirting, so I kept our conversation very casual.

I sat next to Debbie, and once the captain's welcome and safety demonstration was over, I pulled my sleeping mask over my eyes. Even if I wasn't able to fall asleep right away, I hoped to remain undisturbed. Debbie stayed remarkably quiet, and I took that as a good sign.

I tried to empty my mind of all thoughts so I could sleep. I had double- and triple-checked my list while packing, so I knew I hadn't forgotten any items. Besides, we were going to a completely modern country, where I could purchase just about anything.

As the plane leveled out from its ascension and the seat belt sign chimed off, I let out a sigh. There was no turning back now. I was really going to Greece.

I thought of the package Maria had given me at the airport for her brother. She had changed her mind at the last possible minute about going. There had been no time to explain, but by the redness of her eyes, I guessed there was some sort of disagreement between her and Gabriel.

I pursed my lips together, thinking of it. Having Maria on the trip would have been great, and now it seemed that Gabriel had said something to dash her spirits. He would be quite surprised to not only receive a package from his dear sister but to also receive a talk from me. I hated saying anything negative to someone, but the image of Maria's expression wouldn't leave my mind. I could understand where he might feel that his sister was overbearing, but she had a wonderful heart and only wanted the family closer.

I hoped that having a purpose as soon as I arrived in Greece would help ease the transition. I knew that if I could make it through the first twenty-four hours in Athens, I'd be fine. I just had to get through the first day.

* * *

I waited for it to hit me—memories, sorrow, nostalgia, something. I even found myself gripping my carry-on until my hand hurt. I waited, but nothing made me want to rush to the bathroom. The Athens airport smelled like any other airport, and nothing triggered my senses.

Debbie and Lark walked in front of me along the terminal, eagerly pointing out the signs all written in Greek. Debbie stopped in front of one, looking back and forth between the Greek words and the other languages.

We made a few stops on the way as some in our little group went to the restrooms, then grabbed drinks at the airport café.

While we were waiting for our baggage, a man with a cigarette dangling from his mouth came in through the doors with a sign that read *Newport Seniors.*

"That must be us," I said.

Those around me turned.

I studied the man for a moment before he looked over and saw us. Could that be Gabriel? If so, he was much shorter than I'd imagined. He was a few inches shorter than my five-foot, six-inch frame. He wore a dark red cap pulled over his dark hair, which looked quite curly.

"Newport Seniors?" he called out in broken English, then smiled when a few people stepped forward, waving at him. I didn't think it was Gabriel. Maria didn't have an accent, so it was doubtful her brother did. Then who was it?

"The bus is waiting, okay? It's red and white." He waved toward the outside doors. "Outside there, okay?"

Just then the first suitcase thumped onto the conveyer belt.

Fortunately, I had tied the handle of my suitcase with a bright yellow ribbon—it made it very easy to find in the mass of dark cases coming toward us.

Lark and the other men were pulling off cases the ladies were pointing out. Debbie's came barreling down right before mine. Lark pulled hers, then mine from the conveyer.

We moved to the outside doors, and the heat blasted in as they slid open. I hadn't realized how pleasantly air conditioned the airport had been. The red-and-white bus was at the curb, and the man in the red cap leaned against it, a new cigarette in his mouth.

As soon as he saw us exit, he sprang into action and opened the understorage doors to load our suitcases.

"Others come in two hours," the man said. "They fly from Amsterdam. Don't worry, okay? I drive you to hotel first, okay?"

We climbed onto the bus; it was a bit cooler inside the bus at least. The man in the red cap settled into the driver's seat when everyone was on board. He spoke into the mic. "I'm Bruno, your driver. Or call me Bruce— like American, okay?" He chuckled into the mic. "Welcome to Athens. Welcome! We go to the hotel now." Static came on for a few seconds while he turned off the mic.

I smiled at the frequency of Bruno's using "okay" at the end of his sentences. He must have thought that was what we Americans did.

We traveled in snarled traffic to the Ariston Hotel. The white marble façade looked very clean and comfortable. I held my breath for a moment, wondering if the memories would wash over me now and leave me staggering.

Again, there was nothing. Just the feeling of wanting to rest before dinner, though I knew I'd first have to face Gabriel. I pulled out the compact from my bag and glanced in the mirror. I smoothed my hair and applied a bit of Chapstick. I didn't want to look too ragged.

Bruno stopped in front of the hotel, then waved us all off the bus and started unloading our baggage with the help of a porter. Once we were all in the lobby, I sat on one of the wide, pale-gray couches while the others checked in at the front desk. One thing I'd insisted on was my own room. Debbie had invited me to be her roommate, but I knew the only way I'd have any time to myself was if I had my own room.

I glanced around casually, waiting for the appearance of Gabriel, but he wasn't to be seen. I tuned into what the bus driver was saying—something about the restaurant inside the hotel and the always-open bar. "Mr. Alexakis will be here for cocktails. Five o'clock, okay?"

Ha. So I'd have to wait to meet Gabriel, and my carefully planned lecture would be delayed. It was just as well. I needed something horizontal to lie on.

A few people asked questions I couldn't quite hear, and after Bruno answered them, he said, "Now I go to pick up the next group."

I was the last to check in, so by the time the porter accompanied me to my room, the hallway was empty.

When the porter shut the door, I crossed to the window that overlooked a small balcony. Opening the sliding door, I stepped outside. The bustle and heat of the city reached me from below, and I watched the traffic for a few minutes, still waiting for something to hit me. But all I felt was tired and relieved that we'd arrived safely. And very grateful that I'd decided to get my own room. The personal space was bliss. Since Phillip's passing, I'd grown used to a quiet, empty house.

A yawn took over my thoughts, and I stepped back into the hotel room, pulling the balcony door shut behind me. I looked at the itinerary I'd printed off before leaving Newport. We'd spend two nights in this hotel. Tonight, at five, like Bruno told us, was the cocktail meet-and-greet.

I wasn't sure how the greeting would go when fifteen of us were American and the rest Dutch. I didn't think I knew a single Dutch word. Phillip and I had never visited Holland.

I pulled the taupe-colored linen drapes closed, and the room was virtually dark. I didn't even mind the street noise coming in as I sank against the pillows. My cell phone alarm was set for two hours from now, and I intended to make the most of those two hours.

* * *

The cocktail meet-and-greet was in full swing when I stepped into the hotel's restaurant. I had taken the extra time to shower and press the outfits I'd be wearing over the next couple of days.

I wore a turquoise linen blouse with matching earrings I'd purchased in San Diego. With white pants and sandals, I felt very much the tourist. Debbie was already pairing up people and taking pictures, and it seemed that, with smiles and drinks in hand, they were more than happy to comply. The other part of our group was markedly sitting apart from the Americans. But as I watched, Debbie made her rounds with a big smile, drawing the newcomers into posing with the rest.

I couldn't help being impressed by Debbie's antics. I released a breath; this wasn't going to be so hard, I decided. I'd made it this far. Phillip had stayed buried back in California. There was nothing of him in Greece, and I hoped to enjoy the vacation without worry.

Debbie saw me and waved me over. I started walking toward her, returning her smile, when her gaze shifted to something behind me.

"Gabriel!" she called out.

I stopped as she rushed past me.

"It's wonderful to see you," she said.

A male voice murmured something, and I turned around just in time to see Debbie embrace the man.

It only took seconds to understand why Lark had been so quiet around Debbie lately and even less time to realize the picture of Gabriel in the Newport travel office did him very little justice. Yes, he had the same dark eyes and the same tanned skin. He was taller than I had assumed, his eyes were warm—like the swirling chocolate in a Hershey's commercial—and he was easily the most striking man in the room. And he was staring right at me over Debbie's shoulder.

I looked down, or maybe to the left or right, I wasn't sure which, but I couldn't exactly meet his gaze. The lecture I had so carefully prepared seemed silly and trite when I imagined delivering it to the man standing only a few feet away from me.

"Oh, you must meet my dear friend," Debbie was saying.

I had to look up—I could only fiddle with my purse for so long. I wasn't even sure why I brought the thing downstairs, except I never entirely felt safe being away from my purse in a foreign country.

Gabriel smiled and extended his hand. I wasn't sure what he said, but his voice was low and mellow, like he had all the time in the world to stand around and chat. I raised my hand and grasped his, then pulled away quickly, ignoring the warmth and confidence I felt in his handshake. It confused me a bit—wasn't he supposed to be a depressed divorcé?

He looked anything but depressed as he greeted the others who came up to him—many of them seemed to be old friends. I stole a few glances as he made his rounds through the entire tour group, welcoming everyone with a handshake and a few words.

I thought of the wrapped package in my room and the sad woman who had delivered it to me. The worry Maria had expressed about her brother didn't mesh with who I saw milling about the room. Maybe there were more reasons why he didn't want her to come to Greece. Maybe Maria was right about what she told us in the office—maybe he had a girlfriend.

Gabriel sure bent to kiss plenty of ladies' cheeks. I knew it was customary in Greece, but I still wondered . . . He seemed awfully at ease with these women, paying them pretty compliments that made them blush and stand a little straighter.

I cleared my thoughts. It was really none of my concern. I'd give him Maria's package, enjoy my trip, and let everyone live their own lives. The more I watched Gabriel, the less I wanted to interfere. Every bit of my courage had fled. I was seriously considering leaving the package outside his door, knocking, and running.

Did he have a room in the hotel too? For some reason, the thought had my pulse racing, and I felt much too hot. I walked over to the bar and ordered something that resembled an American piña colada.

Had I really planned to give Gabriel, a virtual stranger, a piece of my mind? I wrapped my fingers around the glass, letting the cold penetrate my hands and spread to my arms.

"Maria has told me so much about you," a man said next to me.

It couldn't be. He was just on the other side of the room. I turned my head and glanced at Gabriel to be polite. Then I looked down at my drink.

"Maria is *wonderful*," I said. It was as close as I could get to a lecture right now—especially with all of these people around.

"I'm very lucky," he said, then paused as if waiting for me to say more.

Why was he pausing? I was about to ask why he'd told her to remain in the States when someone else came up. Carson.

He put his hand on my arm, moving between Gabriel and me. "Ruby, I was wondering when you were coming down."

I just smiled. As much as I didn't want to be the object of Carson's flirting, this particular instance was convenient. I sensed Gabriel looking back and forth between us, but I wasn't about to explain why I was late. If I was going to mind my own business, then I'd make others mind theirs as well.

"We have room for one more at our table," Carson said, his hand on my arm increasing its pressure.

"All right," I said. And just like that, I was away from Gabriel. I didn't talk to him the rest of the evening, and by the time I was back in my hotel room, I'd neglected to tell him about the package from his sister.

* * *

One positive aspect of jet lag was that you got to watch the sun rise. Although, waking up at 4:00 a.m. was a little early for even the best of the sunrise enthusiasts.

I dressed in a public-approved jogging suit (not that I ever actually jogged) and grabbed my new iPad. Tori had talked me into making the purchase and had come over a couple of days ago before the trip to show me how to use it. It had also been the perfect opportunity to get her alone to drill her about the on-goings of the set for *Vows*. I'd never really cared for bachelor-bachelorette-type shows, but with Tori's inside information, I'd become hooked. From a purely technical viewpoint, of course.

Entering the deserted lobby, I told the desk clerk I'd like some tea delivered. The woman picked up the phone to place the order, and I settled on one of the couches. It was pleasantly quiet; the only sound was that of a few passing cars.

I sent a quick e-mail to Kara and Tony, as well as the book-club ladies, informing them of my safe arrival and a few bits of trivia. My fingers hovered over the miniature keyboard as I considered mentioning Gabriel. I decided there was no harm in it, so I simply typed, "Met the tour guide,

Gabriel. He's very personable, like his sister Maria, who heads up the travel agency in Newport."

I had the sudden urge to pour out my thoughts about how he was treating his sister, but instead, I hit send. I didn't want to have to field multiple questions from everyone—since I didn't have the answers anyway.

Exiting out of my e-mail account, I opened the Kindle app. I marveled at the technology that could let me carry so many books with me. I had downloaded a few Georgette Heyer novels; it was like a small-measure comfort from home. I had started reading one of them on the plane ride, but at the moment, I figured I should get started on the next book-club selection. It seemed to be a bit of a heavy-hitter.

The War of Art by Steven Pressfield. Well, Tori had said it was a wonderful, fast read, but nonfiction was always a little slow-going for me. The first page told me immediately that this book was for the creative types—writers or artists. Definitely something that would interest Tori. She'd confessed her dream of becoming a writer when she helped set up my iPad. She was such a sweet woman, though, that I knew I shouldn't complain and should be more open-minded.

I read a few pages, mildly interested—this Steven fellow did have an engaging narrative voice—then I stopped. "Most of us have two lives. The life we live and the unlived life within us. Between the two stands Resistance."

Something warm spread through me, not comfortable warmth but prickly, uncomfortable warmth. Like the knowledge that if anyone had ever lived two lives, it was me. I scrolled back to the beginning of the book to check the complete title again: *The War of Art: Winning the Inner Creative Battle.* It was for artist types—not me. This Steven fellow couldn't possibly be talking to someone like me.

I let out a sigh, louder than I'd intended.

And that's when I heard footsteps hitting the tiled floor behind me. My tea was here, but when I turned, it wasn't the desk clerk.

I found myself staring into Gabriel's dark eyes.

"Bad news?" he said.

Confused, I said, "What do you mean?"

He rounded the couch I was sitting on. "Your sigh. I thought you were reading something unhappy." His gaze landed on the iPad. "Is that an iPad 2?"

"I think so," I said, although I wasn't entirely sure. Were there two types of iPads? "I'm just learning how to use it. Bought it right before the trip."

I noticed he held a rather tattered paperback in his hand. "Nothing bad happened. I'm just reading for my book club. It's not really my favorite genre."

Gabriel nodded like he understood and had read plenty of books that weren't his favorite genre.

He settled on the couch across from me and opened his book. I glanced down at the iPad, expecting him to continue the conversation he'd started. When he actually began reading and didn't say anything else, I was surprised. And miffed.

Now that he was effectively minding his own business, or ignoring me, depending how I looked at it, I realized I wouldn't mind talking to him a little more. I wanted to see if my assessment of him was true. So far everything I had thought about him on the flight over wasn't exactly matching up to the actual person.

For instance, he was reading a book at . . . I checked the time on the iPad . . . nearly 5:00 a.m. Breakfast for the group wasn't until 7:00 a.m., and *he* didn't have jet lag. I realized I was studying him quite openly and quickly focused on my e-book before he caught me staring.

My tea arrived, and when the desk clerk asked Gabriel if he wanted anything, he politely declined. He continued to read as if completely absorbed in his book and completely without the need to drink anything. My curiosity increased, and then I suddenly realized something.

"I have a package for you from Maria."

That made him look up.

"Oh, well, thank you for bringing it." He glanced around me.

"It's up in my room. I'll go get it." I bookmarked my page.

"You don't have to go right this moment," Gabriel said, but I was already standing. "I'll come with you, then you won't have to bring it down to me. I have to make a few phone calls anyway."

The back of my neck tingled. As long as he didn't set foot inside my room, I supposed it was okay. Not that I thought the tour guide was ready to assault me—especially on the first day. We walked toward the elevator together, and I couldn't think of a thing to say. Even the speech I'd prepared to tell him about his sister was completely gone.

Gabriel didn't seem to feel the same urge to make conversation. In fact, he looked perfectly at ease as he leaned against the wall in the elevator with a slight smile on his face. He didn't look at all worried or depressed or like the heartbroken man Maria had painted him to be. Maybe there was much more to the divorce than Maria had let on. He wasn't really her poor brother; he was her happy and newly freed brother.

My stomach twisted to think that I was in the confined space of an elevator with a man who might possibly be like my husband. I was relieved when the elevator door opened, creating more space between us. Thankfully, he waited out in the hall while I went into my room, and I didn't have to pointedly tell him to remain outside.

By the time I met him again in the hall, I had steeled myself. "Maria was very upset when she gave this to me." I handed over the rectangular package wrapped in floral paper.

Gabriel raised an eyebrow and opened his mouth to respond when someone exited their room down the hall. It looked like a couple of ladies from the Amsterdam group. As soon as they saw Gabriel, they called out a greeting and started walking toward us.

He looked back to me, his expression questioning.

There was no time to explain anymore, and I waved at the oncoming women, then stepped into my room and shut the door. My timing was terrible. Even at 5:00 a.m.

Chapter 8

By BREAKFAST, I WAS YAWNING. Traveling seemed to be catching up with me much quicker at sixty-two than ever before. I hadn't traveled any farther than Arizona since Phillip's death, and the last few years of his life, traveling had been more and more infrequent too.

Debbie and Carson both snagged me at the same time, and I sat with them. Lark was with a couple of Dutch ladies; it seemed he was trying out some rusty Dutch on them. Who knew Dutch anyway? Debbie kept glancing over at Lark's table, and I wanted to tell Lark to stop sulking around her.

I decided no matter how old a person was, they never really left high school behind.

When it came time to load the bus, we all sat in our sections, the Americans versus the Dutch. Only Lark seemed determined to infiltrate the Dutch members, greeting them with an exuberant "Hallo!" every chance he got.

I met Gabriel's gaze as he climbed on the bus, but then I looked away quickly. There was definitely a curious expression on his face, and it probably had something to do with our unfinished conversation. I was glad he was curious. Let him mull it over for a while—all day if necessary. I didn't foresee much of a chance to discuss anything with him alone while the tour was in full force.

We were starting the tour off with a bang and visiting the Acropolis first. A new museum had opened in 2009, so I was definitely looking forward to that.

Gabriel's low voice washed over me as the bus lurched through traffic. "We don't want to overschedule anyone, so each day there will be one main attraction we'll visit, combined with other optional sites. Most are in walking distance of our hotel, but if you do get tired, you can always elect to hop the Metro. Just don't forget the name of our hotel."

Scattered laughter erupted around me. Still, I kept my gaze averted, staring out the window, looking for anything I might recognize. The country as a whole was familiar, although everything seemed more crowded, more modern, and sleeker. The beauty was startling with all of the white buildings set against the brilliance of the blue sky. It must have been the bluest in the world.

I realized I was searching for something—but I wasn't sure what. Something that would trigger my memories here with Phillip. Really, all I remembered was spending a lot of time by myself, jumping on buses to different sites, and reading in my hotel room at night. The memories in Greece were mostly those of wishing my husband weren't so busy and that I had brought our son after all. The painful truth hadn't hit until after we'd returned home.

So maybe I was worrying for nothing. Maybe I could finally relax, forget about the box of memories hidden in my closet, and enjoy this trip for what it was. Gabriel's voice came into focus again, and I relaxed into my seat. It was nice to have someone in charge who wasn't me. I could let Debbie lead me around by the hand, and she'd be content. I had my books on my iPad, and the sun was warm in the brilliant blue sky.

Even with my interest in the scenery we were passing, I kept glancing at Gabriel despite myself. He smiled once when our eyes met, but he smiled at everyone. I could ignore the increase in my heart rate and chalk it up to our future conversation—one he probably wouldn't care much for.

The bus dropped us off at Syntagma Square, and we walked through the Archaeological Park to reach the Acropolis. The tourists were out in full force, but it was a pleasant day, and everyone appeared to be in a good mood.

It seemed Gabriel was taking it slow but somehow managing to keep everyone happy. Those who wanted to spend extra time in the museum did so, and others just sat people-watching.

We ate at the Platanos Taverna, and I was impressed with the quick service and simple yet delicious meal. The roasted lamb and yogurt sauce were even better than I remembered. Carson had followed me to where I sat by a couple of the Dutch ladies. I attempted to make friendly conversation with a lady wearing a huge sun hat and another lady who looked like her sister and was wearing a slightly smaller hat.

"How are you?" I said and told them my name. We exchanged names and seemed to understand each other well enough. The older woman was Hilda, and the younger one, Helda—at least that's what it sounded like. Goodness. I wasn't sure I could keep that straight. After a moment, Carson went to sit by someone else. I guess he couldn't keep them straight either. I noticed Debbie and Gabriel sitting next to each other, seeming to be in a serious conversation. By their glances in my direction, I knew it had to do with what I'd said about Maria.

Sure enough, after a few minutes Gabriel headed my way, his pita sandwich and cappuccino in hand.

"You like Greece?" Hilda asked, tugging at my attention. Her huge sun hat practically shaded everyone around her.

"Very much," I said. "Is this your first time?" I held up one finger.

Both ladies nodded vigorously, then their eyes widened and smiles broke across their faces. It seemed that Debbie wasn't the only one who was all smiles around our tour guide. I knew Gabriel was headed our way but had hoped that he might pass us by.

He sat next to me, with Hilda/Helda across from us. He stuck his hand out. "Hilda and Helda. How's the sandwich?"

So it *was* Helda after all.

"Sand-wich?" Helda said, her eyes absolutely full of adoration for her tour guide.

"Lunch, the food," Gabriel clarified.

She smiled. "Oh, yum, yum."

I couldn't help laughing, which made Hilda/Helda laugh, their mouths full of meat and other things I wished I hadn't glimpsed. Gabriel winked at me. Winked! He didn't seem quite so concerned about his sister now.

He didn't direct any personal comments to me but just talked casually, making sure we were all included in the conversation. As people finished their lunches, a couple more women wandered over and entered into our conversation. They gravitated to Gabriel, who seemed to bask in the attention, which set my back up for reasons that annoyed me. He was certainly surrounded now.

* * *

I was up early the next morning, and with my book in hand, I ventured down to the café to order tea. Gabriel was already there. I hesitated and was about to sneak back to my room when he looked up and saw me.

"I hoped to see you this morning."

For some reason, I suddenly felt breathless. Which was ridiculous. I couldn't possibly be nervous about speaking to my tour guide. And it was definitely time to let him know about how upset his sister had been.

I smiled briefly and sat on the chair across from him. Far enough away to keep my distance but close enough so as not to seem too rude. "Are you set for today?" I didn't know why I was stalling. I noticed he held the same ratty paperback from the day before. I opened up my iPad and selected my own book, waiting for him to speak.

"The tour is like clockwork now," Gabriel said. I felt his eyes on me as he set aside his book. He leaned forward and clasped his hands together, his elbows on his knees. I told myself I didn't notice that his khakis looked nicely pressed. He probably had room service do it.

"I was hoping to talk with you for a few minutes—without everyone around," he said, his gaze practically burning into me.

I looked up. "That's almost impossible."

One side of his mouth lifted in amusement. I hadn't meant to be funny or even remotely clever.

"One of the downfalls of a tour," he said, "is that it's not conducive to really getting to know a person."

What did he mean by that? I refused to ask. I just nodded as if I commiserated with him, although it couldn't possibly be his goal if he were truly trying to recover from a divorce.

"I talked to Maria last night," he said.

This did surprise me. And I couldn't restrain myself any longer. "How is she?"

Gabriel chuckled. "She asked about you too. It seems you made quite an impression on her."

I thought of the tears in Maria's eyes when I last saw her and the fact that the culprit was sitting across from me. "She was really upset. I hope you apologized." My hand flew to my mouth. It was too late to take it back now.

Gabriel simply nodded. "I didn't realize how upset she'd be. When I talked to her several days ago, she said she really didn't have time to come over, so I encouraged her to stay. I guess she really wanted me to beg her."

"I wouldn't exactly say *beg*."

"I'm not too savvy about interpreting the hidden meaning behind a woman's words," Gabriel said, his tone a mixture of sadness and regret.

This surprised me as well. The two-dimensional Gabriel I had pictured was becoming far more complicated. "I don't think there's much to interpret about Maria. She loves her brother, and she misses him." Now I'd put my foot in my mouth.

But Gabriel didn't seem offended or angry. "We've always been close. I think sometimes it bothered Rhea, my ex-wife."

I froze and wanted to look everywhere but at Gabriel. Talking about his ex was getting way too personal. Should I excuse myself before it went any further?

"I'm not sure what Maria said to you . . ." he said.

"Her feelings were plainly hurt, so that probably explains some of the things she told me."

"Like about me seeing other women in Greece while I ignored my duties at home?"

His voice wasn't hostile or defensive, just sad. I nodded.

"It sounds like I probably have some explaining to do."

I was feeling increasingly uncomfortable. Over the past twenty-four hours, I had seen several sides to Gabriel, and I wasn't as motivated to give him a piece of my mind. "You really don't have to explain anything to me."

His gaze held mine as he said in a quiet voice, "We'll be stuck together for a while, and I don't want you thinking I was deliberately mean to my sister."

I let out a breath of air. "I didn't think—"

He held up his hand. "I know—you've been very generous, and I appreciate that you brought the package from . . . Maria. In fact, Maria encouraged me to talk to you about my ex-wife. My sister seems to think I need all the support I can get—although I'm not sure I'm going in the direction my sister wants me to. Maria seems to think Rhea and I should get back together, but my sister only knows part of the story." He reached down below the couch and picked up a bag I hadn't paid attention to before. Gabriel pulled out a book and what looked to be a photo album. Without a word, he handed both of them to me.

I took them reluctantly. The book had a bright orange cover. It took only a glance at the title to tell me it was one of those "save your marriage" books. My mouth went dry. At one point in my marriage, I had read at least a dozen marriage self-help books but had found that if my husband wasn't willing to work on our marriage, it was pointless for me to keep reading advice about how a marriage could be turned around. It wasn't until the very end—the last weeks of his life—that Phillip had begged for forgiveness.

My eyes burned, and I blinked rapidly, trying to dispel the memory of my husband's pleading voice and outstretched hand. I set the orange book down and looked over the photo album. On the cover were two names embossed in gold: Gabriel & Rhea. Was this a wedding album? I really didn't want to open it. I looked up at Gabriel.

"Go ahead," he said. "The pictures will explain more than I can. I think after this you'll realize I'm not hiding from my sister and I'm not secretly dating women in Greece."

My eyes flew to his.

"Oh, yes," he said with a grim smile. "I know everything Maria thinks. She has a hard time holding her tongue." He nodded toward the book in my hands.

With quite a bit of trepidation, I lifted the cover. The first page had the same lettering as the cover, just in black. What was I doing? If this was a wedding album, I'd look at one page, then hand it back to Gabriel. I really didn't want to look at pictures of someone's painful past, especially a stranger's.

My jaw dropped as I turned the page. It was of a lovely dark-haired woman, or what could have been lovely, but her long hair was in snarls, and her eyes looked practically sunken into her face. If no one told me a thing about her, I'd say she looked like a concentration camp victim. Her thin arms seemed to poke out from her shapeless sundress, and her collarbone was so prominent it cast a shadow.

She seemed to be staring right through me, as if whoever had taken the picture hadn't really been there. Despite her garish appearance, what was even more shocking was the picture of Gabriel. It was obvious he wasn't present for the original photo, but his picture had been cropped in, like a bad Photoshop job. Gabriel's looked pretty close to what I'd seen on Maria's desk—in fact, I wouldn't have been surprised if it had been copied from that picture. He was smiling into the camera, but instead of his arm around his sister, it was around his wife.

My stomach tightened, and a feeling of dread seeped through me. Who had created the picture? Maria?

I looked up at Gabriel. "Go ahead and turn the page." His voice was calm, as if the strange picture didn't bother him.

The next page was another Photoshopped picture. This one of Rhea sitting down. But as I looked closer, it was the same photo as the first page, though the legs had been cut and repositioned. Gabriel wasn't right next to her anymore; a couple of inches separated them now. He still had that smile on his face, and Rhea still looked terribly emaciated.

I turned page after page, and I realized it was a message, or a story. Gabriel's and Rhea's pictures were positioned farther and farther apart until Gabriel was missing completely. Rhea's picture was pasted on by itself. Someone had penned in tears running down her cheeks and drawn dollar signs on the page.

The final page contained smiling Gabriel right next to his wife again. There were no drawn tears, but a phone number was scrawled on the page, over and over. It must have been rewritten dozens of times.

Sufficiently creeped out, I closed the album and handed it back to Gabriel. He slipped it into the bag at his feet and leaned back with a sigh.

"What's wrong with her?"

I expected him to tell me she had cancer or even anorexia disorder, but he simply glanced down at his hands. "She has a mental disorder called intermittent explosive disorder."

Chapter 9

I STARED AT GABRIEL. I wasn't sure what intermittent explosive disorder was, but it sounded vastly unpleasant. And violent. The woman in the album looked too frail to harm anything.

"It's linked to several other mental disorders," he said, "but it's kind of a catchall when one can't be specifically assigned. As you might guess by the name, she has periods where she goes into uncontrollable rages. Sometimes with no provocation."

I could only shake my head.

"It started soon after we were married, at least as far as I know, and seemed to get worse every year." His voice went quiet. "But now . . . she says she's starving herself until I come back to her."

"*Starving* herself?" My mouth dropped open. "Why?"

"It's part of her disorder. If she doesn't get what she wants, she goes into destruction mode of either herself or others in order to manipulate." He lowered his head, staring at his hands. "I gave in to her demands for years . . . for more years than I care to remember. But this is by far the most extreme thing she's done." His eyes were on me again, almost pleading for me to understand. "She found out Maria was coming over here—I don't know how she found out—but she was determined to come as well."

"That's why you told Maria to not come."

"Yes," his voice sounded defeated. "She was prepared to follow Maria. She must have brought the gift over on a pretense of sending it with Maria. But she left a phone message of her real plans. I was reluctant to share all of . . . this . . . with Maria." He waved to the bag at his feet. "I've only told her what's necessary. She gets so worried about me and thinks that she can fix things—fix Rhea. But Maria doesn't know the whole story.

I don't know why I've felt obligated to protect Rhea so much; maybe it was the marriage vows."

I knew all about marriage vows and protecting secrets of a spouse. My mind spun. I couldn't grasp the enormity of what he must have dealt with in his marriage. I wished I knew more about the disorder and could offer some consolation. But I couldn't very well start the Google process on my iPad with him sitting across from me. Of course, my biggest question was what he planned to do about it. Or if anything could be done.

He leaned back against the couch and scrubbed his hand through his hair. I knew he was younger than me by a couple of years, but at this moment, he looked at least ten years older. The faint but distinguished lines in his face even seemed deeper.

"I didn't divorce her because of the disorder," he said in quiet voice, so quiet I almost didn't hear him.

"Gabriel," I started, then took a deep breath. "You don't owe me any explanation." I was curious on one hand, but on the other hand, I saw the defeat in his eyes and could practically feel the pain radiating across the space between us.

He stood and crossed over, sitting on the couch by me. "Look, we hardly know each other, but when I saw the mistrust in your eyes yesterday . . ." He looked down at the save-your-marriage book sitting between us. "She had threatened divorce pretty much since the honeymoon. It threw me for a loop at first. But as time went on and I realized each threat was empty, I tried to not let it hurt me."

Instinctively, I put my hand on his arm. He didn't pull away, but he didn't acknowledge it either.

"I convinced her to come with me to a marriage counselor, and that's when he recommended she go through psychiatric testing," he said. "She was angry, flew into a terrible rage at home, then, of course, completely denied she had any disorder. She refused to come with me to counseling after that. It was a couple of years before she was finally diagnosed—the hospital ran some tests when she suffered a miscarriage."

I breathed out; there was so much to take in. "When did Maria find out?" I asked. I felt like I had to say something.

"Not until we were in divorce proceedings. Even then, Maria begged me to stay—it's against the church, she said. I'd burn in hell, she said." He inhaled and looked down at my hand on his arm.

He stopped talking. My eyes started burning. I had only a small glimpse of his marriage, but the pain still seemed fresh.

"I think there are exceptions when a divorce can be acceptable." I had contemplated a divorce more than once with Phillip. Well, many times more. I didn't want to ask, but we'd come this far. "So what was the final straw for you?"

Gabriel was quiet for a moment, and at first I thought he wouldn't answer. It was personal, and maybe I shouldn't have asked.

Then he spoke. "Rhea tried to kill me." A thick pause. "More than once."

My heart froze. I felt like I was listening to a bad CSI episode. These things didn't happen to real people.

"The first time . . . there were so many ways I justified her actions. The disorder. I'd provoked her without meaning to . . . The next time put me in the hospital." He leaned back on the couch, staring across the room. "I've never told anyone about the hospital trip. Not even Maria knows."

I was stunned. I didn't even know what to say. It was nothing like I imagined.

"The doctor who treated the stab wounds counseled me to leave her, to put her in an institution permanently. He wanted me to press charges against my own wife." His voice was bitter—over his wife or the doctor's advice, I wasn't sure which. "She wouldn't have survived in prison."

"Gabriel," I said, putting my hand on his shoulder. "If this is too hard . . ."

"It wasn't until the next . . . attack . . . that I decided enough was enough."

"Did she stab you again?"

"She tried to run me over," he said. "Her license had been revoked several months before, but that hadn't stopped her from driving. I pressed charges, and they put her in lockdown. She refused any sort of medication or counseling. Four weeks later, she was transferred to another institution and was begging me to take her back. By then I had started the divorce papers, and I told myself I couldn't change my mind."

"So you came to Greece?"

"So I came to Greece."

I stared at Gabriel. His dark eyes were hiding great wells of pain—I felt it to my very core. It was unusual to hear about a grown man being abused by a woman—or was that what had happened?

The fact that he told me and hadn't even told his sister the whole story astounded me. The lump in my throat grew. I was at a loss for words. The phone at the registration desk rang, and the receptionist answered it, but the sounds seemed distant, like they belonged in another sphere.

"Now you know the dark side of my life," he said. "I hope you can forgive me and still enjoy your vacation."

I shook my head, and a real look of worry crossed his face. "I think whether or not I'm having a great vacation is the last thing you should worry about."

He looked down at his hands, and I suddenly had an urge to grasp them, to show him there was some kindness out there in the world. But I kept my hands to myself this time.

"I don't know what I can do from here," he said in a faint voice. His gaze went to the bag with the demented photo album in it. "About this new development."

"First of all, you can't do this on your own," I said. "If you're interested, I can help you."

He looked at me, surprised. "You would help me? You hardly know me."

I nodded. "I know more about you than I know about the neighbors I've had for twenty years."

With one hand, he scrubbed his jaw. "It's just so overwhelming sometimes, but you're here to have a great vacation, not get caught up in my mess."

"It might help me out with some of my own things as well," I said.

Surprise, then relief crossed his face, and soon he was nodding. "That would be wonderful," he said in a quiet voice.

I exhaled. I could do this. "All right. First thing you need to do is call social services and tell them everything."

He drew his brows together. "What can they do, force her to eat?"

"Actually, they can. At least with an IV. Rhea needs to be back in an institution getting professional help."

He blew out a breath. "I've been through the rounds many times. They keep her about a week, then discharge her with another round of medications—which she always refuses to take once she's home."

I picked up the bag, taking out the photo album. Using my iPad, I took a few pictures of the photos of Rhea. "What's your e-mail?" I asked him. "I'm sending you these pictures so you can forward them to the social worker as evidence of her deteriorating state of mind. No one should be allowed to starve to death. You shouldn't have to return to an abusive marriage in order to help your ex-wife."

Gabriel just stared at the iPad as I logged into my e-mail and selected the attachments. "How many years were you married to her?"

"Twenty-four."

I blinked back the burning in my eyes again. I knew all about long and miserable marriages. But I knew I could help Gabriel. I pressed send and then went to the Google page and started a search for the family social services agencies in Newport Beach.

"You don't have to do all of this, Ruby," Gabriel said, his voice starting to sound normal again.

"I know," I said. This man needed someone to help him—even if it was a small thing like contacting social services. "I think it's been a long time since you had a friend." I smiled at him, even though I really wanted to cry for him.

The haunted look in his eyes faded a little. "Thank you."

"You are most welcome." I started dialing. It might have been too late for me to rectify my marriage to Phillip, but it wasn't too late for Gabriel to salvage some happiness for himself.

* * *

Day two of the tour seemed a bit subdued, at least on my part. I vacillated between feeling sorry for Gabriel, feeling angry at myself for judging him harshly, and feeling frustrated that it was so hard to get his wife some help.

During the phone conversation with family services, he'd answered a lot of questions, many of them financial. Even though Rhea was now his ex-wife, he'd be paying for her care. And a tour guide in Greece who also owned a business back in the States couldn't exactly be rolling in the dough.

The important thing was to get Rhea to stop harassing Gabriel and to get the proper help. I had also encouraged him to tell Maria everything. He seemed to be considering it.

Climbing onto the tour bus, I noticed that Debbie and Lark were still in a who-can-ignore-each-other-more battle, but I didn't really want to know the specifics. After hearing Gabriel's heartbreaking story, their spat seemed meaningless.

As we drove to the National Archaeological Museum, I pulled up *The War of Art* again and started reading. It seemed I read everything with new eyes now, with Gabriel's situation in mind.

When I turned to the "Resistance and Fear" chapter, I slowed down. This was exactly what Gabriel was facing. He feared his ex-wife's death and that it would be on his shoulders. He was afraid to do the best thing for his wife—but that just emphasized that it *was* the best thing. My eyes pricked with tears as I turned the page and read about "Resistance and Love." It couldn't be more applicable. The reason it was so hard for Gabriel to take action was that he still felt love for her—even if it was buried deeply.

With these things in mind, I watched Gabriel closely as we visited the museum.

He seemed just as friendly and just as gracious toward everyone as he was the day before, but now I noticed a bit of darkness beneath his eyes and a slight strain in his voice from time to time. Every so often I'd catch him watching me, and I'd feel my pulse thud. I told myself it was nothing. I was just concerned for him now that I was privy to his greatest secret.

Debbie caught up to me as we left the museum and headed for the National Gardens. "What's going on between you and Gabriel?" she asked.

I slowed my step, letting a couple of the Dutch tourists pass by—not that they could understand what we were saying. "Nothing is going on." I swallowed hard. Had it been so obvious? "Why?"

"He's been watching you like a falcon."

"Do you mean a hawk?"

She linked her arm through mine, ignoring my correction. "I think he likes you."

I about choked out a laugh. She knew he was recovering from divorce, and she was even friends with his sister. Besides, if she even knew half of what I did, she'd realize he was too emotionally taxed to think about having a relationship with another woman. I decided to come clean—the last thing I wanted was for her to say anything to the others. I slowed down even more, until we were standing at the very back of the group. Gabriel had stopped the group and was explaining our afternoon options—stay in the gardens and enjoy the weather or take the cable car up Mount Likavitos.

I waited until people started to spread out. We had three hours before we were all to meet up again. I led Debbie toward a fountain, pretending to inspect it. "I told Gabriel that his sister was really upset at him because he didn't want her coming over to Greece," I said.

"Oh, how did he take that?" Debbie said.

"He told me things are very complicated with his ex-wife, and having Maria over here would make it worse." I couldn't say more.

"He told you about Rhea?" Her eyes widened significantly. "He does like you."

"No, you're wrong," I said, feeling irritated now. I was a sixty-two-year-old widow and didn't want to discuss crushes with anyone—especially if they had to do with me. Gabriel had just shared something very private, so he was probably watching to see my reaction throughout the day. I knew what would distract Debbie. "Are you speaking to Lark yet?" I noticed that he and Carson had wandered off somewhere together.

She pursed her lips.

I suppressed a smile and moved back toward the main group that was planning on taking the cable car. Gabriel was standing with Hilda and Helda. He looked over at me as I approached, and I met his gaze straight on. I wanted him to know his secret was safe with me. He gave me a slight nod, and I didn't care if Debbie noticed it or not. I had a friend, and I was set on helping him.

I didn't speak to Gabriel the rest of the day or even at the dinner in Kolonaki at the base of the mountain or the social hour back at the hotel. I escaped to my room as soon as possible and continued reading *The War of Art*. I scrolled back to the chapter on "Resistance and the Choice of a Mate" and read the differences between the supporting partner and the partner who overcame resistance.

I wondered which Phillip fit into. Then I read, "If we're the supporting partner, shouldn't we face our own failure to pursue our unloved life rather than hitchhike on our spouse's coattails?"

I paused, thinking that this fit me more than Phillip. I had definitely followed along on his dreams, or "coattails." In a way, so had Gabriel with his wife. Gabriel had been controlled by the whims and illnesses his wife endured.

Putting the iPad down, I closed my eyes. Gabriel and I made quite the pair of friends . . . both of us taking care of others' needs without much thought for our own. My chest pinged. I really didn't want to face my own needs because then I might discover how deep they were. It was easier, and I believed it made me happier, to focus on others' needs anyway.

Just getting those pictures sent to social services earlier had filled me to the brim, and feeling the camaraderie when Gabriel looked at me made it overflow.

Chapter 10

LIKE CLOCKWORK, I WAS UP early the next morning anticipating another discussion with Gabriel. As I pulled a comb through my hair, I thought about Debbie's comment on Gabriel liking me.

"What's not to like?" I said to my image in the mirror, then laughed at myself. There were plenty of things not to like, at least according to Phillip, or why else would he go to such lengths to meet up with other women?

I turned away from my image and finished packing up my bags. We'd be checking out and taking a boat to Mykonos to spend a couple of days on the beaches. Whoever organized this tour sure knew how to spoil us. I went downstairs to scout Gabriel and have a cup of tea. He wasn't there yet, so I settled onto a couch with the tea and let the steam warm my face.

After a few minutes, I started reading again but kept glancing at the hallway, wondering when Gabriel would show. We'd only met twice down here—but it felt like an old routine. Thirty minutes into spending more time watching the hallways than reading, I finally stood. He was probably just packing or making arrangements for today's travel.

Something tugged at the back of my mind. I walked to his room, determined to knock on his door. I stopped when I realized what I was doing. How could I justify showing up at his hotel room? And what was I about to say? "Why didn't you show up for our unscheduled meeting?"

I walked down the hall and knocked softly on his door anyway, half hoping that he wouldn't hear my knock and wouldn't answer it.

Before I could escape, the door opened. If Gabriel looked surprised to see me at 5:30 a.m., he didn't show it. He wore a plain T-shirt and what looked to be either sweatpants or exercise pants. He stepped into the hall and shut the door behind him.

"I wanted to check on you," I said in a rush. "To see how you're doing."

He rubbed his forehead and closed his eyes for a few seconds, then he looked at me. "Ruby, how did you know?"

"Know what?"

"Meet me downstairs. I'll be there in a couple of minutes." He disappeared back into his room.

I stood in the middle of the hallway, trying to decipher how the tone of his voice sounded. I didn't want him to come out and find me rooted in place, so I went back to the lobby and waited on a couch.

He showed up about ten minutes later, wearing pressed pants and a button-down, short-sleeved shirt. I had caught him in an underdressed state. He walked toward me with long, purposeful strides, then sat across from me. "Has anyone told you that you have a sixth sense?"

"Not exactly, at least not in those words," I said, wanting him to get to the point.

"They found Rhea . . ."

My heart thumped, expecting the worst.

"You were right," he continued. "They gave her an IV, and she'll be in the hospital for a couple of days for observation. Then they'll transfer her to an institution. Which, of course, she'll hate."

"Isn't it better than the alternative?" I breathed out.

His complexion looked brighter, as if some weight had been lifted. There was still enough darkness behind his eyes that I knew the pain remained.

"Yes," he said, but his voice wasn't too convincing. He buried his face in his hands.

I couldn't just sit there and let him suffer. I moved next to him and put an arm around his shoulder. "You did the right thing. She'll be taken care of now."

He nodded, his face still in his hands.

"Don't blame yourself either. She would have done something rash with or without the divorce."

He lifted his head. "How can you know? How can anyone really know?"

I knew he wasn't criticizing me, that it was just frustration speaking. I had plenty of experience feeling guilty for the things my spouse did.

"Just believe that someone does know," I said in a quiet voice. "Even if you don't believe it yourself yet."

He straightened, and I moved my arm from his shoulders. With a sigh, he leaned back. "Sorry to be such a downer. You're here for a vacation, and I've dumped all of this on you."

"It's perfectly fine, Gabriel." He looked over at me like he was trying to decide if he believed me. "Really," I added. "I'm just glad Rhea is getting some help now and your burden is lighter."

"Much lighter, thanks to you," he said. "I took the plunge this morning and called Maria. Told her pretty much everything."

"Wow," I said, because there weren't any other words. He'd told his sister—that was a really big step in this process.

"Yeah, wow."

"What did she say?" I asked.

"After chewing me out for about ten minutes for not telling her all along, she broke down and cried."

"Poor Maria," I murmured.

Gabriel chuckled. I stared at him; this was far from funny.

"She actually said the same thing about you." His eyes were warm now. "She says I need to stop dumping all of my problems on you. That is, she told me that after she got over being offended that I told a near stranger about my miserable marriage before I told my own sister."

"I can see how she'd be a little miffed," I said, hiding a smile. "Sometimes it's easier to confide in a person who's not emotionally invested." Or to never confide at all—that was my method, and it had worked pretty well for me.

I was in Greece, after all, facing the past—well, almost.

"Thanks for everything, Ruby," he said, reaching over and squeezing my hand.

Something zinged through me. I didn't have time to put a definition on it, though, since his cell phone started ringing. An early call probably wasn't good news. I moved to the other couch to give him some space.

The conversation was in Greek, and it sounded all business. When he hung up, he said, "The bus driver is running late, but we should still be able to make the boat. At least there will be plenty of time for breakfast." We were back to business and discussing matters of the tour.

"I should finish packing," I said, standing.

Gabriel rose too and extended his hand. I shook it, with that zing going through me again. I pushed away any possible meaning for why I was suddenly feeling strange around him. Maybe he had revealed too much, and I *was* becoming emotionally involved in his life. Maybe Maria had been justified in her frustration.

As he released my hand—a bit slowly—he said, "By the way, Maria wanted your e-mail."

"Oh. All right."

"I can put it into my phone and let her know."

I rattled off my e-mail address just as his cell rang again. I took the opportunity to leave while he was on the phone and hurried back to my room. Once inside, I leaned against the door to catch my breath. What was wrong with me? Yes, Gabriel was handsome, and I could appreciate that in any man—before and after I was widowed. But I'd touched him casually before, and now . . . I looked down at the hand that had shaken his. It was like I could still feel the strength of his fingers against mine as they'd pressed around my hand.

His hand had been warm and comforting and reassuring somehow. It had been a long time since I'd felt truly safe around a man . . . If I had to count, it would be over thirty years, I was sure. I wasn't going to count.

I looked around the hotel room. Everything was cleaned up and packed. I'd even made the bed and wiped down the sink. I knew the hotel staff would come in and take everything apart, but I didn't want them to see a mess.

To stay busy until breakfast and to stop thinking about Gabriel, I typed up an e-mail to the book-club ladies. A couple of them had already responded to my first e-mail. Shannon said she'd checked on my house and everything looked great. She wished me well on the trip. The other e-mail was from Daisy.

When I opened it, I was surprised at the length. Daisy definitely had a little more time on her hands with her forced bed rest. What was most interesting was how many times she'd mentioned her ex-husband, Jared. Apparently, he'd been over to her place quite a bit, helping her with odd things, even cooking some meals for her. I sat back with a smile. I knew Daisy and Jared had a volatile history, but I also knew they'd both matured over the years.

At 7:00 a.m., I went down to the hotel restaurant and ordered fruit and yogurt. Debbie joined me at my table, and Carson sat down with us a few minutes later. I tried not to notice when Gabriel entered the room.

That was pretty much impossible when he stopped at our table, resting his hand on the back of my chair as he chatted with everyone.

Debbie wiped her mouth quickly and grinned at him. "Ready for the big boat ride?"

Gabriel laughed, and I noticed how warm and full it sounded. Sharing his burden with his sister must have really helped. "I hope no one gets seasick.

If you do, I have some Dramamine. You'd just need to take it right away so it can kick in before departure."

Always the prepared gentleman. I shook my head slightly, which only directed his attention to me. "How about you, Ruby? Do you ever get seasick?"

Debbie jumped in. "I should doubt it. She's been all over the world, on cruises and everything."

"Really?" His voice held genuine surprise—not so much that I'd traveled but more likely because I'd never mentioned it in any of our early-morning discussions. Gabriel moved to the side of my chair so our gazes locked. "I'd love to hear about your travels sometime."

No, you wouldn't. "Sure." I smiled at him, then returned to shuffling the food around my plate.

Debbie started a rundown of the places I'd traveled, never giving up an opportunity to talk to Gabriel. No wonder Lark had been sulking the entire trip.

I felt my face heating up and took a long drink of the iced juice I'd ordered. What was Debbie doing? I'd been careful to keep my friendship with Gabriel all about him and steer it clear of me whenever possible.

Now Debbie was giving him a laundry list of my life—what little I'd shared with her. Finally, it clicked. Debbie was bragging about me in her own disjointed way. Thankfully, someone came up to greet Gabriel, and they moved off together. I focused on not looking in his direction, but I definitely heard everything he said.

Debbie leaned over the table and whispered, "Did you see how his face lit up when I talked to him about you? I really think he likes you."

I put a hand on hers. "Please don't, Debbie. I can't explain now, but it's better that you don't think of us as a couple."

Debbie's mouth formed a tight line. I was afraid I'd offended her, and I didn't dare look at Carson to see what he thought. Maybe Carson would say something to Lark about how Debbie was trying to set up Gabriel and me. Lark might be happy to know that. Conversation buzzed around us, making the silence feel more awkward.

A time or two, I sensed Gabriel was looking at me from the table where he was eating, and I brushed it off. He didn't need my intervention anymore. Rhea was taken care of, and Maria could now be his confidante.

Debbie had gone overboard in her enthusiasm, so I hoped I'd made myself clear. It was time to distance myself from Gabriel—and leaving this hotel was a perfect way to start. I didn't want to deal with any more zings. Zings weren't on my vacation list.

* * *

I soon found out that the information Debbie had so adamantly handed over to Gabriel had only piqued his interest—in a friend sort of way, of course.

About half an hour into the boat ride, I found a quiet place on deck to watch the aqua waves churning beneath. The wind felt delicious, and I truly felt that I was shedding my previous memories of Greece and replacing them with better ones. Although having to be firm with Debbie and avoid Gabriel weren't exactly ideal.

"It's beautiful, isn't it?"

Gabriel's voice washed over me, and I steeled myself against any potential zing. He rested his forearms on the railing next to me, and I looked away after noticing how the hair on his arms glinted against his tanned skin.

"You didn't tell me you'd been to Greece before. I thought I had a whole group of first-timers."

I laughed, trying to keep the irony out of it. "Sorry about Debbie."

"I'm not sorry. It was actually nice to learn something about you for a change."

The wind wasn't doing its job anymore; I felt too hot now.

"When were you here last?" he asked, his voice floating over me somewhere.

I should have prepared myself better for this question—it wasn't like I hadn't answered it before. It wasn't like it wouldn't ever come up . . . "Years ago, I think about thirty."

"And you haven't been back since?"

I stared at the waves capping. "No."

He was silent for a moment. "You didn't love it enough to come back sooner?"

"It was actually pretty great. My husband was doing a lot of business, so I spent the time exploring the sights on my own. Sometimes that can be better than an official tour where you are beholden to an agenda," I said.

"What line of work was your husband in?"

"The antique business—international antiques were his specialty, high-end items."

Gabriel nodded and clasped his hands together. "I'll bet you have some real finds in your home."

I thought of my home—it was beautiful—and Gabriel was right; there were many priceless objects. Which, of course, made me glad I had Shannon to check on the house once in a while, although the security system would probably do the job well enough. Still, I hardly noticed the collectibles anymore, and I'd sold a few that had more potent memories.

"How long have you been a widow, if you don't mind me asking?" Gabriel said.

I was a bit surprised at the question. Maybe there was some truth in Debbie's observations. Maybe he did like me—but if he did, I knew it was misdirected. He was still hurting from his divorce, still plagued by his ex-wife.

If there was one thing I'd learned so far about being around the seniors group, it was that two years of being a widow made a woman a target for the dating scene. "Just over two years," I said. "He had ALS the last eighteen months."

"And I'll bet you were his nurse along every step of the way," Gabriel said in a reverent voice.

A nurse who resented every moment, a nurse who cried herself to sleep at night. If that was what he meant, then, yes, I had been a nurse to Phillip. I lifted a shoulder in a shrug. "Even when you know someone is going to die, it's surreal when it really does happen."

"I can't imagine." His hand covered mine.

I was sure that others in the tour group could see us talking, but for the moment, I didn't care. I closed my eyes, feeling the warmth of his hand on mine, the wind blowing around us. For a few minutes, I allowed myself to be comforted for once. Gabriel could never imagine what those last months had been like, and no one ever would, because I'd never tell them how I had turned against my husband. How I'd withheld my forgiveness even when Phillip had begged.

As the familiar coldness rushed through me, I focused on the feel of Gabriel's hand and pushed with all my might against that coldness. When it faded, I remembered that I was supposed to be avoiding Gabriel. As much as I detested being curt, I knew I had to address it head on.

"Gabriel . . ." I pulled my hand gently away.

He shifted so he was standing a little farther away—he took the hint well.

"For some reason, Debbie has it in her head that you like me." I put a hand up to stop him before he could reply. I couldn't look at him directly—sure I'd just completely embarrassed both of us. "I had to be quite firm with her, even to the extent of maybe hurting her feelings."

When he didn't say anything, I glanced over at him. He'd turned and was leaning against the rail, facing me. His gaze was open but didn't seem all that embarrassed, and the corners of his mouth turned up.

I hurried on. "I want to reassure you that I don't have any designs on our illustrious tour guide—unlike some of the other lady guests."

His smile broadened, and I had to look away again. The waves were only a partial distraction. "But I think it's better we don't spend time together—at least with just the two of us—anymore. If Debbie is speculating, there may be others." There. I'd said it. I took a deep breath and met his gaze.

He was still smiling.

"What are you smiling about?" I felt perspiration break out on the back of my neck. "I thought you'd be at least a little offended."

Gabriel laughed and leaned forward. I wanted to back away, but I didn't.

"Would it be so terrible, Ruby, if I did like you?" he said into my ear.

My heart was beating much too fast to be good for any sixty-two-year-old. I pulled away and stared at him, at his smile, at his brown eyes. There was a definite zing now, but I couldn't dwell on it. He was just a nice man—that was all. "There's nothing wrong with *liking* someone. I mean, I like you too, but not in the way Debbie's implying. She's gotten ahead of herself, and all of her meddling has caused some hurt feelings with Lark."

Gabriel's smile remained as he leaned on the railing again, crossing his arms. "Ah. That explains some things."

"She loves to speculate."

He laughed.

I laughed too, even though I wasn't intending to become conspiratorial buddies. "I'm sure you're used to it." I waved my hand toward a group of Dutch women not too far from us. "Being around all of these ladies fawning over you."

He lifted a brow. "Fawning? I suppose some are just thrilled to be in Greece on vacation."

"And fawning over you."

He shook he head, his expression serious. "I suppose I have grown used to superfluous friends and not really getting to know people. Two weeks on a tour group together basically tells me who gets tired early and what type of wine a person prefers. And then it's time for the next tour." He paused, his eyes on the waves. "But maybe that's for the best."

I found myself nodding. "Two weeks with a person might be the best solution anyway."

"Two weeks," he said. "I like that. I thought I knew Rhea when we got married, but I turned out to be dead wrong."

I had been dead wrong in the person I'd married too, but I'd never admit it. I would admit that I liked talking to Gabriel. I liked having a friend, even though he was handsome and charming and gave me zings every time we happened to touch. Of course, it could never go past that, but what was wrong with having a friend? Here I was talking myself out of my own resolve. "Well, it's not really common practice to do background checks or psychoanalysis on fiancés."

"Maybe they could make it a new law in California—in order to get a marriage license, all parties must agree to a psychoanalysis."

We laughed together. It felt good to laugh, even though there was so much underlying pain in both of our marriages.

"Look, Ruby," he said, scooting closer and dropping his voice. "I like having you as a friend, and you've helped me so much, but I'm not going to infiltrate your carefully arranged space."

Carefully arranged space? What did he mean? He was either talking gibberish—maybe learned in his counseling appointments with his ex-wife—or he knew me more than I thought he did.

He nudged my shoulder. "I don't think we should worry about what other people think of our friendship."

I let out a breath. So he did only consider me as a friend. I knew it deep down, despite what Debbie had said. Excellent. I could live with that. "All right, Gabriel, I'll trust you on this one." *Trust? Who am I kidding?* "You're the expert on two-week friendships and all."

He stuck out his hand. "We have an agreement? Let's make it official."

"Okay." I grasped his hand in mine, and we shook on it.

Zing.

Chapter 11

DESPITE THE SERIES OF ZINGS, I felt more relaxed around Gabriel now. After we settled into our new hotel in Mykonos, I scouted out Debbie and found her in her room. Her expression was a bit wary when she opened the door—she must have looked through the peephole. Her usual bright smile was absent, and I realized how much I missed it.

"I just wanted to apologize for saying what I did at breakfast." I stood awkwardly in the hall, hoping no one would pass by. "I had a talk with Gabriel, and he agreed that we're only friends. There's nothing more. I just didn't want you to feel like I was mad at you or anything."

Debbie hugged me. "Oh, Ruby. You can say what you want. I know he's interested in you, but I'll keep my mouth shut because obviously *you* aren't interested." She pulled back and winked.

My smile diminished a bit. This tour was going to be longer than I thought. "Well, let's just drop the whole subject so we can enjoy ourselves at the beach. Should we walk down to the bus together?"

Debbie's eyes lit up. "Let me grab my bag and spice up my lipstick."

The Ornos beach was beautiful, smaller and quieter than the one I'd been to with Phillip when we'd visited Mykonos. But that was just as well and perfect for a senior group. It was also nice not to be here in the high tourist season, although there were plenty of people. Gabriel had reserved several areas for the group so we'd have shade beneath the wooden umbrellas. Debbie and I dumped our bags on two blue beach chairs, then kicked off our shoes.

I couldn't wait to get my feet in the water. As we walked to the lapping surf, I was surprised to see both Carson and Lark come toward us. Lark had kept separate from our group since the tour began, but now he seemed determined to join us. He wore an obvious, touristy straw hat that covered the baldness so only white scruffs of hair were visible. It was quite endearing, really.

"Hello, ladies," Lark said, acting like he hadn't been avoiding Debbie all week.

Soon, she was responding and smiling at him as usual.

I shook my head at the pair and cast a sideways glance at Carson. Had he said something to Lark? Carson seemed intent on finding the most intact shells possible and studiously avoided my pointed gaze. Then I realized what I'd said to Gabriel earlier, and sensing his presence I turned toward the shore. He was standing about a dozen yards away, his hand shielding his eyes, looking out to sea. The smile on his face was unmistakable.

He'd somehow reunited Lark and Debbie. I knew it. I covered up a laugh and waded farther into the sea, leaving Debbie and Lark to their conversation and Carson to his shell hunt. The water was cool but refreshing. After about a half hour, I went back to the beach chair and dragged it into the sun. Debbie and Lark were sitting together, catching up after more than four days of avoiding each other. Carson had wandered off somewhere. I put more sunscreen on my arms, then wrapped my legs and feet in a towel so they could warm up. Glad the beach chair kept my iPad out of the sand, I started to read *The War of Art*. For the most part, it was interesting, but I felt a bit hammered on. I tried not to apply the things too closely to my own life so I didn't start feeling miserable.

A shadow fell across the iPad, and I looked up.

Gabriel stood there, wearing a T-shirt and board shorts that dripped onto his sand-covered legs. I refocused to his face before I paid too much attention to his nice tan and muscular legs. He had to be a runner. There was no other explanation.

"Did you enjoy the water?" he asked.

"Yes, thanks. It looks like you did too."

He sat down in the sand next to my chair without waiting for an invitation. "I figure I have a good five minutes before anyone gets suspicious."

I laughed. "Maybe six minutes, tops."

"Even better." He checked his watch, then opened up the book he was holding.

"So we're just reading together?"

He looked over at me. "If that's okay with you."

I smiled and leaned back. Phillip would never have just sat and read with me. He was always on the phone or in a meeting. The word *relax* was buried in some foreign language dictionary Phillip didn't have access to. I started reading my e-book before I could analyze why I was comparing Gabriel to Phillip. Gabriel and I had agreed to a two-week friendship, and it was already day four. I didn't have time to waste on comparisons.

While I was reading, I could see why Tori loved this book. She was extremely ambitious in her goal to get a screenplay produced, but sometimes I sensed an insecurity there—a book like this could only be motivating. The "Resistance of Fear" chapter had certainly been interesting. "Hmmm."

I hadn't realized I'd mumbled aloud until Gabriel said, "Something you care to share?"

Was he really interested or just being polite? "I'm reading *The War of Art* for my book club. It's all about following your creative dreams." He wasn't snoring yet, so I continued. "It talks about overcoming resistance in order to do whatever it is you love. One of the ladies in my club is a screenplay writer—although she doesn't have anything sold yet."

"I've heard of that book," Gabriel said. "Or maybe it was the *Art of War*."

"Probably. This one doesn't have to do with Chinese warfare."

Gabriel earmarked a page in his book and closed it. Apparently, he really was interested.

I went back to the chapter I'd highlighted a few days ago. "So this part is about resistance and fear." I cleared my throat. "'Fear is good. Like self-doubt, fear is an indicator. It tells us what we have to do.'"

He nodded but didn't comment. I hoped he didn't think I was being pointed about his problems with his ex-wife. "I found this part the most interesting: 'The more scared we are of a work or calling, the more sure we can be that we have to do it.'"

Gabriel leaned back in the sand and stretched out his legs, elbows propped up behind him. "That reminds me of when I decided to come to Greece and start the tour. I was pretty nervous about it, and knowing it was the best thing didn't really make the nerves go away."

I was glad Gabriel was talking about his work instead of his ex. He peered up at me. "Have you ever had to do something you were afraid of at first?"

A million things, but I didn't want to talk about Phillip. As far as Gabriel knew, I had been the exemplary, caring wife until the very end. "I was pretty scared to go through birth with my son. Of course, once I was pregnant, I really had no choice but to face it."

"How many children do you have?"

"Just one—Anthony. He's married and living in Illinois. No grandkids yet."

Gabriel was quiet for a moment. I knew he and Rhea had never had any children, and I wondered if it was a medical issue that had caused her miscarriage or if it was her mental condition.

"So how did you feel about becoming a mother?" he asked.

His question surprised me. Phillip had never delved into my feelings like this . . . *Stop*, I told myself. I wasn't going to compare the two men. "It was actually quite terrifying. But it was also the most wonderful thing."

Gabriel smiled a bit wistfully.

"Of course, raising a child comes with a lot of ups and downs." I let out a sigh. "But I survived, and I wouldn't take it back for anything in the world."

"I've heard women say that before," he said in a quiet voice.

"Yes." I thought of the fulfillment that raising a son had given me. Completely different from my failed marriage. I smiled at Gabriel. "Tell me about your book. You've been carrying around that ratty copy since I met you."

He laughed and held it up. "Are you mocking my beat-up paperback? Not all of us are caught up with the twenty-first-century technology, madam."

"Believe me, I'm still learning. Another lady in my book club talked me into this, then showed me some basics."

Gabriel took off his sunglasses, his brown eyes on me. "Your book club sounds very intriguing."

"Oh, no you don't," I said. "We probably only have about two more 'proper' minutes left of being together, and you're going to tell me about . . ." I looked at the cover. "*Zen and the Art of Motorcycle Maintenance?*" I snorted. "It definitely sounds like a guy book."

"It's actually a philosophy book—which may or may not surprise you." His eyes bored into mine.

"I'm not surprised. In fact, I think it fits you perfectly."

I couldn't tell if Gabriel was pleased or not.

"It was published in the early '80s, but it will take me much longer than two minutes to tell you what it's about," he said.

"Oh, really? It's that complicated?"

"It's *very* complicated," he said in a faux-serious voice. "In fact, we'll have to set aside another six-minute meeting in order for me to even begin describing it. After that, we'd need another follow-up six-minute meeting." He looked toward the water, then stood and dusted off his board shorts.

"Looks like your friends are about to join you. Maybe we can do the next six minutes tonight."

I turned my head. Debbie and Lark were walking toward me, apparently done with their tête-à-tête. Before I could stop Gabriel, he'd waved good-bye and was headed in the other direction. I'd forgotten to ask him what he'd said to Lark.

I pulled the towel off my legs. It really was too warm now, especially while thinking of the next six-minute meeting.

* * *

I scrubbed my face once, then again, harder. It didn't hurt—I hadn't burned. So why was my skin so flushed? After drying off with a towel, I walked out of my hotel bathroom. It was ridiculous, frankly, that I couldn't quite catch my breath, yet I felt I could run a marathon.

I sat on the bed and pinched my arm. Hard. Still, I felt I could run forever. What was going on with the energy coursing through me? And why couldn't I get Gabriel out of my mind? I opened the window and leaned out, catching the cooling night air, hoping to drive some sense into my mind. Instead of seeing the pristine white-and-blue landscape of Greece, I could only picture Gabriel. I snapped the window shut and went into the bathroom to fix my hair and makeup. I had to be overtired. I hoped in the morning I'd be back to my normal self. All I needed was a good night's sleep to talk sense into my brain.

A knock sounded on the door; Debbie was here for our dinner plans. I let her in, then finished up in the bathroom. When I came out, she was gazing out the window, her arms wrapped around her torso. "Isn't it just incredible? That we're here in Greece?" She turned to face me, her brilliant smile back. I decided Lark had a lot to do with its brilliance.

I folded my arms and smiled at her. "So, you and Lark are speaking again?"

"He's wonderful," she said. "I was silly to brush him off. But he knows now that I don't have a crush on Gabriel."

"Did you tell Lark that?"

"Well . . ." Her smile faltered. "He actually asked me about it. I was quite impressed with his forwardness, but I'm glad he asked. I didn't want him thinking the wrong thing."

"A lot of women find Gabriel charming, so I'm sure he didn't blame you."

"Oh—Gabriel is charming. But he'd never be the one for me." She waved a hand. "Too Greek."

I arched a brow. "He's an American citizen."

"Oh, you know what I mean. You're a world traveler too. Gabriel is perfect for someone like you." She crossed to me and took my hands in hers. "I know you hate to hear it, but you should be more open-brained about him."

"You mean open-minded?" I pulled away, feeling stiff. "Please, Debbie. I know you might not think I was serious before, but I'll never marry again. *Ever.*" My voice trembled, and Debbie's eyes widened.

She looked down at her hands and clasped them together.

I hated that I had to be so firm with her, but I hated even more that she was so persistent. It would have been nice to spend time with the book-club ladies back home—none of them ever brought up the subject of remarrying. I broke the awkward silence. "Tell me about Lark. Do you see a future with him? He was absolutely doting on you today."

Her head snapped up, her eyes a bit shiny. "He seems to, doesn't he? We haven't really discussed anything that serious. He's actually quite shy when it comes to personal things. Much different from my first husband."

I didn't think Lark was shy at all. Maybe it was just Debbie's way of making an excuse for him. "Well, there's no rush. He's been a great friend to you."

Debbie nodded, although I could see the hope in her eyes. If Lark would just get on with it, he'd have one happy woman at his side.

We walked together to one of the restaurants on the hotel's list of recommendations. Dinner was on our own tonight. Music blared from inside, and the place looked packed with a young crowd of people. I hesitated on the sidewalk. "This looks more like a young people's bar than anything."

"Oh, come on," Debbie said. "Lark is meeting us here." She grasped my arm and leaned close to me. "He said there's dancing."

Exactly. "Debbie—"

"It will be fun. We can leave anytime." She practically dragged me through the entrance where we were besieged by the pumping music.

I was definitely out of my element. I assumed the music was popular somewhere, but I'd never heard it. Debbie shouted over the noise to a young woman with spiked hair sporting pink streaks, who happened to be wearing a name tag, "Table for six."

"Six?" I asked. "Who else is coming besides Lark?"

Debbie followed a waiter, pushing through a group of women wearing extremely short skirts and high heels. I tried not to stare. How did they walk in those things? They must also have shaved way above the knees.

I pulled my sturdy linen jacket tightly around me. I had always prided myself in dressing stylishly, but I felt absolutely dowdy next to these beauties. Fortunately, our booth was in a corner and not right next to the dance floor—if you could call what the young people were doing dancing. I kept my eyes averted as best I could and opened the menu.

Debbie immediately ordered red wine, and I ordered a lemon-water—I didn't want anything to mix with my planned sleeping pill I'd take later. It was my only hope of getting my mind to shut off.

"Here they come," Debbie said, facing the entrance.

I turned to see Lark coming through the crowd, followed by Helda and Carson—at least I thought it was Helda. I was a bit relieved to see Carson paying attention to a woman other than me. I almost did a double take when I saw Gabriel bringing up the rear of the group. I whipped around to look at Debbie, but she was grinning at Lark, completely oblivious to what I might think of Gabriel joining us for dinner when it was so obvious that everyone had paired up.

I did not approve.

Debbie scooted over, so I did too. Before I knew it, Gabriel was squished right in next to me, Debbie on my other side. When everyone was sitting, adjustments were made but not very much. I was still sitting too close to Gabriel. If I moved at all, our shoulders would touch.

"This might take longer than six minutes," Gabriel said into my ear, his arm pressing against mine.

I almost melted against the seat. I was grateful that I'd ordered only water. With my thoughts completely scattered tonight, I needed to stay as alert and as separate from Gabriel as possible. But I was stuck— literally. "Looks like our quota for the rest of the tour will be filled by the time our dinner comes," I said, wishing I didn't have to talk so loud over the thrumming music.

He turned his head, his eyes extremely captivating in the subtle light. "I hope not. Maybe we can pretend tonight never happened."

"Just cross it off our list?"

"As tour director, that's what I'd recommend."

"Deal." I hid a smile and completely hid my pounding heart. I took a drink of the lemon-water, wishing it had more ice in it.

Carson and Helda seemed chummy, despite the obvious language barrier, and I wondered where her sister was. Carson and Helda were becoming quite inseparable. The music was too loud to ask questions across the table, so I didn't. I wanted to tell Debbie I wasn't too happy that this turned out to be a "couple" gathering, but each time I looked at her, she was staring at Lark. I didn't think she would comprehend anything I'd said.

So, really, that left only Gabriel and me if I wanted to have any semblance of dinnertime conversation. I decided not to worry about it. The dancing, the rushing waiters, and the piles of food on our table were all distraction enough. It seemed that Gabriel ordered a little of everything—platters of unidentifiable fish and pickled vegetables. I didn't dare ask what kind of seafood we were sampling; I was afraid to discover exactly what I was eating. I planned to add Imodium AD to my sleeping pill.

When Debbie and Lark rose from the table, I had a little breathing room. But my breathing nearly stopped when I realized they meant to dance—among all of those gyrating, sweaty bodies. I had to admit to myself, they made a cute couple. People would probably think they'd been married forever.

I scooted over, putting some much-needed space between Gabriel and me. By now, I knew exactly what he smelled like—spicy soap—and that he loved oranges squeezed on his fish. Also, that he was left-handed.

"Which is your favorite?" Gabriel asked.

I pointed to a plate of fish covered in some sort of creamy dill sauce. I'd missed the official name. "I could eat that every night. I wonder what the calorie damage is."

"If I tell you, it would ruin it."

I laughed but quickly sobered when Carson and Helda got up to dance too. What was wrong with these people? We were seniors at some trendy bar/club/place. Couldn't they see we didn't fit in with our pressed khakis and starched linen?

Loading another serving onto my plate, intending to eat very slowly, I hoped that would prevent Gabriel from asking the question. It didn't.

"Are you up for a dance?" He leaned on one hand, his gaze on me. "Or will that start the timer ticking?"

"I can't," I said. "I'm still eating." I shoved a mouthful of food in as if to demonstrate.

Gabriel pulled my plate away, and I stared at him, slowly chewing.

"Come on, Ruby." He took my hand that wasn't holding the fork. "Everyone's dancing. It will look strange if we don't join them."

His hand was warm in mine, and I looked down at our hands clasped together. My throat felt tight, and I couldn't think of a word to say. But I knew I couldn't possibly dance with him. Not now, not ever. No matter how many zings were shooting through me at once.

I couldn't remember the last time I'd danced with a man. It was certainly Phillip at some point—maybe it had been as long ago as our wedding reception. But having Gabriel's arms around me, even in something as innocent as a casual dance, would certainly send my heart into overdrive. And I'd been too careful to keep it in neutral. I wasn't going to let that change now.

I pulled my hand away and saw something shift in his eyes. Concern, or maybe questions. Let him wonder. I owed no one an explanation. I took a sip of water to wash down the lump of fish I'd just swallowed. "I'm exhausted," I said, trying to sound nice but tired at the same time. "I think I'll head back to the hotel. Tell everyone I'll see them in the morning."

But Gabriel didn't move, and I was trapped beside him. His gaze was intense. I *felt* what he was about to say. "Ruby—"

"Don't say it," I said. Panic bubbled up inside of me, and the resolve I'd held on to that was keeping me from bursting broke. "I can't do this. The hand-holding, the dancing . . . it's too much."

His gaze stayed on me for another moment as if he was trying to figure out how to change my mind. Then, like the gentleman he'd been all along, he said in a quiet voice, "Have a good night," and he moved so I could leave the table.

Before the tears could fall, I hurried back to the hotel, dodging locals mixed with tourists, all laughing, drinking, and enjoying themselves. Here I was, running from it all, and I couldn't blame jet lag this time. I could only blame myself. I'd been the one to hide the truth, to cover up for my husband, and then to withhold forgiveness from a repentant man.

Tears burned hot in my eyes, and I brushed them away before stepping into the hotel lobby. I found my room quickly and undressed in the dark. I didn't want to see the streaks of makeup on my face or remember how I'd turned down Gabriel for a dance.

It was just a dance—one single dance. I couldn't even allow myself that one small bit of pleasure. But touching a man again, when it had been so long since I'd had any genuine affection . . . Gabriel probably thought I was nuts.

Something in the back of my mind said I was punishing myself too much. There was a possibility of happiness, even for a woman my age. I could fall in love at sixty-two.

But that path to happiness had too many twists and potholes lurking on it. Besides, Gabriel and I were too much alike. We were both pushovers. Our relationship would be one unvoiced expectation after another until one of us simply collapsed along the way.

I climbed into bed, hoping the sleeping pill would send me into oblivion very soon and that the face I could still see in my mind would fade completely.

Chapter 12

WE DIDN'T SPEAK FOR THREE days. Which would have been fine in and of itself, but it seemed that we were always in the same space, part of the same group. More than once, I caught Gabriel looking at me. All right, it was dozens of times, and he could definitely say the same about me.

After turning him down for the dance, it seemed that something clicked in his mind. And I could guess what it was. He realized I was completely serious about not crossing the boundaries we'd set together. Whether we called it the six-minute boundary or not, there was an invisible wall between us now. Even though I'd been the one to create it, I didn't know how to break through it.

We'd left Mykonos and taken a ship to gorgeous Santorini, with its high cliffs streaked with lava. Gabriel and I didn't talk on the ship, nor did we talk when we toured Akrotiri, the "Pompeii of Greece." I didn't join in the sampling of the local wines at the Boutari Winery but stayed at the back of the group, inspecting the extensive vines.

On day six, we visited the black-sand beach, and as I scrubbed my toes through the warm granules, I thought of the last time Gabriel and I had visited a beach. We were like two pals that day, reading our books together and discussing them. I had never heard his synopsis of the Zen Motorcycle book. Laughter floated over to me, and I turned my head to catch a vision of Gabriel surrounded by some of the tour ladies.

Above their heads, his gaze met mine, and I turned away quickly. How did he sense every time I looked his way? Maybe they were laughing at me. I didn't even try to decipher his broken Dutch as he spoke with them. I gathered up my bag and moved down the beach a ways, out of hearing distance.

I opened my iPad and used Pages to type up a letter to the book-club ladies that I'd send later by e-mail. I told them where I was in *The War of*

Art book and how I couldn't wait until the next meeting to discuss it. I'd definitely gained new insights on the tour.

I didn't make any mention of Gabriel or anyone else, for that matter. I wondered if any of the ladies would see through the sparseness of my letter.

* * *

The next day we arrived in Athens and took a chartered bus to the site of ancient Olympia. Since it was now the second week on the tour, small cliques of friendships had been solidified, and everyone automatically organized into them. Debbie and Lark had become inseparable, as well as Carson and Helda. It was actually quite amusing to listen to them communicate, combining the best of both Dutch and English, which amounted to a mishmash of words and gestures.

I sat behind the glued-together Debbie/Lark and settled in for the long bus ride. I was nearly finished with *The War of Art* and looked forward to sneaking in a Georgette Heyer later. Absorbed in reading, I didn't even look up when someone sat next to me, until I smelled the familiar spicy soap.

Out of my peripheral vision, I saw Gabriel flipping through that tattered paperback. He stopped about halfway through the book and started reading, not speaking a word. The bus hummed as it moved along the street, and my pulse hummed along with it.

Why was he sitting next to me? Didn't he know he wasn't talking to me? Of course, he wasn't actually talking, just sitting, but there should be some rule against it. If you weren't speaking to a woman, then you definitely shouldn't sit right next to her so your arms were practically touching, and you shouldn't smell nice and have your sleeves rolled up to show off your tanned arms that flexed when you turned a page.

You most certainly shouldn't lean over and whisper in her ear.

"Do you have six minutes to spare?" Gabriel's breath was warm on my cheek.

"I thought you weren't speaking to me." I kept my gaze on the iPad.

His shoulder touched mine. "I thought *you* weren't speaking to *me*."

"I'm obviously speaking to you now."

He laughed. Loudly. I was sure everyone on the bus heard, at least those who were awake or not lost in each other's eyes like Debbie/Lark.

"What do you want?" I hissed a bit too harshly, but I blamed it on my racing pulse. I wasn't exactly accountable for the emotions flying through me at the moment.

"I want"—he picked up my hand and kissed the back of it like he was some Duke in a Georgette Heyer's book—"to tell you about my book."

A million zings screeched through me, but I proudly didn't move a muscle. "Is kissing women's hands a new part of the tour director job?"

"Just yours," he said with a quiet chuckle. Still, I refused to look at him. My face was at least several shades darker than pink. His hand tightened around mine, and I thought I might stop breathing right there on the bus. He'd have to call an ambulance. Heaven forbid he knew CPR.

"Haven't you listened to *anything* I've told you?" I whispered.

"I've listened to *everything* you've told me." His breath was touching me again. So were his arm and shoulder, not to mention he was still holding my hand. "And I've considered it very carefully."

"But you chose to ignore it? To mock me?"

He didn't flinch, didn't pull away like I thought he would. "I'd never mock you, Ruby." His tone was serious. "I think friends can dance once in a while or even sit together on a bus."

"Is that why you're holding my hand?" I sneaked a peek at him; he was grinning.

"Does it bother you?"

"Gabriel . . ."

"All right, it's probably too much." He released my hand. "I just missed you."

I thought my heart would leap out of my chest. What was it with this man? I exhaled slowly and closed my eyes.

"Holding my hand is that bad, huh?" he said, laughter in his voice.

I couldn't stop the smile that emerged. "Just tell me about the book. People will start to wonder what their tour director is doing."

Gabriel leaned to the left, looking up and down the aisle. "I don't think anyone is wondering anything. Most of them are asleep." He leaned back and flipped open the paperback. "The author, Robert Pirsig, actually wrote the book in the '70s. He's an avid motorcycle rider—goes all over the country, mostly with his son Chris. Of course, he blends plenty of philosophy and life advice, although he doesn't claim to be an expert."

As he talked, I could breathe again. This was an ordinary conversation, nothing about holding hands or him missing me. Because really, I had missed him too. More than I would allow myself to admit. It was nice to have a friend, especially now that Debbie was enraptured with Lark 24/7. It wasn't that I couldn't make new friends; there were plenty of nice people on the tour, but none of them was like Gabriel.

There, I had admitted it. No one was like Gabriel. Or more accurately, no one could match up to him. Not even Phillip—in our early years together, of course. I'd always had to try too hard with Phillip, to mold myself into what he'd expected, or who I'd thought he'd expected me to be. Now I wasn't sure what he'd ever expected but knew I had never amounted to it, couldn't have prevented him from seeking out other women to fulfill those expectations of his.

With Gabriel, I was just me—a woman on the tour. A woman who could be his friend for two weeks. I liked being Ruby-the-friend instead of Ruby-the-jilted-wife. I didn't know what Gabriel would think if he knew the truth about my marriage. But that didn't matter right now. I was in Greece, making new memories and purging the old. A week from now, I'd say good-bye to Gabriel and return to my life, with all of my secrets still intact.

For the next week, I could have a friend.

Gabriel told me more about his book, and I found some connections to *The War of Art* that we discussed as well. The hours on the bus passed quickly, and before I knew it, we'd arrived at the Hotel Europa in Olympia. After checking in, I took a refreshing swim in the hotel pool. It was nearly empty; it seemed most people went out sightseeing or went looking for a place to have dinner.

I'd agreed to meet Debbie and Lark at the hotel restaurant. By the time I'd showered and changed and made it to the restaurant, they were already seated. No table of six this time, and I was grateful to be in a quieter place after a long day on the bus.

"Is Carson joining us?"

"No, he and Helda went off to explore the town."

I nodded. It seemed Carson had a whole other level of energy around Helda.

"Oh, there's Gabriel," Debbie said, making my heart skip a beat.

She hadn't said anything about Gabriel and me sitting together on the bus. She had probably been too wrapped up in Lark to notice.

I turned my head. Gabriel was at the cashier desk, talking to the hostess.

"We should invite him to join us," Debbie said, smiling directly at me.

"Perhaps he'll see us and come over," I said. I wanted him to sit with us, but I didn't want Debbie to know that. Ever since the refreshing swim, I'd realized our time was running out. The tour would be over too soon.

I turned to look over at Gabriel, but he was gone.

"Oh well, maybe we'll see him later tonight," Debbie said.

Opening my menu, I pretended to read it. Sitting with Gabriel on the bus had been really nice—talking and laughing as if we'd had nowhere else to be or nothing better to do in the world—like a balm. I knew he was still worried about his ex-wife, but for a few hours, at least, we were able to forget all of that.

I ordered a familiar-sounding fish platter and the usual lemon-water. Debbie told us about a phone call she'd had with her daughter and the antics of her grandkids. I listened but wasn't paying too much attention. Lark's laughter more than made up for both of us. When dinner was finished, Debbie said, "Do you want to come browse the shops with us?"

"I think I'll read by the pool for a while."

Debbie hugged me. "All right. We'll come find you when we return."

"I won't wait up," I said.

Lark winked at me, making me glad I was staying back. It seemed he wanted some time with just Debbie.

I grabbed my iPad from my room and settled by the pool. It was still quite warm outside, even though the sun was nearly set. The gorgeous oranges and pinks bloomed exquisitely against the surrounding white buildings. Sitting alone in Greece this time was far different from the last time I'd sat alone in Greece. I didn't have a husband to wonder about, and I didn't have to find out later what he'd really been doing with his time.

"Do you want to take a walk?"

I looked up to see Gabriel, his hand outstretched toward me.

"Around the pool?"

He smiled. "I thought we'd be more venturesome than that. I have a place I'd like to show you."

"Oh, a *place*? Your own hideout?" I put my hand in his, and he pulled me to my feet.

"Something like that." He didn't let go of my hand.

This was different from the bus. When he held my hand on the bus, it was flirtatious and even a bit humorous. But now . . . it felt a little more serious and deliberate.

"Come on," he said, guiding me past the pool. We went out the gate and, instead of heading toward the street of shops, turned in the opposite direction.

We walked up a hill that was mostly deserted. We passed a few tourists on their way down but no one from our group.

"There are the ruins of Chlemoutsi castle," Gabriel said, stopping at the top of the hill. He let go of my hand and gestured ahead of us. I immediately felt a sense of loss, or companionship. "What do you think?" He turned and pointed off the hillside.

The castle looked more like a fortress.

"And there's the valley of Ilia below us and, of course, the Ionian Sea beyond that."

I stepped up next to him to take in the view of the valley and the sea below, leading to the horizon. The sky was a deep violet, with just a few streaks of deep orange, and lights twinkled below us like a reflection of the multiplying stars.

"It's a beautiful view," I said.

It was so peaceful up here, like we were overlooking the whole world. The breeze was slight and didn't feel cold at all, making the temperature absolutely perfect.

"We'll tour the castle ruins tomorrow as a group. It's too dark to explore them now." He shoved his hands in his pockets. "I like to come up here when everyone has left."

We stood for a few silent moments gazing at the flickering lights that grew brighter as darkness descended.

"Let's sit over here," Gabriel said, walking to a low wall that looked several hundred years old.

I found a place to sit that wasn't too sharp-edged and watched the orange streaks darken until they disappeared into the horizon.

Gabriel was quiet, but the silence wasn't awkward, just companionable. I couldn't remember companionable silences with Phillip—at least not after I found out about the first woman. Once I knew about that, the times we'd shared before that day seemed fraudulent.

I folded my arms, telling myself I had to stop comparing Gabriel to my husband. There was no point. I couldn't change anything about my marriage now, and in a week, I'd be saying good-bye to Gabriel. For some reason, the thought of saying good-bye to my new friend made me sad. Maybe it was because we weren't surrounded by the others and we were sitting, looking at a beautiful view and I was feeling like my life in Newport was a completely different world. I let out a sigh a little too loudly.

"Are you all right?" Gabriel asked.

"The tour has been really great," I said. "I think you've done an excellent job with our group."

He was looking at me in the moonlight—I felt his gaze on my face.

"How has it compared to your last trip?" he asked.

"There's no comparison so far." I laughed, and bitterness rose up. I closed my mouth, hoping that he hadn't noticed the change in tone.

"Did you visit Olympia when you came before?"

I couldn't answer him out loud, so I just shook my head. I hadn't been to Olympia, although I'd asked Phillip to come with me. He had spent most of the time right in Athens where he'd had his "meetings." The day trips had been on my own . . . Now that I thought about it, there were at least three nights he hadn't come back to the hotel until early in the morning, saying things had run late and it had been hard to get taxi service. At the time, I wasn't even suspicious—that's how much I'd trusted him.

Perhaps Phillip *had* come to Olympia; it had just been without his wife.

Then it hit me. What if Janelle hadn't been the first affair? What if there had been a woman in Greece he was seeing? I had prided myself in finding out all about Janelle, in discovering her through her phone number listed over and over on our phone bill. What if I'd missed another woman because I simply hadn't been looking? The Greece trip had been a last-minute excursion. Phillip had actually discouraged me from tagging along. I remembered scrambling to get his parents to watch Tony for us because I didn't want him to miss school in the middle of the year and he had an upcoming class performance—one Phillip had said *both* of us shouldn't miss.

My eyes started to burn, and I stood up, walking a few feet away from Gabriel. Even in the moonlight, my tears would be visible, and I didn't want him to see. Had Phillip stood here with another woman, looking at the same view, holding hands? I knew I was being overly dramatic, but it seemed the dark night and the memories were twisting around me and not letting go.

I felt as if something had slammed into my stomach, twisting until a coldness rushed over me. It traveled to my heart, squeezing until it was literally painful. I tried to keep my breathing steady and tried to keep the tears from falling and tried to keep my chest from constricting. But the coldness expanded, spreading its numbness until I wondered if I could even hold myself up.

My blindness had been so complete. I might not have any proof, and it would probably be impossible to find, but I felt sure Phillip had spent his time in Athens with another woman. Hot tears dripped onto my cheeks. He had been cheating on Janelle too.

"Ruby?" Gabriel's voice filtered through the cold embalmment that had covered my body. "Ruby?" His hand was on my arm, thawing it a little. His arm went around my shoulder, and I leaned against him to prop myself up.

I closed my eyes. It was fruitless to stop the tears now, and it was too late to hide them from Gabriel.

I knew I'd sound like a mess when I talked so I whispered, "Do you want to know why I couldn't dance with you the other night?"

"Tell me," Gabriel said, his fingers stroking my shoulder.

"I was afraid."

"Of what?"

I took a deep, steadying breath. The tears were still coming, but the cold was easing. "That dancing with you would make me feel something."

Gabriel pulled away from me and took my hands in his. "Would that be so awful?"

I looked into his eyes, which were even darker in the moonlight. "You've said that to me before." He looked puzzled. "And my answer is, yes, it would be so awful."

"Why? Because you've sworn off getting married again?" His expression turned sheepish. "Debbie told me."

I was sure she had. What Debbie did or didn't say hardly mattered right now. She didn't know much of the truth anyway. "That's only part of it. The last time I let myself truly trust a man, he betrayed me, and I'm afraid I have yet to recover from it. In fact, I don't know that I ever will."

He was quiet for a moment, staring at me. "Are you talking about your husband?"

My throat tightened, and I could only nod.

He pulled me into his arms and murmured, "I'm so sorry." He stroked my hair and held me close. I practically melted against him, then wrapped my arms around his waist and buried my head against his shoulder. He felt so steady, so warm, but at one time, I'd thought that about Phillip. I realized I didn't really know Gabriel. A week was hardly time to get to know anyone, but here I was, pouring out my heart to him.

I drew away from Gabriel. He was looking at me intently, but I avoided his gaze. I couldn't allow myself to rely on someone I didn't know well. I'd never relied on those I *did* know well. "I'd like to go back to the hotel."

I turned away from him, but his hand brushed mine. "Ruby, you can talk to me anytime. About anything."

Tears threatened again, so I could only nod. I walked around the wall, toward the path, with Gabriel following close behind, not saying anything. I felt sure he would hold my hand if I reached it out to him, which is why I made sure not to.

We were about halfway down the hill when I stopped. Gabriel stopped too, his hands in his pockets.

"I've never told anyone that. *Anyone.*" I looked down at the darkened path. "Not my brother or my son. None of my friends know, not even Debbie." I stared into his eyes; they were nearly black in the moonlight. "Phillip cheated on me so many times that I stopped counting. And now that I'm back in Greece, more memories have been triggered."

Gabriel ran a hand through his hair and let out a breath of frustration. "And you stayed married to him?"

"I did." I brushed away the tears that fell onto my cheeks. "At first, it was because I didn't know what to do—I didn't know if I had the courage to be a single mother. My son was still young, still enamored of his father. I didn't want to destroy that relationship. Later . . . I was just too tired to make a fuss."

"It must have been awful living like that," Gabriel said in a quiet voice. "I know a little bit about unrealized expectations, but even with Rhea, nothing like that happened."

"I was in denial for a long time. I thought if I did things differently, he'd change. I blamed myself for most of it, and still do sometimes."

"You can't blame yourself." Gabriel touched my face, his fingers absorbing the moisture on my cheeks.

"I know that, but knowing something is different from truly taking it to heart." His touch was warming parts of my body that hadn't been warm for a long time.

Gabriel's other hand came to my face. "You have to believe it, Ruby. You're beautiful, intelligent, and fascinating." He leaned down, his face only inches from mine. "Your husband was a nightmare of a husband."

"I know," I said, and then I started laughing. An ugly half laugh, half sob, but hearing Gabriel tell me Phillip was a horrible nightmare was probably the best thing anyone had ever said to me. One single phrase said it all.

I leaned against Gabriel, and he gathered me in his arms. He felt too good, too safe, and I was becoming too comfortable with him. I couldn't believe I'd told him about Phillip—not all of the truth, of course, but more than I'd ever told anyone else.

It felt deliciously soothing to share some of the hell Phillip had put our marriage through. I supposed I shouldn't even think of it as an actual marriage—just an arrangement to live in the same house while we raised our son.

Gabriel drew back a little and cradled my face in his hands. "Ruby, do you realize how lucky I am?"

"Lucky . . . how?"

"Lucky to have met you just when I'd given up." He leaned closer, and I supposed I knew what was about to happen. I was a widow, but I wasn't dense. I could have pushed him away or even ducked, but I didn't do either one.

I let Gabriel kiss me.

Chapter 13

I HAD NEVER REALLY CONSIDERED what it would be like kissing a man other than Phillip. With him, our intimacy had been rushed at the beginning of our marriage, which had always left me feeling a little bereft. I figured it was that way with plenty of newly married couples until they became more comfortable with each other. Then there had been the stretches where he'd worked late or had been out of town or I hadn't been feeling well due to pregnancy or being up half the night with a baby. Still, I'd written it all off to the normal pattern of life. Later, of course, there had been no affection at all between us. I'd had a few miserable experiences in the bedroom after finding out about his "first" affair. I had thought if I dressed like a lingerie model, tried new things, he might redirect his interest toward his marital partner.

But it had left me feeling used and unwanted, like I was an object or a means to an end. There was no cherishing between us, on either of our parts. No matter how much I wanted to forgive Phillip in those early days, the innermost part of my heart eventually hardened completely. As the years passed, my heart had given up on ever feeling any sort of passion.

So it was with great surprise I found out two things when Gabriel kissed me: first, that he was quite the romantic kisser. Second, that I wanted to do much more than kiss him. Gabriel's hands moved from the sides of my face to behind my neck, his fingers threading through my hair as he kissed me. I let my arms move up his chest and to his shoulders.

Gabriel's mouth moved against mine, slow and careful as if he was testing the waters, and I kept telling myself, "You can put a stop to it now," but apparently I wasn't listening to myself. Instead of pushing him away, I kissed him back, my fingers gripping his shirt and pulling him closer. He responded by sliding his hands down my arms, then around my back, and intensifying his kisses. It was no longer gentle.

Finally, I had to breathe. "Gabriel."

"What?" he said, then started kissing me again.

I forgot what I was going to say, and I decided it didn't really matter.

At some point, we made it back to the hotel and discovered it was later than I'd thought. No one was in the hallways, and I was sure I looked a fright after crying . . . then kissing. At my door, Gabriel smoothed the hair from my face and kissed my forehead. "See you in the morning."

He stepped back, and I went inside my room, shutting the door quietly. How could a true gentleman like Gabriel be such a great kisser? I climbed into bed without changing my clothes. My mind was whirling, and the doubts started to creep in.

What had I done? Kissing Gabriel was nothing to be taken lightly. He was divorced, I was widowed, both of us completely available. But both of us emotionally wrecked. Gabriel was still dealing with his ex-wife, and I had a closet full of failed-marriage reminders. What I'd told Gabriel tonight was only a small part of it. And his response had been . . . to kiss me? To make me feel things I hadn't felt with my husband? Things I wasn't sure how to make sense of now.

I pulled the pillow over my head and groaned. How could I face him tomorrow? What would he do when he saw me? Were we now an instant couple, and would he hold my hand or put his arm around me in front of everyone?

A woman who'd just been kissed by a completely handsome man shouldn't be worried about these things. But I wasn't an ordinary woman. I was afraid. Afraid because when Gabriel had kissed me, I'd realized I had, for the first time in as long as I could remember, let myself enjoy a man's touch. The zings pulsed through me even though Gabriel was at the opposite end of the hotel—it was like I still felt his touch. Remembering the feel of his kisses and his whispered words kept me awake far into the night.

* * *

Much to my relief, Gabriel didn't rush over and dip me into a swan-dive kiss when I saw him the next morning. He was surrounded by the busyness of the tour group as usual, but he made it a point to come over to where I stood by the hotel doors when he could get away. I tensed as he grew closer and clutched my bag tightly in my hand and wondered if my heart had ever beat so hard in my life.

"How are you?" he said.

Simple.

"Fine," I managed to croak out.

Then he smiled, and the way he looked at me practically set my neck on fire. He was about to say something else when someone came in through the doors next to us and greeted Gabriel. His attention was diverted, and I was left wondering what he might have said.

People started exiting through the doors; the day had started. Gabriel was caught up in the mass exodus, and I waited until the end of the crowd before I left the hotel. Debbie and Lark were somewhere in the middle of the group, but I didn't hurry to catch up with them. I contented myself with staying toward the back and creating a little space. It wouldn't do to have my face turning red every time Gabriel was near.

In the light of the day, the streets looked different than they had on my sojourn with Gabriel the previous night. But that didn't dispel the fluttering in my stomach each time I thought of what had happened on our walk back to the hotel. Not only had I confessed the truth about my sham marriage, but Gabriel had kissed me after. Really kissed me.

Another zing passed through me, and I took a drink from my water bottle, wishing it was much colder. I'd need to have ready access to cold drinks all day if I were to retain some semblance of normal Ruby.

I hadn't been able to eat a bite of the breakfast buffet, so by the time we reached the Temple of Zeus, my stomach felt pinched. I discreetly took out a fruit bar from my purse and nibbled the end. I had no desire to eat, but I knew I'd get light-headed if I didn't eat soon, especially with the approaching heat.

I found a shady spot to listen as Gabriel explained the site and gave us an overview of the museums we'd also be visiting. It seemed to be uncommonly hot, even in the shade, but as I looked around, no one else was sweating profusely.

Maybe I could escape back to the hotel and swim. But even as I thought it, I didn't want to leave. I successfully avoided Gabriel at the Museum of Excavations, though I wasn't as successful at not staring at him. I felt like a silly teenager staking out a young man. What had I been thinking to allow him to kiss me? Gabriel still hadn't said anything to me except for the morning greeting. Maybe he just considered me a damsel in distress, and by kissing me, he was helping me.

My eyes narrowed as I watched the woman he was speaking with— one of the Dutch tourists. I wasn't sure what her name was. She was a few years younger than I was and wore stylish jeans and a blousy top. Her hand rested on Gabriel's arm as he leaned forward to catch her words amidst the chatter. Maybe Gabriel was nice to all the women. I'd seen him kiss plenty of women in greeting.

I wanted to slap myself—twice. First, for thinking Gabriel could be anything like Phillip. Second, for letting myself get jealous of another woman speaking to Gabriel. We'd shared a kiss—that was it. Gabriel hadn't declared his love or proposed.

My breath caught, and I grew hot again. I turned away and examined a group of nineteenth-century photos. I had actually thought the word *proposed.* I took another quick drink of my water bottle. It certainly wasn't cold enough now.

And just like he knew I was thinking about him, Gabriel crossed over to me. We stood side by side, not talking, as we looked at the photos. I sneaked a glance at him, and the side of his mouth turned up. I started to smile too—I couldn't help myself.

"Would you like to sit at my table for dinner tonight?" he asked.

My heart was working overtime, and we'd only climbed one hill today. "I don't know."

Gabriel turned to face me. "You don't *know?*"

I looked around; he hadn't exactly said it quietly. No one seemed to be paying attention, but I still lowered my voice. "Do you *want* me to sit at your table?"

He cocked his head, his half smile back. "Are you flirting with me, Ruby?"

My mouth dropped open. "Uh—"

He squeezed my hand and leaned down to whisper, "It's all right. I like it." Then he winked at me and turned away just in time to answer some questions for a couple of tourists who'd become separated from their group.

I floated through the rest of the day. I hadn't really understood what that meant, but now that I realized what it meant, I couldn't remember what we saw, what I said, and what I ate. Back in my hotel room, predinner, I walked out onto the balcony. Energy thrummed through me, and I was surprised I wasn't exhausted. Being around Gabriel was absolutely exhilarating. But I was a realist. I was going back to California, to my real life, in a few days, one that didn't involve Gabriel. I couldn't let this attachment I had with him keep growing.

Rubbing my forehead, I groaned. *If only it weren't so hard.* I decided I'd be grateful for this small period of romance with Gabriel. I knew it wouldn't last—there certainly wasn't any proposal in the future, nor did I want there to be. Marriage to one man had been enough to last me the rest of my life. I valued my independence above everything else, and besides, Gabriel would not be so interested in me if he learned the truth of how I had done the most cruel thing possible to my husband.

I walked slowly over to my bed and sat down, the weight of my husband's final weeks returning once again. The quiet moments were what I feared. They were the moments that I could see Phillip's watery gaze directed at me, pleading. His eyes had once been a deep blue but had faded to a dull gray with his illness. His thick head of black hair had grown sparse and gray with the years, although it had always managed to look debonair on him. Men were lucky that way.

In those last few months, he'd lost a lot of hair, as if his body were finally accepting its terminal diagnosis. I'd admit that there were many times I did feel a pang of regret for our silent years together, but it was not enough to melt the steel wall I'd created between us. It had taken only one look inside my memory box, and my resolve had come back stronger than ever.

"Ruby, please," Phillip had said. "Can you ever forgive me? Can you love me again?"

I'd heard that a dozen times by then, and now he was literally weeks from dying. Even as the tears had dripped down my cheeks in regret, I'd shaken my head and turned away, walking out of the room. Away from my feeble and dying husband.

I had stopped questioning God long ago. Now, with the brilliance of Greece surrounding me, I lay down on the bed and closed my eyes. My heart hurt as it thumped, like it was trying to get outside my body to find another place to reside. Inside mine, it only found pain.

"Gabriel," I whispered. "I don't think even you can stop this." Telling him about Phillip had made me feel wonderful and alive again, but it was only for a short time. I had left out the most incriminating parts. As the room grew darker, I squeezed a pillow against my chest, trying to keep all of the pain in one place.

* * *

A knocking sounded at my door, and it seemed to go on forever. I tried to call out—to housekeeping, I assumed—that I was still sleeping. My body felt heavy, but I was too tired to turn over and check the time. It was completely dark, although it could have been night or early morning. Why would housekeeping be knocking on my door in the middle of the night?

The knocking stopped, and I sank back into the void of sleep, only to be startled awake with renewed knocking. I pulled myself out of bed, feeling shaky on my legs, and cracked the door open.

Debbie stood in the hall, and right behind her was Gabriel.

She started right in. "We were worried when you didn't come down to dinner. I even called your phone a couple of times."

My mouth felt too dry to answer, and Debbie rambled on. I looked past her to Gabriel. He shook his head slightly, and I hoped that meant he hadn't told her about *us*. My breath caught as Gabriel's gaze soaked into me. How could he even look at me like that when I was completely disheveled?

The level of worry in Debbie's eyes was much less than that in Gabriel's. She continued to talk, and I continued to watch Gabriel. He really did look like he'd been worried.

I gave both of them the best smile I could, mumbled an "I'm fine. I just fell asleep" and closed the door on them. I couldn't handle Debbie's questions right now.

Leaning against the door, I could hear Debbie still talking—now to Gabriel. The clock on the nightstand glowed 10:30 p.m. So it wasn't quite the middle of the night. I sighed with relief when her voice faded away. I was wide awake now, and I realized I felt grimy from the day's activities. Instead of taking a shower, I decided to swim. The pool should be empty, so I'd have it to myself.

I quickly changed, then grabbed two towels. I looked forward to the pool; I used to take Tony all the time when he was growing up. I left my room, and by the time I reached the pool, my eyes were burning with tears again, but I was tired of feeling sorry for myself. Coming to Greece had been important, and although right now it was painful, I was glad I'd done it. It made me realize the depth of Phillip's treachery and also that not all charming men were creeps.

The pool was empty, and only a young couple occupied two chairs near one of the tables. They were too immersed in cuddling with each other to even greet me. I draped my towels over a chair close to the pool and slipped into the water. It still held warmth from the day's sun, but it was cool enough to make me shiver. I pushed off from the edge and stroked through the water. After two laps, I was already out of breath, but the water slicing around my body felt soothing and, more importantly, numbing. I spent a few minutes resting at one end of the pool and noticed the young couple had left.

Normally, I might have been a bit nervous to be completely alone in a foreign-hotel pool late at night, but for some reason, I had no qualms. I plunged through the water again and completed two more laps before stopping to rest again. That's when I noticed someone else in the pool area. A single person, sitting a little farther back from where the couple had been. By his silhouette, I could tell he was a man.

Had he been there all along? Or had he just arrived? My heart started to pound. Maybe he'd come out to smoke, but there was no burning cigarette in his hand. I chided myself—he was completely harmless.

I plunged back into the water and swam to the other side of the pool. The chill started to set in, and I decided I'd had enough. I'd probably be sore in the morning as it was. My muscles were long overdue for a workout. I climbed out of the pool and wrapped up in a towel, then used the other towel to dry my arms, then face.

"Ruby?" The man who had been sitting was now walking toward me.

"Gabriel," I said in a breathless voice, mostly from swimming.

"I didn't realize you were the one swimming." His voice was hesitant, cautious.

"Well, it is dark and . . ." My voice sounded thick.

Gabriel smiled, which looked wonderful on him in the dim pool lighting. How could this man look so good in any circumstance? As for me, I probably looked atrocious. Now I was asking myself why I cared so much. I was too broken for Gabriel anyway.

"You're a great swimmer," Gabriel said. "Did you swim competitively?"

I laughed. "You—you say the funniest things." I pulled the second towel around my shoulders to ward off the slight breeze.

"How is that funny?" he asked, his voice genuine.

If he only knew—Phillip never paid attention to any of my activities. I don't remember him coming a single time with Tony and me to the pool. I had actually bypassed swimming lessons for Tony and taught him myself. It had paid off when he'd passed the lifeguard test and worked as a lifeguard for the summer months during high school.

Gabriel was still looking at me, quite intently, and I smoothed my dripping hair.

"I just swam recreationally, like all the other California girls I grew up with." I wondered if he was trying to make conversation—about anything other than why I had missed dinner.

"I'm glad to see you're feeling better," he said, his voice growing soft.

The kindness in his tone nearly killed me. I wanted to throw my arms around him and feel his warmth and strength. To forget everything except for him for just a few minutes. Instead, I stepped back. "Thanks for checking on me earlier. I guess I really needed a nap."

Gabriel didn't smile. His eyebrows drew together as he studied me. "I haven't been fair to you."

"What do you mean?" I asked, although I knew exactly what he meant. He regretted kissing me. It was hard to digest, but I should have known better. I wasn't familiar with dating—it had been too long—and I'd let myself get too carried away over a single kiss. The good news was that I didn't have to worry about hurting his feelings.

"I've pretended that I've been all right with our friendship," he said. I let out a sigh. It was worse than I'd thought, but I'd be strong. This wasn't the worst thing that had happened to me.

"I really like you, Ruby."

Of course, but we aren't a match. Not even for friendship.

"And I want to be completely honest," he said. "I like you much more than a friend."

I stared at him as disjointed thoughts tumbled through my mind. More than a friend? He liked me *more than a friend?* The compliments he'd given me the night before . . . before our kiss . . . came flooding back. Maybe he had really meant them. Maybe he wasn't just being his charming self.

I took a step back, catching my breath. "The tour is almost over—"

"Forget about the tour. Forget that I live in Greece and you live in California." He closed the distance between us, his hand touching my arm. Even though there was a towel between my arm and his hand, I felt his warmth burning through. "I want to date you. I want to take you out to dinner. I want to know everything about you—what you love, what you hate. And then I want to take you out again on another date." He was leaning so close that his breath touched my face, warm and minty sweet.

"How will that be possible?" I asked, pulling away slightly. "How can we go on a date? Through e-mail?"

"I'm going to figure something out." His hand slid up my arm and rested on my shoulder, his fingertips brushing my neck.

My chest tightened. This was too fast. Yes, I liked him, but this was way too fast. "You can't leave your job. Think of all the disappointed ladies."

He laughed softly, and his other arm went around my waist. I should have resisted. I was in my swimsuit and a towel, for heaven's sake. "I'm a mess, Gabriel. I can't let you make extreme changes in hopes that I'm even capable of what you're talking about. I'm not sure I am."

He didn't seem to be listening as his mouth pressed against my neck.

"I'm a mess," I repeated. "I don't know if I could really trust a person again."

He lifted his face, but his breath was still on my cheek. "I'm a mess too. Maybe we can learn to trust together."

I wanted to believe him, and I wanted to believe there was a second life for me out there somewhere. But it all seemed too good to be true. Which meant it was.

I leaned against him. He just held me, not moving. I was sure I was getting him wet, but he didn't seem to mind. I was just glad he'd stopped kissing me; I was about to break all the rules that a dignified widow should keep.

"Ruby, have you ever let anyone take care of you?" he asked.

I lifted my head. "What do you mean?" I played dumb, but my eyes burned with tears. I'd given up on that long ago. I'd decided that I'd take care of myself.

"You know, let anyone be there for you, to listen. Or anything?"

I shrugged. I really had nothing to say. There was no point in bothering others with my minutia.

"That's what I thought." He released me, took my hand in his, and pressed a kiss on it. It reminded me of that day on the bus. Something so simple yet so intimate. The zings were back in full force.

"Come on." He tugged my hand, and we walked out of the pool area. "You need to get some sleep."

At the door of my hotel room, Gabriel kissed me on the cheek and said good night. I wanted to tell him to not waste his time, that even if there wasn't an ocean to separate us, it would be useless. But the exertion from swimming was taking its toll, and I let him leave without any more protests.

Chapter 14

I AWAKENED WELL BEFORE THE sun rose, but I stayed in bed. I couldn't remember the last time I'd lain in bed doing nothing—not sleeping, not reading, not typing an e-mail. It felt strange to allow my hands and mind to be idle. Maybe Gabriel was having this strange effect on me.

Waking up and thinking of Gabriel before anything else crossed my mind was certainly new. An unchecked smile spread on my face. Gabriel had been very clear: he liked me—really liked me—and wanted us to date. Which, of course, was impossible but very sweet. And it didn't hurt to soothe some of the pain that had arisen since I'd begun suspecting that Phillip had had even more affairs than I'd first thought.

Someone knocked on the door at 6:00 a.m. Now that I was used to the time change, it felt way too early. I pulled on a robe and went to answer it, surprised to see a young woman wearing a hotel name tag and holding a bouquet of white daisies. She smiled and said in broken English, "Thees for you."

I reached for the flowers, and she held out a card. "Thees for you too."

I took the card. It was a voucher for a spa treatment.

"Come now," she said, motioning with her hand.

Looking at the daisies, I searched for a note to see who they were from, although I thought I already knew. "Who sent these?"

"Nice man," she said. "Come now."

The next hour was bliss. I'd had plenty of massages before, but this one seemed different somehow—knowing it was a gift from Gabriel. I brought the flowers with me so I could smell them as the masseuse worked. When she finished, my mind felt completely active, but I wondered if my body would ever move again. It took a full ten minutes to get enough life back to sit up. Was Gabriel trying to wear me out before the day even started?

When I returned to the room, a notecard sat on top of the bed.

Meet me for breakfast on the pool terrace? —G

I turned the card over—there was no time listed. I crossed to the window, where I could see one corner of the pool area. The pool looked empty, but beneath one of the umbrella tables, I could see a pair of legs extended, crossed at the ankles. Gabriel.

I flew through my morning routine, and by the time I reached the terrace, everything inside of me was fluttering. Gabriel lounged in a chair next to a table that looked like it had been set for dignitaries. The glasses looked like real crystal and the utensils, silver. The only thing that seemed out of place was the book he was reading—that ratty paperback. It was so . . . Gabriel.

I laughed, and he looked up. My step nearly faltered as our gazes met. His hair was slightly damp and curled against his neck. He stood and pulled me in for a hug. I didn't think I'd ever smelled anything as nice as Gabriel fresh out of the shower. And I made myself not look around to see if any of our tour group happened to be nearby.

"Did you have a good morning?" he asked, drawing away but not releasing me.

What if he kissed me right here in public, in broad daylight? I realized I wanted him to, really wanted him to, which meant it was time to put some distance between us. I stepped back and looked at the artfully arranged food on the table. "I had a wonderful morning, and it looks like it's not over yet."

He grinned. "I hope you're hungry."

"Starved." I shook my head, trying to let it all soak in. "You're spoiling me." I touched his arm. "Thank you for the spa massage. It was amazing."

"You're welcome," he said, taking my hand. He leaned down, and I caught another spicy waft before he kissed my cheek. He lingered, and I was sure my face turned bright red.

I cleared my throat. "Aren't we on some sort of schedule?"

"Yes," Gabriel said, his eyes teasing. "But I'm the one who sets it."

"Oh really? And what time is the bus coming to pick us up today?"

"Eight thirty."

I nodded. "Just as I thought." I pulled my hand away, which he reluctantly released, and sat down. There were at least a dozen different cheeses, a platter of fruit—which we could never finish eating—and exquisite-looking pastries layered with jellies and creams.

"I wasn't sure how you liked your coffee." Gabriel poured it into a cup from a silver pot. He had everything on the table: sugar cubes, cream, whole milk, and lemon.

"Actually, I prefer tea."

His face flushed, and I laughed. "It's all right. I'll have juice this morning."

"I'll order some tea."

"No, I'll survive. We're on a schedule, remember?" I said with a smile.

He looked chagrined as he scooted his chair in. "I should know that you prefer tea by now."

I took a sip of orange juice. "It's not like we've known each other very long."

"Long enough." He was staring at me, creating those zings. He seemed more interested in talking than eating.

I ripped off a piece of a still-warm baguette and spread cheese on it. "Aren't you hungry? All that planning in the middle of the night must have interfered with eating."

He smiled, grabbed the baguette from me, and took a bite.

"All right, I'll let you have that one," I said, tearing off another piece of bread for myself. At home, I'd never eat bread for breakfast, but in Greece it seemed perfectly natural. It was also feeling perfectly natural to spend more and more time with Gabriel.

"Are you ever going to finish that book?" I nodded toward the paperback he'd set next to his plate.

"Not anytime soon. It's my third time through."

"*Third* time? Who reads the same book that many times?"

He slid it over to me, an eyebrow quirked. "You might like it." His hand touched me, and his fingers tangled with mine.

Trying not to feel too distracted by his touch, I thought of the books I loved, but I'd never read any of them three times. "I'm just impressed you found a book you like to read over and over."

"It's the second edition, actually. The ending is revised from the original version, as well as a couple of other corrections."

"I'll take your word for it," I said, smothering a grimace.

He laughed, his fingers trailing over mine. "Someday you'll read it—I'll convert you."

I smiled and looked down at our hands together. This "thing" with Gabriel was getting quite public. Here we were, holding hands on the pool terrace.

"Can I sit by you on the way to Delphi?" he asked, leaning toward me.

There was no hesitation this time. "Of course."

His head was really close to mine, and I think my heart rate tripled. A beeping sound broke into my heady thoughts.

Gabriel checked his cell phone. "Time to go." He pulled me to my feet. "Do you need me to carry your bags down?"

"That would look really great in front of the tour group. You go be the director, and I'll find a porter."

Gabriel touched my face with his fingers, his eyes nearly melting me. "See you in a little bit."

I could only nod. He strode away, hands in his pockets, like he'd just been on a casual walk. I wondered if he knew that he carried part of my heart with him.

I finished the last few swallows of orange juice, then picked up a section of grapes to take with me. I'd definitely need my stamina today. The ugliness of the previous night, of dwelling on Phillip, had faded, replaced by a sliver of hope. Maybe it wouldn't be too terrible to enjoy the next few days with Gabriel and get to know him better. I could leave Phillip back at home, in his grave, for that long, couldn't I?

The drive from Olympia to Delphi was breathtaking as we passed the bridge that stretched across the Gulf of Corinth. We stopped at one of the beaches for lunch. A few people swam, but Gabriel and I just walked the shore together. He didn't hold my hand, and I didn't reach for his. It was enough to be side-by-side, and it was just fine to keep things between us fairly private.

I knew that when I returned home and spent time at the senior center, I'd endure unending questions if Gabriel and I were more obvious. Although I was pretty sure Debbie sensed enough of what was going on, even in her enamored state with Lark.

After we checked into the hotel, there were no real plans for the rest of the evening. Gabriel had given everyone a list of things to do. I'd wanted to find out what Gabriel was doing, but we hadn't had any private moments after the beach.

When I came out of the shower, there was a note on the floor by my door.

Meet me in an hour in the lobby? Wear walking shoes. —G

I brought the note to my nose and inhaled. That's when I knew I had lost it . . . lost my ability to think sensibly. I didn't think I'd ever smelled anything of Phillip's—unless I was checking to see if a shirt needed to be laundered. There were a few times I'd checked for distinctly female perfumes. Here I was comparing the two men again.

Well, I'd given myself permission to enjoy the rest of the tour. And going on a walk with Gabriel sounded quite enjoyable right now. I dressed in a pale-peach blouse and navy slacks, accompanied by my navy Converse shoes.

Gabriel was leaning against the reception counter, talking to the desk clerk, when I came into the lobby. It had been only an hour since I'd last seen him, but my heart jolted anyway. Watching him when he didn't know I was there was kind of intriguing. He laughed at something the clerk said—a pretty woman with long dark hair—but I didn't have the ugly twist of envy for some reason. Like I would have had with Phillip.

I'd seen Gabriel be gracious to everyone, men and women alike. And I was grateful to get to know such a kind man. I wondered why he was so different from Phillip. They were both nice-looking men, could even be considered "ladies' men," since women seemed to congregate around them, but Gabriel's kindness wasn't uncomfortable. It was genuine and pure.

I exhaled. That was it, I realized. Gabriel was genuine.

With Phillip, there was always an underlying motive to his charm. And most of it was directed at getting the woman of his current attention into bed. The coldness was starting to creep in again as I thought of Phillip. I couldn't allow it to happen. I focused on Gabriel, the way his arms rested against the counter, his sleeves partly rolled up, the tanned color of his skin, his dark hair just touching the collar of his rust-colored shirt.

My breath thawed a little, and I forced one foot in front of the other as I walked toward him. Gabriel laughed again, followed by the clerk's higher-pitched laugh. She looked up at him, adoration in her eyes. My stomach hardened. She had to be half his age—what was she doing flirting with Gabriel? I knew I was being ridiculous, but I couldn't stop the cold from spreading, from numbing any reasoning I might have. If I could just reach him before it grew worse . . . if I could just touch him.

I was a couple of feet away from Gabriel when he saw me. He immediately smiled, but then it faltered. Could he see the darkness in my eyes? Should I turn around now, before I dragged him down with me?

He reached for my hand and squeezed it tightly—as if he *knew*. Although he couldn't possibly have known what was going through my mind, the warmth of his hand started to do its magic. He was introducing me to the clerk, and I smiled at her politely, not hearing anything in their conversation. All I could see were her long eyelashes, the tiny mole by her mouth, and her smooth, flawless skin.

Finally, it was over, and Gabriel was leading me outside, still grasping my hand. It was a like a lifeline—an anchor—as we moved out into the evening air. Gabriel led me down the street, not saying anything, as if he knew I wasn't up for talking. He just kept hold of my hand, strong and sure.

Eventually, I started to notice our surroundings. We were walking in a massive grove of trees—olive trees. They were gorgeous, and many of them were ancient, but there were also plenty of younger trees whose limbs looked young and strong. The contrasting trees mirrored Gabriel and me, even though we were only two years apart—I was the ancient broken woman; he was the young strong man.

Then I noticed something unusual. "Where is everyone?"

"Ah. You're back," Gabriel said. "This is private land. I got permission to walk among the groves."

Through the trees up ahead, I caught glimpses of the ocean. "It's beautiful."

Gabriel just nodded, and we kept walking. It was peaceful, quiet—exactly what I needed. It seemed he always knew what I needed.

I owed him an explanation. "I'm sorry about that . . . back there."

Gabriel glanced at me. "You looked a bit pale. I thought you might be sick, but then I remembered I've seen that look on your face a few times before."

"What do you mean?"

"The look that you'd rather be anywhere but where you are."

"You've seen it before?" I asked in a quiet voice.

He stopped walking and tugged my hand so I was standing close to him, facing him. "Look, I know you've had a tough time, and there are a lot of things you don't want to tell anyone." He ran his other hand through his hair and looked past me, not meeting my eyes. "Believe me, I know what a troubled marriage is like." His gaze found mine again. "Although I'm not saying I went through what you did. Not even close. But you can *trust* me, Ruby."

I blinked my eyes against the stinging. "I don't think I even trust myself."

"The first step is admitting it," he said in a soft voice.

"Are you a therapist on the side?"

"Hardly." His eyes were full of tenderness. "I've been to plenty of sessions though—mostly by myself, of course."

"Of course." I stared at him. Could I truly trust another person? Myself? Gabriel? My son? Anyone? I wasn't sure.

"So next time you see me talking to a woman and you think you might pass out, remember that I'm just talking—and it's probably not about anything even remotely interesting."

I laughed, although I wanted to cry. I wanted my hotel room—four walls and a door with a lock on it. "Well, it's not like we're . . . married or even really dating," I choked out, my voice sounding hoarse.

Gabriel ran his fingers along my cheek. "Oh, we're definitely dating."

My next smile was tentative. "All right. I'll try not to pass out when you speak to another woman, even if she's gorgeous and flirting with you."

The edge of his mouth turned up. "She wasn't flirting, and she's young enough to be my granddaughter."

I scoffed. "Daughter, maybe, but definitely not *granddaughter*."

"Okay. Daughter." His other hand released mine, and both of his hands now cradled my face. This time I met him halfway. I think I surprised Gabriel by kissing him with such force. In fact, I surprised myself. He definitely didn't seem to mind.

* * *

The next morning in Delphi was busy and kept Gabriel and me apart most of the time. We toured the Sanctuary of Apollo and the Delphi Museum. Then we left Delphi and headed toward Kalambaka to visit the site of the monasteries in Meteora. The buildings perched on top of massive pinnacles were breathtaking.

We took a tram to the first monastery, and after Gabriel's general lecture to the group, he found me sitting on a bench by the entrance. I enjoyed watching Gabriel from afar. I'd never been to Kalambaka before, but I felt I knew quite a bit about the life of a monk. I'd lived it myself plenty in Newport, although for me, it wasn't a badge of honor. Living like a nun in your own home was nothing that would earn a woman heavenly salvation or the title of a saint.

"If I were a monk, I'd definitely want to live here," Gabriel said. He'd broken off from the group. Most of them had wandered into another room.

"Your hordes are appeased for the moment?"

He sat down next to me with a laugh. "I might have fifteen minutes, twenty at the most."

"So you're going to use them up sitting next to me?"

"Unless you're going somewhere else." He looked over at me. "I can follow you around like a stray dog."

I smiled. "It feels great to sit for a while."

"Last night was fun," Gabriel said. "Sorry I got you in so late."

It had been fun, and my cheeks warmed as I thought of our private dinner at a café by the freshwater springs. We had eaten quite late after our walk through the olive groves and had made it back to the hotel after midnight. "I'm not too tired," I said, then right at that moment, yawned.

Gabriel laughed. "Yeah, I can see that."

I nudged his arm, and he grabbed my hand. Looking down at our intertwined hands, I said, "This is quite public." A few members of the tour were still in the room.

"That makes it all the better."

It was my turn to look at him. He'd never been affectionate around the tour group—only when we'd been alone together. My heart hammered—this felt like a whole new step for us. I couldn't remember the last time Phillip had been publically affectionate with me.

"Are you okay, Ruby?"

I blinked, realizing I had been staring at Gabriel. "Am I fading again?"

He squeezed my hand. "You can fade anytime."

"This is still . . . so new. It feels not quite real."

Gabriel's gaze was intense. When he looked at me like that, everything else seemed to disappear. "What doesn't seem real, Ruby?"

"The way you're looking at me—as if you're really interested in what I have to say." I looked past him; it was hard to concentrate when he was staring at me. I felt like all of my flaws were exposed, like he could see right into my heart.

"I *am* interested," he said, his tone gentle. He squeezed my hand. "Can you feel this?"

"Yes."

His voice dropped to a whisper. "That means it's real."

I nodded, my throat feeling too tight to speak. I wasn't ready to have another relationship talk—we'd had plenty of those. But what he'd said made me feel better; he had a talent for that.

"Let's go see some monk rooms," he said. "I would be neglecting my duty if I let you sit this one out."

"All right," I said. He pulled me to my feet and released my hand as he drank from a water bottle. We turned in the opposite direction from the rest of the group, which was more than fine with me.

When we entered a room lined with human skulls, I gasped.

He chuckled. "You didn't listen to my lecture, did you?"

I shook my head, staring at the empty eye sockets lined up against the wall, staring at us.

"This is called the Ossuary."

"Are these all the monks who used to live here?" I asked.

"Yes, burial grounds are limited on a cliff."

I shuddered, and he draped his arm around my shoulders. Even after a long day, he smelled nice but not nice enough to block out the rows of decaying skulls.

Gabriel steered me out of the room, and I let out a full exhale. "This place is incredible, but that room was a little too much," I said. "It's amazing how they could build something like this so long ago. I can't imagine climbing up a rope ladder to get to my home."

"Some men will do anything for tranquility." The hall narrowed, and he dropped his arm from around my shoulder, leading the way.

"What did fourteenth-century men have to escape from?" I asked.

Gabriel chuckled, the sound echoing off the stone walls. "It sounds unbelievable now. I wonder what they'd think about the twenty-first century?"

"They'd probably never leave their cliffs." We entered another room that looked to be a food storage area. "I don't blame them for wanting to get away from it all. Maybe they had a nagging wife."

"Or their wife became a stranger."

I felt the meaning of his words deep inside, and I met his gaze. "Maybe living on top of a cliff was preferable to working on a relationship back at home." It wouldn't be hard to completely cut yourself off from the rest of the world in a place like this. I walked to the far end of the room, marveling at the flagstone floor. The work that had gone into the construction of this place was incredible. The monks certainly hadn't been idle.

"I think I would have stayed to work it out." Gabriel's voice reached across the room like a caress, making goose bumps break out on my arms.

I turned to face him. He had a half smile on his face, but his eyes were serious. "I have no doubt you would," I said.

"You would have done the same," he said, crossing to me. "We make a grand pair." His fingers brushed my arm. "Why didn't we meet thirty years ago?"

I was saved from answering that question by a group of people coming into the room.

"There you are," Debbie said. Her voice was unmistakable above the chattering. "Lark says there's a nunnery in one of these cliff things as well."

Gabriel turned in full tour director mode. "There is. We can head over there next if you'd like."

When we finished the tour of the monasteries, we traveled to Dion and checked into the Palace Resort Hotel—a spectacular place that looked like the backdrop for a *Vogue* magazine photo shoot. A group of us had dinner together, and Gabriel didn't make it any secret that he wanted to sit by me. I don't think anyone noticed too much. Across the table, Carson and Helda were in their own cozy world. Debbie seemed unusually bright and cheerful, whereas Lark acted nervous and high strung, and the reason soon became apparent.

After our meal was cleared and thick, delicate baklava was placed on the table, Lark tapped the side of his wine glass, capturing everyone's attention. Gabriel slid his hand into mine under the table.

"I'd like to propose a toast," Lark said. His gaze traveled around the table, then settled on Debbie. "To the most wonderful woman, Debbie."

Her face flamed red, and the rest of us laughed, then touched glasses. But Lark wasn't finished. "And to the woman who I hope will honor me by becoming my wife."

We all went silent, and Debbie's mouth fell open. "You're asking . . . You . . ." She looked over at me, and I grinned.

"Did he . . . ?" she said mostly to me, then turned to Lark. "Yes!"

Lark laughed and hugged her, then drew back and gave her a sound kiss on the lips.

Gabriel squeezed my hand, and I realized I had been gripping his. I let go and joined in the clapping.

The heat crawled up my neck as I felt Gabriel's gaze on me. Caught up in the moment of celebration, my mind was opening up to newer and more daring possibilities. Maybe I could have the same sort of happiness with Gabriel. Maybe the end of the tour wouldn't be the end of our relationship.

I steeled myself against the intruding thoughts and shoved them away. I couldn't let the wine, the music, the laughter, and the handsome man next to me cloud my judgment. No matter how good it felt to have his arm draped around the back of my chair and to have someone to turn to and talk to. When the congratulations died down and the conversation turned back to its normal buzz, Gabriel leaned over.

"Want to get out of here?"

My heart started to pound, and I nodded. It would be good to get some fresh air. We said our good-byes and offered another round of congratulations, then slipped outside the restaurant. We were directly across from the beach, and without a word, we walked in that direction. Gabriel had his hands shoved in his pockets, and I made no effort to change that.

We slowed when we reached the sand. The waves were gentle tonight, barely making a sound beneath the bright moonlight. I waited for Gabriel to say something, but when he didn't, I said, "Debbie looked so happy. She's been following Lark around for forever."

"Much longer than two weeks?" He stopped, looking over the water.

"Much longer." I folded my arms. The breeze was just a tad on the chilly side. "Although I'm not certain *how* long, I'm sure it was before I met Debbie at the beginning of February."

Gabriel ran a hand through his hair and let out a sigh.

I stiffened. Was he upset at something? I didn't know him well enough to read all of his moods—especially this one. He was practically brooding. Maybe this was the beginning of the end. The countdown to the last couple of days—in which we'd have to face the inevitable separation.

"Does it really matter how long two people know each other?" Gabriel asked, startling me. His tone sounded so serious, much different from the usual.

"I think it matters a little," I said. "We both know what it's like to marry someone who turned out quite different than expected."

He was gazing at me now, a thoughtful look on his face. "So what do you think the appropriate time would be to . . . declare one's affection?"

My hands felt sweaty and my throat dry. I was sure a relationship expert somewhere had spent years researching this very topic. I thought of how long I'd known Phillip before we'd started talking marriage—it had been a couple of years of on-and-off dating. Had that been too long? Had that been a warning signal in and of itself? "I'm sure it's different for everyone."

Gabriel nodded as if he were considering my answer very seriously, when it was really a cop-out.

"How long did you know Rhea before you married?" I asked, wincing at my boldness. Why I had to ask him that, I didn't know, but I preferred to talk about him instead of where I thought this might be leading . . . to us.

"A couple of months. Rhea wasn't one to waste a moment of life back then. She pushed quite heavily, in fact. Maybe that should have been a red flag." He turned away again, looking out over the mellow water.

Phillip had been the opposite. So what was the balance? Was there one? Or were we back to background checks? I chuckled to myself.

Gabriel turned again to look at me, eyebrows raised.

"Sorry," I said. "I was just thinking we should have had a time statute in addition to background checks for our spouses."

A smile touched his face, but his expression was still serious. His hand moved toward mine and grasped my fingers. "I guess that's why there aren't any hard and fast rules. I don't know if any relationship could operate under so much scrutiny."

"So you're saying love is blind?" I cringed when I realized what I'd just said—the *L* word.

"It's probably more blind the first time around but much less blind the second time around." He turned toward me, and his other hand moved to my cheek. "But I think it's better to have your eyes open wider."

He was looking at me like that again—I knew this expression by now. He was either about to kiss me or about to say something that would dig our relationship even deeper. I wanted to melt against him, but I couldn't let myself. I started to realize this infatuation I had with Gabriel was lurking dangerously close to that *L* word, which was totally impossible.

The sooner I got back to the old Ruby, the better off I'd be.

Gabriel's lips brushed against mine, and I closed my eyes. "Gabriel—"

"Just pretend like you aren't leaving in two days and that kissing me in the foothills of Mount Olympus is an everyday occurrence," he whispered, his arms pulling me close. "Don't start the countdown yet."

Chapter 15

SOMETHING WAS DIFFERENT WHEN I woke up the next morning. Then I remembered. Debbie and Lark were engaged. But it was more than that. I had let go. I had let my heart open a crack—and for better or worse, it had happened.

I moved slowly through my morning routine, in no rush to see Gabriel. I knew he'd be there when I came into the lobby, looking for me and smiling. It was a calm feeling to have *someone* there for me. Someone who cared. And I knew I was going to miss that. I had promised not to start the countdown, but my heart wasn't listening—it was scheming and plotting how I could see Gabriel again when he finished his next round of tours. Maybe I could come to Greece again. Maybe he could come back to the Newport office.

By the time I'd made it to the lobby, the tour bus had arrived and people were settling in. I scoured the faces for Gabriel but didn't see him. After the driver loaded my bags beneath the bus, I grabbed a pint of yogurt and a bottle of juice from the café. Still no Gabriel. I took a seat near the front of the bus since I felt foolish not sitting down—looking obvious about waiting for him.

Debbie and Lark were several rows back. Her eyes were closed, her head resting on Lark's shoulder. They must have stayed out much later than us. The bus driver was speaking Greek into his cell phone, and I wondered if something had gone wrong with our plans or upcoming reservations.

Finally, I saw Gabriel hurry out of the hotel entrance. He looked neatly pressed as usual, but as soon as he climbed onto the bus, I noticed the dark circles beneath his eyes. He greeted everyone as cheerfully as ever and apologized for running late, but he didn't give us any reasons. There was a slight hesitation before he took his seat next to me. Was he not planning on sitting by me but felt obligated since I was near the front?

As the bus pulled forward, he leaned into the aisle to answer some questions. I studied his hands, strong and tanned, and found myself blushing. Why was I looking at his hands? Pulling out my iPad, I opened to the Kindle app to browse through books, but I couldn't concentrate on any book with Gabriel next to me. He wasn't carrying that ratty paperback either, that I could see.

When his conversations ended, he settled back into his seat with a sigh.

"Are you all right?" I asked.

He seemed hesitant to tell me anything. My stomach clenched. What could have possibly changed between last night and this morning?

"Just tell me, Gabriel," I said in a quiet voice, trying not to sound desperate.

His eyes searched mine for so long that I wasn't sure what he was looking for. "What's wrong?" I said again.

"I need to talk to you in private."

"Of course," I said automatically, though my stomach felt sick. Talking in private? And the look in his eyes wasn't exactly warm or humorous. More like serious and anxious.

Somehow I survived the visit to the royal tombs at Vergina and Pella. I was proud that I didn't lose my mind when we walked through the museum at Vergina and listened to Gabriel describe the gold artifacts from Alexander the Great's tomb.

It wasn't until we reached Thessaloniki, a quaint harbor town, that there was a remote possibility of any privacy. But Gabriel still didn't make an effort to pull me aside. We all ate lunch in a group, and while Debbie and Lark were discussing whether they wanted to explore the Aristotelous Square and its vendors, I excused myself and told them I'd meet them at the hotel later.

I headed for the harbor, grateful for the stiff wind. My stomach was so knotted up that I'd hardly been able to eat. Gabriel had been gracious but distant today—opposite of how he'd been the day before. I didn't know if I could handle this type of roller coaster that every relationship seemed to endure.

Were we still even in a relationship? If not, then the countdown had already ended. Just as soon as it'd started, it was over, faster than I could have imagined. I didn't know if I was relieved or even more depressed when Gabriel caught up with me. "Ruby."

I turned to see if anyone was with him, but he'd come alone. I just nodded at him and waited for him to say something—although it was practically killing me to not beg him to put an end to my misery.

"Maria called this morning," Gabriel said.

I slowed down and looked over at him. "Is she all right?" Hope renewed itself. Maybe this was just a family matter, nothing to do with us.

"Maria is fine." A brief smile crossed his face, but the worry was close behind. "It's Rhea."

I held my breath. What if something had happened to her? Would that be good or bad? I immediately berated myself for thinking that Rhea having trouble could in any way be good.

"Rhea needs an assigned guardian. If she doesn't have someone as her advocate, she'll be turned over to a state representative and made a ward of the court." He took a deep breath as if it were hard to talk about. I could only imagine the emotions rocking through him. "Maria is very upset with the idea that a stranger could make decisions for Rhea—as if she were less than human or could be treated like a child."

I nodded. I could understand. "What about her family?"

Gabriel's eyebrows went up. "I was her only family. Her parents are both gone. She doesn't have siblings, and her extended family isn't an option."

Suddenly it hit me, and the twisting in my stomach was back. Maria was asking Gabriel to step in. Was he looking for my approval? I didn't understand all the ramifications of Gabriel being his ex-wife's guardian, but it sounded like he had no other option.

"You should definitely do it," I said, trying to hide the trembling in my voice. "You know her so well and would be her best advocate."

He was nodding, relief in his eyes. Had he doubted my support? It was saying something that he thought he needed it, but there was still something dark in his expression.

"I thought you'd say that, Ruby. You always put others before yourself." He shook his head. "But I don't know if I can do it. I'd be pulled into her vortex again—and that wouldn't be fair to you."

"To *me*?" I asked. "How would it not be fair to me?"

"Rhea can be all-consuming."

I stared at him. He was putting our dating above the needs of a helpless, mentally ill woman, even if she had been a terrible wife? *I* shouldn't be a factor in this decision. He'd been married for over twenty years. He'd known me for only two weeks. "She knows you're her ex-husband, so she can't expect any higher level of commitment. Besides, you'd just do the paperwork or whatever goes along with being a guardian."

"You don't understand." He let out a sigh and looked away. "She'd be given all of my contact information. She'd be able to call me day or night, and I'd have to assist in all of her requests. If she decides to throw a tantrum and stop her medications, I'm the one who will be called. If there are evaluations with a psychiatrist, I'll be expected in the meetings." His eyes were back on mine again, searching. "I'd have to move back to California."

I stared at him, a million thoughts flooding my mind. Gabriel in California? My heart equally soared and plummeted. We could continue dating . . . but then there would be Rhea and . . . And I didn't know what else. I touched his arm. "It may only be some of those things, but what's the other solution?"

He looked down at my hand on his arm. "I can't go back to Rhea—not in any form. If I do, I'll crack. I told Maria no. I told her I wasn't leaving Greece anytime this year—maybe ever."

My breath caught at the resolve in his eyes but, more significantly, at the pain and darkness. I knew about pain and darkness and how I'd spent so much time and energy keeping them at bay. Gabriel knew where his was locked up, and in order to survive, he would avoid it at all costs.

"What did Maria say?"

"She screamed at me, then hung up." The circles beneath his eyes looked darker. "She called back a few minutes later and screamed some more." His gaze absorbed me in its sadness. "I'll call her in the morning, when she's had the day to get over the . . . shock of her brother's cold heart."

I rubbed his arm. "You have to do what's best for *you*, Gabriel."

"Then why does it make everyone else so miserable?"

I laced my fingers through his. His hand felt like a dead weight; there was no returning warmth. Had this decision come between us after all? I blinked against the burning in my eyes. I could see it in his face . . . He'd started to close off. I let go of his hand.

"You haven't made everyone miserable," I said, forcing a smile, although my heart felt like it had been run over.

He looked down at me. "Ruby—"

"You don't have to say anything," I said. "Forever in Greece is a really long time."

He scrubbed his hand through his hair, then grabbed my hands. "I thought there was a chance I'd return. No, a really good possibility . . . and you and I could keep seeing each other—"

"Really, Gabriel, I understand completely." I squeezed his hands, trying to reassure him, but inside, I wanted to run straight into the ocean and sink until I could no longer feel anything. "The countdown was just a bit shorter than we thought."

He pulled me into a fierce hug, and I clung to him. People walking past us probably wondered what was going on, but I didn't care. I knew that after this moment, everything that had been Gabriel and I would be over. Closing my eyes, I inhaled his scent, creating a new memory box around this moment.

"Ruby, I don't know if I can let you go," he whispered.

I wanted to say, *You don't have to. I'll stay in Greece.* But I said nothing. I couldn't make that kind of decision when I hardly knew the man—no matter what my heart was saying. When I pulled back, I'd blinked away a good portion of my impending tears. Gabriel's eyes were moist, and I almost hugged him again.

Instead, I smiled with false brightness. "I think I'll finish my walk along the harbor. I'll see you at dinner?"

"Ruby—"

"I'll be all right. You need to focus on doing what's right for yourself for once. It's about time you did." Another weak smile. "I'll be your cheerleader from afar—that I can do well."

His hand touched mine, but I wouldn't let him wrap me up again. I didn't want to hear him ask me to stay in Greece. Or tell me how much he'd miss me. I dragged my fingers from his and gave him a half wave. "See you at dinner."

Before he could say anything, I walked away, trying not to run. After several dozen steps, I turned to see him watching me. Not moving, not following, but just watching. Thank heavens, I was too far away to see his expression.

So this is it, I told myself. Things hadn't ended in exactly the manner I'd thought, but when did life ever do the predictable? I'd be his friend from afar, just like I'd said. I tried to find a little comfort in that. We'd e-mail back and forth. He might ask me to check on some California law for him.

I could do a bit of research and e-mail him about it. I'd report on Debbie and Lark's wedding and tell him how great it was. I'd think about stopping in to visit Maria to give him an update. There was a possibility he might even say he missed me a time or two over the next couple of months, but after that . . . our e-mails would become less and less frequent, until one day, they'd stop completely.

But that was all right. I would return to California in the same state I'd left: a single woman, a widow who had plenty of things to occupy her time and mind. I had a great niece who lived close by and definitely needed support with her busy schedule, a brother I needed to do better at keeping in touch with, and a son and daughter-in-law I should plan a summer trip to visit.

Then there were the book-club ladies. Daisy would need help when her new baby arrived. Paige could always use any sort of break. Athena would be delighted if I accompanied her on visits to her father. Ilana would need some assistance as her arm continued to heal, Tori would probably enjoy escaping her hectic job to have lunch with me, and Olivia and I could swap some recipes. I could even help Shannon by spending time with Keisha.

By the time I reached the far side of the harbor, I had refueled my resolve. My life could go on without Gabriel, full of purpose and ways that I could make a difference in other people's lives. It was what made me truly happy anyway. I watched a couple of gulls pick at a discarded wrapper. I wasn't a scavenger like those birds. I had a full life, and with or without Gabriel, it would continue to be filled to the top.

The pain that twisted inside of me would fade, like most painful things did. I wiped at the tears that had collected on my cheeks. Tears were fine for now, but by the time I reached the hotel again, they needed to be a thing of the past. Just like Gabriel.

* * *

I never made it down for dinner but instead opted for room service. I knew it was some sort of huge faux pas—room service in Greece—when I could be at a great café surrounded by friends. Instead, I stared at the iPad screen, trying to write an e-mail to the book-club ladies. They'd all sent cheerful replies to my last e-mail and had asked a bunch of questions. It had been a couple of days since I'd sent any updates. Surely they were anxious to hear the latest. But everything that had happened since my last e-mail had Gabriel front and center. I could barely envision the places we'd visited, let alone remember any names or interesting facts. I had truly been in a fog—a very thick, dense fog.

Finally, I turned off the iPad and took a sleeping pill.

The following morning, I woke feeling tired, but at least I had slept—that, I hadn't expected. Thank goodness for sleeping pills. Now *there* was a scientist I wanted to hug. The tour schedule had today listed as a relatively open day. A list of sights and activities were included, so I decided to set off on my own.

When I reached the lobby, a group of Dutch women, including Hilda, was just leaving. Helda was probably off with Carson, so I joined Hilda's group, enjoying the fact that I wouldn't have to answer any probing questions as to why I was wearing my sunglasses inside the enchanting Byzantine churches. Nobody needed to witness my swollen eyes.

We climbed into a couple of cabs and headed to the Turkish quarter above Thessaloniki. Every moment, I wondered what Gabriel was doing, what he was saying, or who he was listening to. Had he already been to the little churches or gazed out over the sea? Had he eaten lunch, or was he even hungry? We stopped for lunch at a café before walking back down to the harbor.

We walked at a slow, casual pace, which I enjoyed, although it was strange to be in any part of Greece without Gabriel nearby. It seemed I had grown used to his presence. Conversation with the Dutch women consisted of short sentences and lots of gesturing, so I was content to let them talk amongst themselves. I let a sigh fill me—I had accomplished my main goal, it seemed. Greece had now become about Gabriel, not Phillip. It was good in a sense that the memories with Phillip had mostly been replaced with Gabriel memories. But not so good that both trips were centered on men who had ultimately broken my heart.

I adjusted my sunglasses as another tear tried to escape. Yesterday had been for crying, not today. I tried to think of how much I looked forward to returning to my regular life. My routine would bring me comfort—it always did—and it would be wonderful to not live out of a suitcase anymore.

Maybe I'd do some redecorating—in celebration for having conquered Greece.

We returned to the hotel for a short break. Later, I headed out with the same group of ladies to Krikelas. It was definitely a hopping place, with a lot of young people, making me feel ancient. But Gabriel was nowhere to be seen, so I was relieved. We wandered through some great boutiques, where I picked out trinkets for the book-club ladies as well as my daughter-in-law. After a bit of agonizing, I decided to get everyone the same thing, including Keisha; I bought silver "evil eye" earrings and matching bracelets. I also bought something extra for Athena—a statue of the goddess. Then I picked up two Alexander money clips for both my son and brother. For myself, I selected a couple pairs of sandals, a gorgeous embroidered tablecloth, and two one-size-fits-all blouses.

One portion of the shop carried tour-guide books and authentic Greek cookbooks. I thought it might be fun to try some Greek cooking with the book club, so I bought one of the cookbooks, then grabbed a second one for Debbie. She and Lark would want to rekindle their memories of Greece in their new home together.

I laughed aloud when I spied a familiar cover: *Zen and the Art of Motorcycle Maintenance.* It was just too perfect not to buy it. I'd find a way to slip it into Gabriel's belongings. It would be my farewell gift—a brand-new copy to replace his torn one.

The store owner was only too delighted with my multiple purchases and thanked me over and over until I had left the shop and was halfway across the street. The other women helped me carry my purchases back to the hotel, exclaiming over them—although I couldn't understand a word they said.

Once inside the lobby, I assured them I could make it to my room fine. Just as the elevator door started to slide shut, I heard an unmistakable voice. Gabriel had come into the lobby. I didn't think he'd seen me, but my heart hammered as I watched the doors close, dividing us. I was tempted to stick my foot between the doors, to stop the elevator and catch a glimpse of him, but I kept my feet firmly planted.

My eyes were watering again by the time I reached my room. I focused on organizing and packing my new treasures. Then I took a sleeping pill for the second night in a row.

Chapter 16

IT WAS LIKE A HAZY dream. We caught a commuter flight back to Athens and were given three hours to visit any final locations. Our plane was leaving at five. We turned in our baggage and only kept what we wanted to carry on the plane. In the chaos of the tour group dividing and deciding what everyone wanted to do in the final hours, I managed to slip the *Zen/Motorcycle* book into Gabriel's bag. I just hoped he wouldn't find it before I left.

I caught him watching me a few times, but I managed to align myself with the Dutch ladies as we set out to walk toward the Acropolis. It would feel good to stretch our legs before the overnight flight.

The last time I'd been in this area had been when I was first getting to know Gabriel. It was strange to be walking through Athens, knowing he was nearby somewhere but not with me. We stopped at several shops, the women with me selecting last-minute souvenirs. I was finished shopping, so I just browsed along with them. When my cell phone rang, I was surprised. The caller ID said unknown number, but that was due to the international calling plan.

I answered, even more surprised to hear Maria's voice on the other end.

"Ruby—you must speak to Gabriel. He must return to California," Maria said, skipping any greeting.

I stepped outside of the shop to hear better, but the noise of the traffic and passersby was worse. "Maria? Is everything all right?"

"Nothing's all right." Her voice sounded high pitched and frantic over the phone. "Gabriel refuses to become Rhea's guardian."

"Yes, he told me."

A slight pause was followed by, "He told you? What did you tell *him*?"

I felt uncomfortable, and my mind was spinning. Why was Maria calling me? Did she know about Gabriel's and my relationship? It was like I was going behind his back. "I encouraged him to be Rhea's guardian." *But . . .*

What had he told her?

"Oh." Her voice sounded defeated. "Gabriel said he couldn't do that to *you*—to your *relationship*."

The spite in her voice made me shudder. I had never heard Maria speak like that.

"Apparently, Gabriel is too caught up in a woman he's known for two weeks instead of his wife, who he was married to for twenty-four years and cruelly divorced."

My stomach felt like a rock. Gabriel told me he'd told Maria everything. Had he not told her the truth about the marriage yet? She sounded like she still disapproved of the divorce. Why would Maria want Gabriel to go back to Rhea?

"Maria," I said, my voice sharper than I'd intended, but it got her attention. "Gabriel and I aren't *seeing* each other anymore. I told him he should take on the guardianship of his *ex*-wife, so you are preaching to the wrong person. And I don't think it's for either of us to tell Gabriel what to do at this point. There are too many things we can't begin to understand. He needs to do what's best for him." Even though I knew what was "best for Gabriel" included breaking up with me, it was the only thing I could tell Maria.

There was a stretch of silence, and I wondered if the call had been dropped. Then Maria said, "Oh," her voice sounding defeated again. "Well. Gabriel isn't answering his phone. I thought you'd be together, and since . . . he's turned his affections toward you . . . I thought you could help me convince him."

I let out a sigh. "I wish I could help you, Maria. Gabriel and I aren't really speaking right now, and I fly out in a couple of hours."

"He must be in one of his stubborn moods," she said, her voice high-pitched again. "You're better off without him, Ruby."

I was stunned. I'd had the impression that Maria adored her brother.

"He certainly doesn't need any distractions from his duties," she said, the spite in her voice again.

My throat hurt, and my eyes were bleary. "As far as I know, Gabriel has made up his mind. With or without any *distraction*." I took a shaky breath. "You should be discussing this with him. It had nothing to do with me. Good-bye, Maria. I have a plane to catch." I pressed end on the phone and waited a moment to compose myself before going back into the shop.

Gabriel hadn't been kidding when he'd said his sister was upset. But through the bitter sound of her voice, I had sensed pain there as well. It was obvious that she wanted her brother home, even if she had to use the guardianship excuse to get him there. But it was hard to understand why Maria wouldn't want Gabriel to have a relationship with another woman. How could she be upset with him over ending such an impossible marriage?

Well, I'd probably never find out. It wasn't something I could exactly ask someone I wasn't speaking to. I went back into the shop and busied myself looking at necklaces, none of which I intended to buy. I didn't want to be a jewelry snob, but I wasn't really interested in the cheap touristy stuff for myself.

When Hilda and her friends were finished, I followed them outside, the sharpness of Maria's voice still rattling through me. I felt a bit sorry for Gabriel as I contemplated how often his sister berated him for something. No wonder he didn't want to return to California.

By the time we made it back to the airport, all of our baggage had been checked in, and we only had to go through security. I was surprised to see Gabriel in line in front of us. He was certainly taking his duties as a tour director seriously by seeing everyone off at the gate. Apparently, security was all right letting him through without a ticket. It would have never happened in Los Angeles.

I caught myself staring a little too much in his direction and pulled my focus back to the group of ladies who were chattering in Dutch. I really needed to learn a little Dutch. "*Hoe gaat het*"—*how are you*—didn't really cut it. We'd spent plenty of time smiling and nodding at each other, not to mention a lot of pointing.

Once through security, we walked to our gate. My heart had started its slow hammer in anticipation of speaking to Gabriel again. There was probably no way to avoid it at the departure gate. Sure enough, he was surrounded by farewells when we arrived, but he immediately looked in my direction as if he sensed me coming.

I don't know if I was the only one to notice, but his warm eyes held a hint of worry. I knew it was for me. I straightened my shoulders and smiled at something Hilda was telling me—about a bird or a chicken, I wasn't sure. Was *vogel* a bird? I didn't want Gabriel to worry about ending our dating. We'd both known it would probably go nowhere after the tour. I couldn't imagine making him feel pressured about one more thing in his life.

Before I knew it, I had migrated toward Gabriel as he said his good-byes to everyone. Most of the women hugged him, several kissing him on the cheek, and even a couple shed tears. I tried not to laugh at that, primarily because I felt that tears were closing in on me as well.

Carson and Helda had been hugging for about five minutes straight, although I was certain they had plans to rendezvous at some point. The American flight would be leaving sooner than the Holland flight. I'd moved down the farewell assembly line enough to be only one person away from Gabriel. It would be impossible to avoid him now.

He grasped both of my hands, looking into my eyes as if there were no one else in the room with us. I wanted to rewind the past couple of days and walk through the sites of Greece, hand in hand with him. But it was over. I had to remember that.

"Ruby . . ." He left my name hanging there as if he didn't know what else to say.

"Thanks for everything," I said, knowing it sounded completely trite. "You were a gracious host, and I only hope the very best for you." I pulled my hands away and clasped them together. I didn't think I could stand it if I let him hug me. I wouldn't be able to let him go and definitely wouldn't be able to stop the tears. "Good-bye."

"Ruby—" he started again, but I stepped away, letting the next person crowd between us. I waved and gave him a small smile. It was all I could manage without making a complete fool of myself.

As I turned away, I felt his gaze on me, but thankfully, the voice over the intercom announcing that seating had begun on our flight drowned out his voice for a moment. Besides, Gabriel had my contact information and could get ahold of me if he really had something more to say.

I forced myself not to look back as I passed the ticket agent. Once settled into my seat, I let out a sigh of . . . what, I didn't know. My hope to survive Greece had been more than a reality. Not only had I survived it, but I'd fallen in love with the country. As I pulled on my eye mask, I admitted to myself the falling in love with Greece part had a lot to do with a certain man.

* * *

It seemed a year had passed since I'd been inside my home, surrounded by my things. The calendar said it had only been two weeks. Everything looked a bit dull and quiet after the vibrancy of Greece. The house felt empty and still, but it was clean—heavenly clean. Not that things in Greece hadn't been kept up, but nothing was like being in my own clean home.

For a moment, I scanned the kitchen, seeing it with new eyes. The expensive wood blinds, the knotty-alder cabinets, the Italian tile . . . I wondered what Gabriel would think. He probably lived more simply than I did. I wasn't sure how much money there was in the tourist industry, but Phillip had always demanded the best products in our home. Would Gabriel think it was pretentious?

I shook my head. I was done dwelling on all things Gabriel. I wished him all the best and was happy that he was allowing himself to move on from his former life, which would be difficult for anyone to manage. I had no expectations to be any part of it. Although, if he happened to e-mail a request to me, I'd be happy to help him . . . as a friend, of course.

I checked my messages first and wrote down the names of people to call back. There were a couple of neighbor calls, a handful of sales pitches—why they left messages, I didn't know—and a call from my CPA. That return call could definitely wait. I needed some vacation recovery time before worrying about my taxes.

I grabbed a cold water bottle from the fridge—which reminded me that I needed to go shopping—but all of that could wait until after a nice, long nap. I'd also wait to power up the laptop until later. The iPad had been nice on the trip, but I could whip things out much quicker on a computer. For now, I turned on the iPad and sent a quick e-mail to the book club letting them know I was home safely and I'd e-mail more details later.

I opened the lower cupboard in the kitchen, where I'd hidden the laptop, and set the iPad in there as well. Then I noticed the laptop wasn't there. I bent down and felt along the shelf. No laptop. And no power cord. I knelt and looked on the lower shelf, but there was nothing.

I had moved the mixer to put the laptop there, hadn't I? Sure enough, the mixer was on top of the counter. The only other place I'd ever taken my laptop was in my bedroom. Most of my work had been done in the sunny kitchen—I loved the natural lighting—and my living room furniture was not as cozy as my bedroom.

Perhaps in the double- and triple-checking of packing my baggage, I'd left the laptop in my bedroom for some reason.

I hurried upstairs and did a thorough check. I couldn't believe I'd forget to put the laptop away. I'd always been so fastidious about putting my things in the same place, even if it was inconvenient at the moment. I sat down on my bed, unsure of what to do. It wasn't like I could dial a number and listen for the computer to ring—which I'd done a few times with my cell phone.

I decided to check every room in the house. I must have been completely distracted while packing and put it somewhere unusual. A search through the house turned up nothing. I even checked my car, all the while my pulse rate increasing with worry. Was I just completely exhausted and not thinking straight?

With my head pounding, I checked the security settings and scribbled down the times that it had been turned off. Four times since I'd been gone—all in the evening when Shannon had likely come in after work to check on the house. Not that I'd expected her to do an actual walk-through, but she was that type of person. It had to be her medical background—always thorough about everything.

Maybe Shannon had borrowed it but had forgotten to tell me. I wasn't sure if she knew where I kept the laptop, but she was a pretty observant person. Yet, why would she need my laptop? She had her own computer, I was sure. I didn't mind, of course, although it had all my financial files on it. I completely trusted my niece, but it was still a bit uncomfortable to consider.

It was much too late to call Shannon; I'd have to wait until the morning.

* * *

The ringing phone woke me, and it took me a moment to realize I was in my bedroom, in Newport Beach. I was startled when a male voice greeted me. It took a few seconds for the fog to clear and for me to realize it was my CPA, Taylor Redd. Maybe he didn't get the message I left with his secretary to reschedule our tax appointment. Still, I was surprised at his persistence in calling me himself.

"Mrs. Crenshaw, I'm glad I finally got ahold of you."

"Oh? I've been out of town. On a tour to Greece, in fact."

He didn't seem impressed or very congratulatory. "Have you cleared things up with your bank yet?"

My mind went blank. What was he talking about? "What do you mean?"

"You haven't spoken to them?"

"No. Please tell me why you're calling. I have a good case of jet lag, and I'm not sure I can play guessing games."

He exhaled over the phone. "Your bank called me—they must have not been able to reach you—but they told me there were quite a few red-flag purchases on your account."

Red-flag purchases? "Well, I have been in Greece." But that didn't make sense either. I'd used my credit card in many countries, and I'd never been contacted by my bank before. Also, why would they call Mr. Redd? Phillip must have set him up as an emergency contact.

"I don't know anything about the purchases," he said. "They wouldn't give me that information, but they were definitely eager to get in touch with you."

"Thank you. I'll call them right away," I said, although a peek at the clock told me I'd have to wait about an hour before anything opened. It was probably nothing—a new intern or something in account security had seen the international purchases and flagged them.

I hung up. I was definitely awake now, and it was only 7:30 a.m. I figured since it was a school day, Shannon was probably awake, but my call went straight to voice mail. Maybe she'd turned her phone off last night and hadn't turned it back on yet, so I left a message telling her to call as soon as possible.

I hoped she wouldn't think it was a real emergency, just that she'd call me as soon as she could.

I slipped my cell into my robe pocket while I went downstairs for some breakfast so I wouldn't miss Shannon's call.

I was warming up hot cereal when she called back. I quickly answered.

"Hi, Aunt Ruby," she said. "I just got your message. Are you sure your laptop isn't there somewhere?"

"I stored it in one of the kitchen cabinets when I left. I know I did because I had to put my mixer on the counter to make room, but I thought a mixer was safer in plain sight than a computer, you know? It's not there. The whole shelf is empty. You didn't borrow it?"

"No," Shannon said. "And I never saw it during the times I came to check on things. I always locked the house up when I left, I swear."

This isn't good. My mind raced to other possibilities. I'd already searched every place I could think of. "The security system recorded each time you disarmed it, and I know the alarm was reset correctly each time too, which is just so strange. How would anyone have gotten in without tripping the alarm? Do you think someone could have bypassed it?"

"I didn't get any notifications." Shannon paused. "Is anything else missing?"

I hadn't even thought to notice if anything else was missing—I'd been so focused on the laptop. My neck started to prickle as worry set in. "Um, I haven't really checked since I thought you'd just borrowed it. I'll go look right now. I don't leave valuables out, you know, especially when I'm going to be gone." I slid off the bed and walked into the master bedroom, my heart starting to pound. "I locked up my jewelry box in the safe, along with some of my more expensive souvenirs I've collected over the years." I opened the door to the master bedroom, then went to the closet. "Everything looks fine . . ." I stared at the closet floor. A couple of boxes stacked in the corner had been moved. They were no longer tucked tightly against the wall but were moved out about a foot and turned on an angle. "Oh, wait . . . someone's been in the master closet—that's where I keep the safe. My shoes are mixed up."

Shannon's voice sounded tight. "Did they get into the safe?"

Panic pounded through my chest as I typed in the combination on the safe. The seconds seemed to drag on until the door popped open. I scanned all of the items; nothing had been touched. The antique wine box was still there as well. "No," I said but fingered some gouges on the edge of the safe door. "But it looks like they tried to pry it open."

"You said you looked at the history and could see that I reset the alarm each time I came over," Shannon said. "How many times does it show I came?"

"Four." I listed off the dates, then, before Shannon could answer, I said, "I'm going to call the alarm company right now and have them check the system. Maybe they'll have a more complete report." I grabbed my home phone and scrolled through the caller ID numbers. There were no phone calls from the security company. There were two calls from the bank, but they had never left messages. I was anxious to get off the phone now to contact the security company.

Shannon's voice sounded very worried now. "Do you want me to come over and stay with you? Do you feel safe there alone?"

She might have thought I was nervous about my safety, but that hadn't crossed my mind. I just wanted answers. My safe hadn't been broken into, and my house wasn't vandalized. The thief had come and gone. "I'll be fine, dear. Thanks for asking. And thank you for watching the place."

"It seems I didn't do a very good job of looking after the house," Shannon said.

"Nonsense." How could I blame this on Shannon? "This is obviously the work of a professional. I suppose no security system is completely foolproof. I'd better go though. I've got more phone calls to make." I had the sudden urgency to get ahold of the bank right away, even before I called the security company.

"I'm so sorry, Aunt Ruby," Shannon said. "If you need anything, I can be there right away." The tiredness in her voice was obvious, and there was no doubt she'd worked a full shift today.

"I'll call if I think of anything," I assured her, "but I'm sure I'll get to the bottom of it."

I used the iPad to look up the number for my bank. Perhaps I could get some answers out of the twenty-four-hour customer service.

While the phone rang, I opened the bank app on the iPad and typed in my account number and password. The international purchases were pretty easy to distinguish, and I skipped over the automatic transfers for utilities and my cell phone bill.

Then I saw it. A series of purchases at Target, all in $50 increments. As I looked closer, my stomach churned. Various stores were listed, each with $50 charges. What in the world cost exactly $50? Maybe gift cards? My heart dropped as I clicked on each link to find out the location of the stores. The purchases were all in the Los Angeles area, and the dates were while I was in Greece.

I had heard about identity theft on the news, but I had always been very careful of where I used my credit card, and I doubled checked my receipts against my statement each month. A customer service representative answered the phone just as I clicked on the last purchase link. I explained why I was calling, and after asking me several pointed questions, she filed an official claim for me. I also cancelled my credit card. Now I'd have to reset all of my automatic payment accounts. This all had to be connected with my missing laptop.

I hung up with the bank and called the security company. They promised to be over within the hour.

I needed to shower so I could be presentable when the security man arrived. I opened my suitcase to retrieve my toiletries. A book sat on top of my things—one with a ratty green cover. I stared at it for a moment, hardly believing what I saw. Then I picked it up—it was real and smelled like . . . Gabriel.

I sat on my bed, shaking my head in disbelief. He'd given me the book I'd given him such a hard time about. I'd given him the same one—brand-new. We did make a pair. I held the blasted thing to my chest and closed my eyes. Gabriel had given me his favorite, well-worn, and well-read book. I let out a laugh, but my eyes filled with tears.

For a moment, it was like he stood in the room and I could see his warm eyes and broad smile. The memories were stronger than I could have ever expected, and all it took was the sight of a book.

"Thank you," I whispered, then smiled at my idiocy.

I was sure he thought it was hilarious when he found my book, and thinking of his laugh made me miss him even more.

I wanted to tell him about the missing laptop and my stolen credit card number. I wanted to tell him how long the plane ride had been, and how, despite the sleeping pill I'd taken, I'd hardly slept at all. I wanted to tell him that I could still hear his voice in my mind and still see his fingers wrapped in mine. Most of all, I wanted him here, right now.

I brushed away the tears and placed the book on my bedside table. I might have to read the darn thing now. I wasn't one to waste a gift.

Chapter 17

THE DOORBELL RANG ON SATURDAY morning while I was going through each room for the second time, scanning for anything else that might be missing. So far, it was just the laptop. I hurried to the door and was out of breath when I opened it.

Shannon stood on the porch, her brow furrowed. "Oh, good, you're home. I was worried—"

"I'm fine, dear," I said, hugging her. Her arms tightened around me a bit protectively. When I pulled away, I noticed the mauve scrub pants she wore with her Walgreens shirt. Her hair was pulled into a neat ponytail—she must have been on her way to work already at 8:00 a.m.

I'd been up since 4:00 a.m. and going strong ever since. "Come in, come in. I'm just making a list of missing items."

"*More* things were taken?" Shannon's hand rested on my shoulder.

"No . . . I haven't actually written anything on the list. It seems the thief was after only one thing." I showed her the blank notepad. "I still haven't done upstairs, although I don't think I'll find anything."

Shannon started to explain her visits to my house and what her routine had been.

"You know what," I cut in, "I think I'll write down what you say, just in case it helps the police investigation."

She looked impressed. "You've contacted the police already?"

"Phillip didn't do *everything* for me, you know."

Shannon's expression fell as she followed me down the hall. "I didn't mean that, Aunt Ruby."

"Oh, I know," I said, although it was well known that Phillip would have handled these types of things, leaving the mundane things like cooking and housework to me. "Let's go sit in the kitchen . . . the scene of the crime." My voice was rather dramatic, and Shannon laughed, although I could tell she felt quite guilty.

I poured us each a glass of juice and settled across from her as she told me the details. Since I already knew the time of her visits to the house, I didn't drill her about those. I asked her to tell me what she checked on.

When I'd written down everything Shannon could think of to tell me, I said, "Let's forget about it for a while and have some muffins." I stood to put together the ingredients.

"Oh, I have to be to work by ten."

"This won't take long," I said. "Why don't you fill me in on your family? How's your son liking his new basketball team?"

"It's taking some adjusting—he's the new kid. We're planning a team party at our house"—her voice was definitely more cheerful—"so I think that will break the ice for him." She paused. "What's this book?"

I turned, but it was too late. I'd forgotten that I'd brought Gabriel's book downstairs this morning and left it on the table while I ate a quick bowl of Cream of Wheat.

"It's . . . from the tour guide, actually. He was reading it over there, and I asked him a few questions." I laughed at myself. "He sneaked it into my bag, so it was a bit of a surprise when I found it."

Shannon was staring at me with a puzzled look on her face.

"Have you ever heard of such a strange title?" I said.

"Gabriel's the tour guide?"

"Well, he's part owner of the travel agency with his sister, Maria." I put another thing on my mental to-do list. I needed to smooth things over with her now that she knew Gabriel was not coming back and that it truly wasn't my fault. Then I continued. "But he also works as a guide on a lot of Greece tours."

"Aunt Ruby, I think you're blushing."

My hand flew to my face. It was warm, but I wasn't blushing. "I— no, I don't think so." I turned back to the counter and started mixing the muffins.

"Do you have a picture of him on your phone?"

My heart raced at the thought of showing Gabriel's picture to Shannon. When I didn't answer, she said in a knowing tone, "Can I see the pictures?"

Because my face was definitely red now, I tried to cover up my pounding pulse by calmly picking up my phone and scrolling through the pictures. "Debbie took most of the pictures, but there might be a few on here." There certainly were, but I wanted to edit what Shannon might see. I clicked over to a group picture that included Carson and Helda as well. We were standing outside one of the monastery buildings. In fact, Gabriel and I were on opposite sides, which was just perfect. I handed the phone over to Shannon. "He's on the left."

"Oh, wow. He's good looking. And look at that smile."

I said nothing but waited for her to hand back the phone. I didn't want her to scroll through any more pictures. There were a few that might be misinterpreted—I had analyzed them plenty on the flight home.

Shannon grinned up at me. "He's not smiling at the camera, Aunt Ruby. He's smiling at you."

"What?" I grabbed at the phone, trying not to be too dramatic, but she pulled it out of my reach. "No. He's smiling at the camera."

"I don't think so . . . He's definitely smiling at you."

I came around the counter and looked over her shoulder at the picture. "Well, he's just a cheerful person. He smiled at everyone." I grabbed the phone and snapped it closed before slipping it into the pocket of my housedress.

Shannon rested her hands on her hips, a silly grin on her face. "He sounds really nice."

"He was nice—nice to *everyone*. He did a great job as our tour guide." I turned away again, the phone safely in my pocket.

"Why won't you let me see more pictures?"

"When I get them all from Debbie, I'll make an album and pass it around at book club."

Shannon was quiet, and I hoped her attention was diverted. I peeked over my shoulder—she was leafing through the paperback.

"To Ruby. All my love, G."

I whipped around. "What did you say?"

"All his love," she said, raising her eyebrows. "Tell me more about Gabriel."

I felt my face warm. "I don't know what you're talking about."

"There's an inscription." She held it open to the front page, her eyes twinkling. "Didn't you see it?"

I couldn't look at his writing. He'd written in the book, to *me*. I pulled out paper muffin cups and placed them into the muffin tin. "Like I said, he was very thoughtful—to everyone."

Shannon just mm-hmmed and continued turning pages. "Have you ever thought about dating again, Aunt Ruby?"

I took a moment before answering to steady my nerves. Shannon was way too observant. It was easier to keep all things Gabriel tucked away in Greece, and the fewer people who knew anything about him, the better. I filled the muffin cups with batter and slid the pan into the oven. After rinsing my hands off, I faced Shannon. "I was married for thirty years, dear. I consider myself retired."

"Why is that?" she asked, setting the book aside and resting her arms on the counter. "You've taken excellent care of yourself, you've got more energy than some women half your age, and you've got a lot of years left. Why not see if there's someone you could share those years with?"

I kept busy by wiping down the counters. "Thank you for your kind comments, but I guess I just had my fill of it."

"Is this about Uncle Phillip's . . . ?" Shannon started to say in a quiet voice.

When she didn't finish, I asked, "Phillip's *what*?" My heart raced for some unexplained reason, but I ignored it. Shannon knew nothing anyway. "What are you talking about?"

"You know . . ." Her voice dropped off.

My neck was hot, which was ridiculous. "Know what?" I breathed out, slow and steady. "What are you talking about, Shannon? This has nothing to do with my husband. A lot of widows remarry. It's just not for me."

She folded her arms, watching me carefully. Could she see my flushed skin or sense the sweat on my hands?

No one knew what kind of husband Phillip really was. Not even my brother. And if my brother didn't know, there was no way Shannon knew. Unless . . . my heart dropped, and I turned away, perhaps too quickly. I couldn't let Shannon see my face.

Suddenly, I noticed a bit of broken egg shell I'd missed on the counter. I didn't want any part of salmonella in my kitchen. I reached for a paper towel and moistened it.

"Ruby," Shannon said, her voice quiet, but I bristled at the knowing tone I heard in it.

I wiped up the egg piece and tossed the paper towel in the garbage. Every small sound seemed to magnify and echo in my kitchen.

Shannon came over and stood by me, and I shut the cupboard door. Then I used another paper towel to wipe down the already-clean stovetop. Anything was better than letting Shannon know how rattled I was.

"Did you know Uncle Phillip had an affair?"

My breath stopped, and all I could see was the coils on top of the stove. The black against silver blurred together like a murky pond. I opened my mouth as questions tumbled through my mind, but I couldn't form the words.

Shannon touched my arm, and I eventually became aware of the slight scent of antiseptic that seemed to accompany her whenever she wore that Walgreens shirt.

"No . . ." I started but couldn't finish. *No, what?* No, there weren't other women? No, Shannon couldn't possibly know about them because that meant . . . I tossed the second paper towel in the garbage. "How did *you* know?" I croaked out, my eyes pooling with tears.

Her hand tightened on my arm. Then she wrapped her arms around me, but I remained stiff.

"I overheard my parents talking the day after . . . Uncle Phillip's funeral. It seems my father has known for a while."

Dismay shot through me. "Your parents know too?"

I felt her nod. "I'm so sorry," she said.

My brother knew *and* my sister-in-law. Jason and Kodi were good people—people who'd never let something this dark be a part of their lives. Yet, they had said nothing. It was too much to comprehend. I melted against Shannon, the tears burning my eyes. Shannon had known for the past two years and had said nothing. I wasn't sure if I was grateful or hurt. I couldn't grasp it—all the hiding I'd done, all the careful steering of conversation away from my relationship with Phillip. I pulled away. Suddenly, the kitchen was stifling, and my legs felt weak.

I walked into the living room and sat down on one of my white couches, then slumped back. Shannon was next to me in an instant.

I couldn't bring myself to look at her—to see if her eyes were filled with compassion or pity or both. I had to know more. "What did your father say?" I asked when my voice regained some control. "How did he find out?"

"When I overheard the conversation he had with my mom, I knew it wasn't something I could pretend not to know," she said. Her gaze seemed to pierce through me, but I refused to meet her eyes. I'd been pretending for decades.

I waited, feeling as if this wasn't really happening to me. That it really wasn't possible, but when I clenched my hands into fists, I felt my nails dig into my skin. That, at least, was real.

"Dad said he ran into Uncle Phillip at a restaurant in San Diego. At first, he didn't think much of it and assumed it was a business lunch. But the woman was dressed very casually for a business meeting." She paused and waited for me to respond, but I could only sigh and blink back tears.

"Dad had a strange feeling when he left the place, so he doubled back and stepped inside a second time." Again, Shannon stopped.

I looked at her. "Tell me."

"It was obvious they were in a close relationship, and Uncle Phillip knew he was caught." Shannon reached out and tentatively touched my hand. I didn't pull away.

"Why didn't your father tell me?" I asked.

"Uncle Phillip made him promise." Her voice grew quieter. "He threatened to leave you with nothing. He said that you already knew and your marriage was all about your son and that was the most important thing . . . that if Dad made a big deal about it, the whole family would be torn apart."

I breathed out. Phillip was right. The family would have been torn apart. By keeping his affairs secret from everyone else, it meant the only one who was torn apart was me. I was the sacrifice for his actions.

"After he died, Dad didn't see the sense in dragging up such painful memories."

"When did your dad see my husband in San Diego?" I didn't want to know, yet I couldn't stand not knowing. I glanced at Shannon. Her eyes were darker than usual, not quite filled with pity but something more like resolution. I guessed the death of an unfaithful man could soften the anger for some.

"It was about three years before he died."

I nodded. San Diego. Five years ago. "Then that was Evelyn."

Shannon's mouth opened. "You know her *name*?"

I pulled my hand away and clasped both of mine together. I knew Shannon had her own challenges in her little family, and she'd always seemed to carry them with grace, especially with her stepdaughter, Keisha. I sensed there was a lot she wasn't telling me, a lot of hurt that she and John had gone through over Keisha, but she'd managed to put on a happy front. Just like her aunt.

I'd felt closer to her more than ever since my son had moved and now with my brother living in Arizona. It bothered me that my brother had wimped out like I had, let Phillip's threats get to him. Yet, how could I blame him?

I looked Shannon square in the eyes. "I knew *all* of their names, honey."

* * *

As Shannon and I walked up the stairs, I took courage in Gabriel's insistence in knowing he had to divorce his wife and let go in order to move on from an abusive marriage. I hoped that by telling Shannon the whole story about Phillip's affairs, it would help me move on as well.

Opening the door to the master bedroom always sent a shiver through me. It was like stepping back in time to a place I had so desperately tried to forget. Shannon didn't say anything.

I went straight to the closet and opened the safe. I pulled out the memory box and knelt on the floor to unlock it, then lifted the lid. Shannon sat down by me. I took out the starfish first. Might as well go in order. Then I removed a rolled-up set of phone bills.

"This phone bill was the first clue—I discovered all of the long-distance phone calls he made right after we returned from Greece on our first trip over there thirty-two years ago." I didn't unroll the billing statements, just placed them on the floor next to the starfish. "I waited a long time before I confronted Phillip; in fact, it gave me a strange sense of power knowing he didn't know that I knew about Janelle." I pointed to the starfish. "Janelle lived in Dana Point, and I kept the starfish as a reminder."

"When did you confront him?" Shannon said, a mixture of dismay and curiosity in her voice.

"After Lisa, who was number two." I pulled out a glass-bead necklace. "Lisa lived in San Clemente and ran one of those touristy beach booths that sold cheap hippy jewelry. Bought this from her myself." I laid the necklace on the floor in an oval shape. "She never knew who I was."

Shannon shook her head, speechless.

"I'd fooled myself into thinking Janelle was a one-time affair and that maybe Phillip was going through a midlife crisis. At thirty-two, no less!" I stared at the glass beads. "I was so wrong. And when I found out about Lisa, I was beside myself. I guess the intense anger gave me the courage to confront him." My hands shook, and I gripped them together in my lap. The argument from so long ago seemed like it'd happened only a few days ago. The hurtful words, the slammed doors, the crying, then the bitter silence that followed all jolted through me.

I didn't realize I was crying until Shannon handed me tissues and put her arm around my shoulders. "Sorry," I said, taking a deep breath. "I haven't told anyone—"

"You don't have to say anything more, Aunt Ruby." She squeezed my shoulder.

I sniffled. "I want to. Really. I know it sounds crazy, but I want to finally tell the truth." Another deep breath, and I removed an ace bandage rolled into a tight ball from the box. "I was a bit crazy when it came to Gina. I could have probably been arrested for stalking."

Shannon took the bandage and set it next to the necklace.

"Gina was a nurse at Mission Viejo Regional Medical Center." I closed my eyes for a second, remembering the peppy brunette. "She was sweet, obviously bright, and very helpful. Especially when I tripped on the curb because I wasn't looking where I was walking while following her."

Shannon was staring at me, and I let out a laugh. "Gina helped me immediately and even wrapped my sore wrist in this bandage. I had to be more careful after that." The tears had faded, replaced by a hollow ache. "Anyway, you're probably wondering about Phillip's and my conversation after Lisa. He said he'd give me a divorce, but that we'd be a broken family, which he knew was my greatest fear. Tony would be shuttled back and forth every weekend. It was like my future flashed before my eyes . . . and I read into what Phillip was really saying. I pictured Tony being paraded in front of all of these strange women and wondering where his mom was. And me . . . not having my son with me every day and feeling heartsick at him having to be around his dad's girlfriends or, heaven forbid, getting a stepmom."

I exhaled. The more I talked to Shannon, the more clarity I had. "As dysfunctional as it sounds, I think he wanted to uphold the image of an intact family as well. He wanted a wife in his home, taking care of things and raising his son. It seems that once he realized I knew about the other women and I *didn't* leave him over it, he took that as permission to continue in his despicable ways."

"Aunt Ruby, he was horrible."

"Yes," I whispered. "But I became quite horrible too." I picked up the ace bandage and slowly unwound it. "We stopped talking. I became obsessed and probably could have opened my own private detective agency with all the skills I honed. I even got a long-range lens and took pictures, although I never developed a single roll of film."

Shannon used one of the tissues for herself.

"When Tony started failing out of middle school, it was my wake-up call. I had neglected my mothering duties to obsess about a husband who'd never love me." I wound up the ace bandage into its tidy ball. "So I became a power mom, joined the PTA, started cooking classes, interior design classes, gardening . . . transformed into the Martha Stewart of the West. I was even pleasant and cordial to my husband, as if he were a platonic roommate."

I reached for the next item—a bundle of postcards, the one on top of the San Diego harbor. "Phillip sent these to Tony and me from his trips. I guess he was keeping up the pretense of a unified family. But they remind me of Evelyn."

"The woman my father saw?" Shannon asked.

"Yes, she was an airline stewardess. Imagine! Like something out of a cheap romance novel." My laugh was bitter. "She lived in Irvine, actually, but I'm not surprised Phillip met her in San Diego. She must have had a layover there."

I set the postcards next to the ace bandage. "The last woman I knew about was Pamela. In fact, she came to the funeral." I removed a dried rose from the box. "When everyone left the house, I drove back to the cemetery to sit and think. A woman was standing by the grave, and when I climbed out of the car, she took a flower from one of the arrangements and started walking in the opposite direction. I didn't know it was Pamela when I hurried after her. When she turned, I recognized her immediately—all of my perfected spying techniques, you know."

Shannon took the dried flower from me and laid it carefully on the carpet.

"I told her, 'Don't steal from my husband's grave. You might have been his lover, but I was his wife.'"

"You said that to Pamela?" Shannon covered her mouth with her hand, eyes wide.

"I did." I smiled. "It worked, and she handed me the rose like it was some official ceremony."

"I wish I could have helped you, done something—"

"There's nothing *anyone* could have done," I said, cutting Shannon off. "Phillip would have gladly divorced me. But I didn't want to hurt Tony any more than we already had with our strained relationship."

Shannon nodded, though I could tell she didn't quite agree with me. Luckily, she was in a good marriage. Not everyone had that.

"Oh, I know what you're thinking," I added. "I just didn't have the courage to test Phillip. I wasn't as strong as Paige."

"Paige's situation was different," Shannon said. "You can't compare yourself to her."

"Yes, but Paige had a lot more guts than I did. She decided to move on, to give herself a chance at happiness."

Shannon was silent for a moment. "It took a lot of courage to do what you did. I don't think you're any less courageous than Paige. Both of your choices were difficult."

My eyes filled with tears, and I willed them away. Had I made the right decision to stay in an empty marriage for the sake of my son? How could two women make two completely different decisions regarding their cheating husbands?

"It must be nearly ten now," I said. "You'll be late for work."

"It doesn't matter. They'll survive without me."

I looked into her red-rimmed eyes. "Thank you for listening, my dear."

Shannon threw her arms around me. "I'm so sorry about all of your pain. Please know that you can tell me anything—anytime." She pulled away and put her hands on my cheeks. I felt like a coddled child now. "And please don't give up . . . Give Gabriel a chance."

"So we're back to Gabriel now, are we?" I blinked back the tears and reached for another tissue. "He's a dear man, but he'll probably spend the rest of his life in Greece, and I'll spend mine here."

"I thought he ran the travel agency here with his sister."

"Well, that's a story for another day, but suffice it to say he is in Greece and plans to stay there," I said, piling the mementos back into the box. I closed the lid, locked it, and stood up. "You've got to get to work."

Shannon gave me one last hug, then followed me out of the room. Walking down the stairs, I felt that the hollowness inside my heart had filled and warmed. It had been healing somehow to confide in Shannon.

After watching her walk to her car, climb in, and drive away, I turned back to the kitchen. Maybe someday I'd tell her about my adventures with Gabriel, but I wasn't ready to quite yet. The memories were still too fresh. I picked up the paperback and opened it to the title page where he'd written the note to me.

To Ruby,
All my love,
—G

Chapter 18

GABRIEL E-MAILED ME FIRST.

Thanks for the new copy of Zen and the Art of Motorcycle Maintenance. *I seem to have misplaced mine. How are you? Any jet lag?*
—Gabriel

I caught myself grinning, and I imagined him smiling as he wrote the e-mail. I had been home three days already and was wondering whether I should e-mail him or not. But here it was, an e-mail from him. I was so relieved. There was nothing in the e-mail about missing me or anything that was too personal. Just what I had hoped for.

I typed a short, cheerful reply, then hit send. My heart felt lighter than it had since I'd returned to find my house broken into. I didn't tell him about the robbery; I'd wait until everything was resolved. So far, I'd canceled my credit card, and a new one was on its way; I'd changed my bank-account numbers, which had proved quite the ordeal, as I had to contact every place where I had automatic payments set up and change over the information; and the bank had their investigation team on the case, and I hoped whoever had broken into my home would be apprehended soon.

Dressing quickly, I decided to wear the sandals and blouse I'd purchased in Greece. I was on my way to a reunion lunch for the tour members at the senior center. I hadn't seen them since the good-bye at the airport.

My phone rang just as I was leaving the house. Seeing it was Ilana's number, I picked it up. I had left two messages in the past few days, and she was finally calling me back.

"Ilana?" I answered.

"Hi, Ruby. Sorry it's taken me awhile to call you back."

"No problem," I said, thinking her voice sounded a little strained. Maybe leaving two messages had been a bit overboard, but she hadn't responded much in the e-mail loops I'd sent from Greece. "I'm sure you've been busy with work and keeping that husband of yours fed."

She didn't laugh like I'd expected her to. "Actually, I'm not working for the convention center anymore."

"Oh? You changed convention centers?"

"Uh, no. I lost my job."

The news stunned me. She'd said nothing on the e-mail loop, and I thought it might be too personal to ask why. "Well, you'll probably find something soon enough." I tried to sound upbeat. Ilana was educated and intelligent.

"I'm taking it one day at time, so we'll see," Ilana said. "I'm just working on getting completely healed."

"Is your elbow still bothering you?"

"I still have a little pain, but that's to be expected. It was a pretty intensive operation."

It had been almost a month since her surgery—and it was an outpatient one at that. Her pain should have been minor, nothing significant. Maybe that was what she'd meant.

"Have you been in for a follow-up appointment?"

"Of course. I've been to several, including physical therapy appointments." Her tone definitely sounded clipped. "I'm working on it, but there's not much more anyone can do."

I was about to ask her if she'd gotten a second opinion, but she was already saying, "I'm glad you're home safe from Greece, and I'll see you at the next book club."

Well. That was that. "All right, dear. If there is anything I can do for you—"

"Quiet and rest is about all I need," she cut in. "I've got to run. Talk to you later."

Then she hung up.

I listened to the silence on the other end and couldn't believe that Ilana had hung up on me. My thoughts were full of Ilana as I drove to the senior center. I had crossed the welcome line with her and had thoroughly annoyed her. Exhaling, I decided to back off. It would be good enough to see her at the next book club. She obviously didn't want any sympathy or even a friendly shoulder to lean on.

I pulled up to the senior center and walked inside. Debbie rushed around the reception desk and hugged me. "You're here!"

"Let me see it," I said, pulling back and grabbing her hand. She'd told me about her engagement ring over the phone. It was single diamond, simple yet elegant. "I love it."

"I had my other wedding ring resized for my right hand."

I surveyed her outstretched fingers. "You are definitely a loved woman."

Debbie laughed. "We've set the date, but I can't tell you when because Lark wants to tell the whole group at the same time."

I smiled at her. I don't think I'd ever seen anyone more excited. "I can wait a few minutes."

"Oh, all right, I'll tell you. Just don't breathe a word to Lark," Debbie said. Before I could protest, she gripped my arm and whispered in my ear. "May 1, which is May Day. Isn't it lovely?"

May was just over a month away, but there was no warning Debbie that it was all moving quite quickly. I just hugged her again. "Sounds perfect."

"We're no longer spring hens, so we didn't want to wait too long."

"Spring chickens," I said with a laugh.

"Yeah, that's what I meant."

A couple of women who'd been part of our tour entered through the doors. We all went in together, and I was caught up in a flurry of hugs and greetings. Yet, despite how nice it was to see everyone, it was plain that one person was missing.

I settled into a chair near the front of the room. Debbie and Lark enthusiastically made their announcement, and everyone clapped and cheered. They'd decided to have a wedding lunch at the center so it would be convenient for everyone to attend. I couldn't help but watch the happy couple. They'd both been married and widowed, yet here they were, all smiles, as if they were in love for the first time. From what I knew, Debbie had had a good marriage and so had Lark. I'd bet they didn't have closed-up master bedrooms with locked memory boxes in the closet.

Were there really people in the world lucky enough to find devoted love twice?

Chapter 19

GABRIEL HAD BEEN QUIET FOR a few days, but I'd kept busy like usual, even deciding to send out my kitchen chairs for refinishing. I sent a long e-mail to Kara and Tony, detailing my trip and attaching pictures. The bank reimbursed me for the stolen money, and I went to the senior center a couple of times. I tried not to dwell so much on Gabriel and the fact that we hadn't e-mailed for a while. I could feel the separation between us growing. All of his previous e-mails had been funny and kind but nothing too personal, which made it easier to think of our continuing relationship as only friendship. Every once in a while I leafed through the photo album I put together with all of Debbie's and my pictures. But only once in a while. No more than once a day, or twice at the very most.

I felt more alive, more in tune, and lighthearted in a way I couldn't remember feeling before. I didn't have the burden of a relationship, yet it was kind of nice to think of Gabriel in a fond way. Perhaps it was better that we'd ended things when we were still so enamored of each other. It kept the perception of our relationship as something wonderful and practically perfect.

If I did see him again, I'd probably feel disappointed to discover that all the memories I'd crystallized in my mind were just a bit inaccurate. The pictures did nothing to dim the enjoyment of my time in Greece. In fact, they added to the whole allure.

* * *

Saturday morning of April book club arrived with a rain shower, but the poor weather tapered off by midafternoon.

I spent most of the day preparing a Greek meze platter—a large array of appetizers so everyone could have a little taste of Greek food. I'd serve it cold, but it would still be delicious. I fixed everything from fried zucchini, mini cheese pies, hummus, and sliced feta to crusty bread. The cookbook I'd purchased came in handy. I couldn't wait to see what Athena thought.

I changed into my lavender blouse, white pants, and Greek sandals. The women would get a kick out of them, I decided.

Athena was the first to arrive, and I was glad we could talk Greek food without boring anyone else. She went for the hummus first. "Delicious. My mother would have loved it."

I flushed with the compliment. Athena's mother, who was Greek, had been known for being an excellent cook.

"It was a lot more work than I thought," I said. "So I'm glad I can share it with everyone." For some reason, my mind went to Gabriel as I wondered what he'd think of the food I'd prepared.

Paige and Olivia arrived nearly at the same time, and they both filled a small plate with the appetizers, exclaiming over them.

"Tori's bringing dessert, so we'll be having a bit of a meal tonight," I said.

"It all looks wonderful," Paige said right before biting into a zucchini piece. "Mmm."

"Do you have pictures back yet?" Olivia asked.

"I'm saving them until the end," I said.

Olivia laughed. "You're torturing us!"

They'd already heard all about my trip through e-mail and phone calls, so they were all waiting eagerly to see the pictures. The doorbell rang, and I hurried out before I was further tempted to whip out the album, despite my resolve.

Ilana had arrived, and I pulled her petite body into a hug. When I released her, she smiled, but it didn't reach her eyes. She looked unusually tired. "Are you feeling all right?"

"Of course," she said, but it didn't sound convincing.

I ushered her into the living room, taking several sideways glances at her. "Have a seat on the couch over there by my usual spot." I didn't want her to sit on the metal chair I'd brought in as backup because my kitchen chairs were still out for refinishing and wouldn't be back from the shop for a couple more days.

Ilana didn't look too interested in the Greek platter but took one of the cups of water. Now everyone had arrived but Tori.

"Shannon won't be able to make it tonight," I said. "She had to fill in for someone at work. Has anyone heard from Tori lately?"

No one had, and now I was getting worried about her being late. She wasn't usually late. She was coming from Los Angeles, so there shouldn't be much traffic this direction on a Saturday night. But maybe there was an event I didn't know about.

The ladies brought up Ilana's injured arm, and she told them she was doing physical therapy. Athena was gracious enough to tell Ilana she was grateful she'd come because Athena enjoyed her comments.

I left to check out the window, still worried about Tori. When I saw her car coming down the street, I exhaled in relief. She was only about ten minutes late, so I didn't know why I'd been so worried.

Tori had just stepped onto the porch when I opened the door. She looked a bit harried but beautiful as always. She wore a tunic-style jacket, which seemed a bit overwarm, but maybe she had it on because of the rain earlier. And she carried a couple of paper bags. I assumed it was the refreshments—I was so relieved she remembered, not that I didn't think my Greek meze platter wouldn't be a hit, but it was always nice to have someone follow through with plans. But what on earth could be in the bags? "Oh, honey, I am so glad you made it. I was worried about you." I hugged her, then ushered her inside.

She seemed relieved to be at book club but a bit impatient to be inside.

"Mind if I borrow your kitchen for a minute?"

"Not at all. Do you need help?" I was quite curious as to what she'd brought in *bags*.

"Nope. But I'd love it if you'd tell everyone I actually arrived and will be right there." Even her voice seemed a bit flustered.

She must have had a bad day. Had she been working on the set today? I'd heard those shows sometimes went into the weekend. Instead of pestering her, I let her find the kitchen on her own, hoping she could relax and enjoy herself tonight.

I sat next to Ilana. The poor girl looked so thin and pale. I put my hand on her knee. "Are you sure you're all right?"

She was adamant that she was fine, so I decided to drop it.

A few minutes later, Tori came in, shoes off. At least she seemed determined to enjoy herself. I smiled at her as she greeted everyone. She carried her iPad, and I couldn't wait to tell her how proficient I'd become with mine.

"Sorry about the metal chair," I said. But Tori seemed game to sit in it. "Help yourself to some Greek hors d'oeuvres."

Tori filled up her plate, though she didn't make an attempt to try anything. Maybe she was a picky eater.

"Thought you'd gone no-show on us," Athena said.

Tori laughed. "Yeah, well, you know how I like to make an entrance."

It was good to hear her laugh. Maybe her day wasn't as bad as I'd thought it was.

Olivia joined in. "It must be a side effect of working with all those egos in Hollywood."

That must have been it, I thought. Work had gotten under Tori's skin.

"You're not lying there, Livvy," Tori said. "You would not believe the egos I've had to deal with recently. Those bikini-bottomed bimbos are killing me."

"I bet," Athena sympathized.

"Want to tell us about it?" I asked, hoping I wasn't prying too much. I had caught up on the two episodes I'd missed while in Greece, and although the program was a bit over the top for me, it was kind of fun to immerse myself in something quite ridiculous once in a while. Also, I enjoyed hearing about anything behind the scenes from Tori, especially about Christopher Cain, who I believed had a lot more in him than met the eye. But a sad look came into Tori's eyes.

"Sorry, guys," she said. "The almighty contract has forbidden me to speak of what I know. Ask me next season about what went on this season, and I'll be able to tell you some of it."

"Dang." I snapped my fingers. That was that. Really, I just wanted Tori to feel comfortable opening up to us. It would have also been nice to know if Christopher Cain had any designs on the women—real intentions, not just what was shown on the television. Debbie had found out that Tori was an assistant director on the show, and it would have been great to have something new to tell her.

"So let's get this party started!" Tori said, looking around at everyone, obviously wanting to change the conversation. She still hadn't taken a bite of anything. "*The War of Art* by Steven Pressfield. I'm really glad I read this book again."

Again. It reminded me that Tori liked to read books more than once, which then made me think of Gabriel. But I had promised myself not to talk about Gabriel tonight—at least not directly.

"Really, the subtitle kind of takes away the mystery of why I was glad to have read it: *Break through the Blocks & Win Your Inner Creative Battles.*

I don't know how many of you know this, but I'm a writer. This is why I work in the film industry. I don't want to direct film or produce it. I want to write it. I want to change people's lives and minds with the words I put into the mouths of good actors."

I, of course, knew Tori wanted to be a writer. She'd shared it when she gave me a tutorial on the iPad. The other ladies looked duly impressed at how deep her ambitions went. I'd definitely be interested in reading something she'd written.

"That's fantastic," Athena said. The other ladies added their encouragement and asked a few questions as well. Even Ilana seemed to perk up a bit. Maybe all Ilana needed was dessert. Sweets had the power to make everything seem better.

"Anyway," Tori continued. "I'm really glad I read it. And this is going to sound dumb, but the thing that struck me the most was something mentioned at the very beginning of the book." She fiddled with her iPad, and I turned mine back on because it had gone to sleep. "There's a line here where it said it was easier for Hitler to start World War II than it was for him to face down a blank canvas every day."

I remembered that line; it had made me shudder.

"That was kind of powerful to me," Tori said, "because I really do let the blank computer screen get to me. Sometimes I worry I won't be able to fill it with the right kind of words or that the world won't see my words the way I see them. So I let that resistance thing get to me and find other things to do. Find my job to do. I tell people I work on *Vows* because I need it to help me break into the market, but really, that's the biggest excuse of them all. I hide behind my job so I don't have to face the blank computer screen. It keeps me so busy and leaves me such little time when I'm actively involved in filming that I can't be bothered with reaching out and achieving my dreams, you know?"

I thought of the things I'd avoided over my life because I was the neglected wife. I didn't think the women wanted to hear my woes, but I loved Tori's honesty. It made me realize that so many of us had unrealized dreams.

Everyone seemed to be thinking about what Tori said, so I answered, "I really liked the book too." Of course, I wouldn't tell them my husband's affairs had been *my* resistance. I'd have to keep it more general. "I liked how it showed resistance for all the things resistance really is. At the very first of the book, I was grabbed by the line"— I looked down at my iPad, where I'd added a highlight—"'Most of us have two lives. The life we live and the unlived life within us. Between the two stands Resistance. How many of us have an unlived life?'"

I looked up at the ladies. Everyone in the room nodded.

"There are lots of things I want to do," I said in a slow voice. "Maybe not artistic things, necessarily, but things I want just the same, and I let resistance get in my way. My whole life, I've let other things define me. I was the spouse who supported her husband in all of his stuff but never had a—" I stopped, feeling my neck warm. Telling Shannon all about Phillip had certainly loosened my tongue.

I looked down at my iPad, searching for a way to recover my midsentence crash. I scrolled to the next quote I'd highlighted, but that one was a bit personal as well.

Thankfully, Olivia jumped in. "I had that same thought," she said. "Joining this book club in the first place was a huge step for me overcoming resistance."

I sighed with relief. That's what I could compare this to—starting the book club. It *had* taken a bit of courage on my part.

I smiled as Olivia continued. "And some of the things I thought had been holding me back were really nothing more than my own fears, insecurities, and excuses. By me taking charge of my own life, I found happiness. I found happiness in my marriage." Olivia laughed. "I mean . . . Not every day. Some days I still want to strangle the man with his own tie, but most of the time, there's happiness where there'd been only silence before. Reading this book reminded me what resistance could be and reminded me to be cautious not to sabotage myself by turning good things into resistance."

Tears burned at the back of my eyes. I knew silence—painful, torturing silence. "I'm so glad you've found happiness in your marriage, Olivia." My voice sounded a bit shaky, and I decided to stop while I was ahead. I felt Tori's curious gaze on me. I had probably said too much already.

"Where's Shannon?" Tori asked.

Relief flooded through me. Tori was only wondering about Shannon, not why I sounded like I was about to cry.

I swallowed, focusing on things that were not sad so my voice would be steady. Tori hadn't been here when I'd explained to everyone. "Oh, she had to work the night shift tonight. She tried to get it off, but you know how jobs can be so demanding."

Athena cleared her throat, a bit of a frown on her face. "You know, I didn't exactly love the book. I mean, it had some good points. But ultimately, it wasn't my sort of thing. As a business woman, I could totally appreciate the way the author gave a real motivation to just sit in the chair and get the work done, but really? Artists aren't all-powerful beings who shape the future of the universe. It's a little egomaniacal to imagine that a bit of poetry or a bit of color on canvas can do all that."

Olivia let out a chuckle. "Actually, I can bet that a lot of works of art do just that. A piece of literature can help reshape someone's viewpoint." She went on to compare it to when we read *The Help* and how it changed her perspective and made her rethink how she treated people who were just doing the jobs they were being paid for. Olivia leaned forward, anticipation on her face. "There is power in the words we find in books. Some paintings have moved me to awestruck silence and sometimes even tears. And so much music has brought me to my feet and forced me to dance. Art creates action in the person participating with the artist."

I nodded at Olivia's words, thinking of the beauty of Greece. "Which is why it's just that much more tragic that some artists face that blank canvas of their work," I said. "If they never express themselves through their art, that means there are people who aren't moved to dancing or to awe over beauty or to gain a self-awareness of literature. That resistance can actually lead to the detriment of the world's future." It was much easier to talk about art and literature instead of relationships.

Athena grinned. "I'm not arguing. I can actually agree with all of that, and like I said, I really understood and appreciated the lessons of how to avoid resistance or wage war on the resistances in your own life. I think that a person learning how to control the friction that opposes them accomplishing the things they desire is a great thing. But it almost feels like the writer is passing judgment on all of those who allow nonart-related activity to continue in their lives. It seems out of proportion to me. He purports that a person isn't really a professional at whatever their art is until they give up everything else in their lives that isn't art. That seems unhealthy and like the author is snubbing those who strive for a balanced, comprehensive life. Keep in mind . . . I was exactly this sort of person a few months ago, but now I can see how it can get out of hand. There needs to be a balance."

Paige added her thoughts. I was grateful everyone was so enthusiastic to share their opinions. "There has to be balance—a kind of moderation to all things," she said. "But sometimes my life gets out of balance the other way, so this really helped me remember to grow that artistic part of myself. My favorite quote in the book was that resistance is directly proportional to love." Paige scrolled through her Kindle until she found what she was looking for. "'If you're feeling massive Resistance, the good news is, it means there's tremendous love there too. If you didn't love the project that is terrifying you, you wouldn't feel anything. The opposite of love isn't hate; it's indifference.' I'd never considered how powerful a little apathy could actually be."

"Absolutely!" I said before I could stop myself. Then I hesitated. I had been thinking of Gabriel when she said that—and the resistance we had faced with his ex-wife and the infidelity of my husband. But still, we'd found happiness beyond that, even if it was for a short time. We had defied resistance. "I mean, that makes a lot of sense. Things that are good and true in this life take a lot of effort to maintain. If they aren't something you are passionate about, you won't care enough to make it work."

My words were probably getting too transparent, and I was grateful Shannon wasn't here. I thought of the way my marriage had been overcome with apathy—it was a survival instinct. In contrast, I'd been willing to travel back and forth to Greece to maintain a relationship with Gabriel. Of course, that was void now, but the pull of resistance had been quite strong with all of my excuses.

Next to me, Ilana started rocking. At first I thought she was going to say something, but she didn't. Was she cold? Tired? Tori was watching her as well, so maybe I wasn't the only one concerned. I was about to ask Ilana if she needed anything when she said, "Hey, um . . ."

Everyone fell quiet, since Ilana hadn't contributed at all up until now. She rubbed her forehead—maybe she had a migraine. That would explain her paleness.

"Can I use your restroom?" she said.

I put my hand on her arm, if only to feel her temperature—was she hot with fever? Cold? Her skin felt perfectly normal. "Of course, dear. A half bath is just down the hall past the kitchen." Maybe her stomach was upset, and a trip to the bathroom would make her feel better.

"Thanks," Ilana said. She grabbed her purse and left the room. If she didn't look better when she returned, I'd discreetly offer some Ibuprofen.

The attention left Ilana as Paige said, "I see apathy a lot at work in certain clients." She continued for a few moments, talking about apathy.

"Very interesting," I said when she finished, although half my thoughts were with Ilana. "At the senior center, there is a class on attitudes. They talk about how apathy can affect your health. When we no longer care about things, we stop eating healthy, exercising, and keeping our minds sharp."

Athena nodded. "The care center where my father is staying had that topic as part of the seminar they presented to family members. I can see how apathy could really stand in the way of simple things—as well as our bigger dreams."

"I see it in my kids all the time," Olivia said. "They have dreams, and then some resistance comes along and—poof—they give up!"

I glanced over at Tori, who had a worried expression on her face. Was she thinking of Ilana too? Tori mouthed, "I'll be right back," and I nodded. It was sweet of her to check on Ilana.

The women continued to explore the topic of following our dreams when Ilana came back in, without Tori. The color was back in Ilana's face, and she smiled at me as she sat down. A trip to the bathroom was all Ilana had needed. She looked much better now.

It was several more minutes before Tori came back, looking like she was in a bit of a hurry. I frowned, wondering why she seemed distressed. Her usual cheerful expression seemed somber all of a sudden.

The conversation had divided up among the ladies, and I felt we'd covered enough of the book. "Well, let's have dessert," I said, clapping my hands together.

Tori seemed to leap to her feet as if she had been waiting for the invitation. When I made a move to stand, she said, "Don't worry, I've got it." A couple of minutes later, she came into the room with a tray of donuts. They were artfully arranged, looking beautiful. Imagine! They looked delicious too.

While the ladies started on the donuts, I pulled out the photo album. Everyone leaned in to get a look as I turned the pages and explained the various sights. I'd taken out the more chummy pictures of Gabriel and me, but that didn't stop Athena from saying, "He's very nice looking, Ruby."

I'd probably told her more about Gabriel than anyone, well, except for Shannon. But she'd been very sensitive to what I'd said. Unlike Shannon, who continued to ask what he said in his e-mails. I tried not to hold that against her because I secretly enjoyed talking about him.

"And," I said, grabbing a package I'd left next to one of the floor plants to keep it out of the way, "I got you all a little souvenir from my trip."

"You didn't have to do that, Ruby," Paige said, but she smiled as she examined the evil-eye bracelet and set of earrings.

"I couldn't resist when I saw this Athena statue," I said, pulling it out of the bag. "So Athena gets something extra."

"I love it," Athena said, laughing. "It's going right next to my bed so I can remember I'm a goddess the moment I wake up in the morning."

We all laughed, and even Ilana laughed along with us. She was halfway through a donut, looking much better.

"Well, let's choose the next book." I looked around at the women, trying to remember who should be next.

"Why don't you choose it, Ruby?" Tori said with a grin. Those donuts had certainly made her perk up as well. *Maybe we should have donuts every meeting.*

"All right—if everyone's okay with that?"

"Sounds good to me," Ilana said.

I looked at her with surprise. I supposed I *could* choose next. A certain book immediately popped into my mind. "How about *Zen and the Art of Motorcycle Maintenance?*"

"I've heard of that book," Paige said. "It sounds great."

I think I was still in shock at my own suggestion, but Paige had just endorsed it, so there was no turning back now.

"I think I've heard of it too," Athena said. "A memoir, right?"

The few things Gabriel had told me came to mind. "Yes, a good friend of mine absolutely loves it. So I guess we'll find out what all the fuss is about."

Athena was on her Blackberry and announced, "It's by Robert M. Pirsig."

We wrapped things up, and Ilana was the first to leave, hurrying out before I could even give her a hug. I made a mental note to call her a little later to check up on how she was feeling. Olivia followed Tori into the kitchen with all the plates, and I walked Athena and Paige to the door.

When they left, I found Olivia and Tori in the kitchen. Tori was putting the last of the donuts back in one of the bags she'd brought them in.

With most everyone gone, I felt braver to ask, "What's been bothering you tonight, honey?"

Tori smiled. "Nothing." Her answered seemed rushed, kind of like when a wife tells a husband there is nothing wrong, yet everything is wrong.

"You seem frazzled, and frazzled isn't nothing," I said.

"And you were frazzled before you walked in the front door," Olivia said from the other side of Tori. "Is something going on at work?"

Her face fell. "I think I'm in love."

I stared at her for a second, then the words sank in. Dear, lovely Tori was in love! "With who?" I practically shouted, clapping my hands together.

"Wonderful!" Olivia said, grabbing her into a hug.

"Yeah, wonderful," Tori said as if it were the worst thing in the world.

I gaped at her. No wonder she looked out of sorts . . . I knew that feeling. "Tell us everything. If you won't tell me about Christopher Cain's love life, I can at least hear about yours!"

Tori seemed to go into la-la land for a moment, then she said, "There isn't anything to tell." She was gripping that donut bag pretty tightly. "He doesn't even know I'm alive."

A gorgeous woman like Tori? "Nonsense!" I said. Olivia made a face and blew a raspberry. "No one could overlook a woman of your beauty and intelligence." Really, I wasn't blind, and I knew most men weren't blind either. Even married men could be painfully observant when it came to a beautiful woman.

Tori smiled, so I hoped that meant she wasn't completely serious about this mystery man not even knowing she existed. But she changed the subject rather quickly.

"Oh, hey, guys. I'll take a rain check on you all telling me how great I am and how lucky he'd be to have me, because I really need to get going. Don't worry about me. I'm a little distracted, but I'll be fine. I promise." She grinned, but I felt she just didn't want to talk about it anymore. At least she'd said that much.

She moved past me, saying, "Thanks for the great book club, Ruby. I appreciate you letting me come to restore my faith in humanity."

"You're welcome, dear." I gave her a hug, wishing she felt more comfortable explaining what was going on. None of us was going to judge her, least of all me. "Though we're certainly not perfect, we are perfectly human."

Tori nodded. "You're more right than you know." Then she turned to Olivia and hugged her.

"Well," I said to Olivia once Tori was gone. "I can't wait to find out who this mystery man is."

Chapter 20

I'D JUST FINISHED REPLYING TO an e-mail from Kara when someone rang my doorbell at 8:00 a.m. I assumed it was Shannon stopping by on her way to work, since no one else visited me this early. It was a week after book club, and strangely, I hadn't seen her. We'd had a couple of phone calls in the beginning, with Shannon asking me more questions about the missing laptop and fraudulent purchases, but then she had backed off, probably wanting more information, just like me. I was frustrated that nothing had turned up, but at least I'd had the funds returned by the bank as part of their security-and-fraud insurance program.

Opening the door, I was surprised to see John, Shannon's husband, instead.

"John," I said, looking past him. He appeared to be alone. "Is everything all right?"

"I needed to talk to you for a minute in private." His normally warm and friendly personality seemed reserved, as if he was worried about something.

My heart sank. I'd seen him anxious before when his daughter had gone off the deep end. But from what I knew and had seen at book club, Keisha was doing wonderfully.

"Of course. Come on in," I said, pulling him into a hug as he stepped inside. John was a good-natured man, tall, gregarious, and a bit on the paunchy side. He worked hard and was probably the most honest man I knew—he once told me a story of how he'd been undercharged at Carl's Jr. Of course he reported it and paid the difference. I would have probably walked away with the discounted cheeseburger—or not even noticed in the first place. Shannon was lucky to have such an attentive husband who cared about the small things.

His hug felt a bit stiff, and as he followed me down the hall, I debated whether or not to go into the living room or the kitchen. Deciding that what he needed was the cheery kitchen, I turned to the right.

"I have fresh orange juice," I said, keeping my tone light.

John scrubbed at his receding brown-and-peppered-gray hair. "That would be great."

I poured a glass of juice in the too-quiet kitchen. I could almost feel his eyes boring into my back.

After setting the juice in front of him, I took a seat across the table and folded my hands together. A dozen curious thoughts ran through my mind—why was John here? Was it something about Keisha? Shannon?

John looked a little lost, staring into his juice. I reached over and patted his hand, deciding to make this easy on him. "Is this about Keisha?"

His eyes lifted, surprise in his gaze. I was equally surprised. If not Keisha, then what? A knot of dread tightened in my stomach. I could deal with Keisha—it was almost expected—but nothing beyond that.

"I didn't think you knew," he said.

"Knew what, John? Is Keisha in trouble with drugs again?"

If possible, whatever light had been left in his eyes dimmed. "You don't know . . ."

Again, that twinge of dread, stronger than before. But something told me to wait, to be patient, to let John tell me what was going on in his time.

A moment later, he finally spoke. "I hoped it would be Shannon sitting across from you, but life can be unexpected." His hand moved to his head again, like he was fighting off a headache. Then he reached into his pants pocket and brought out a receipt. With his eyes on the receipt, he shook his head.

The suspense was about to give me my very first heart attack—or stroke; I wouldn't be surprised about either scenario.

"This is a receipt from a pawn shop." He held it out to me, and I gingerly took it from his fingers.

The transaction was for about $400, with one word, *Laptop*, written in the item description. I caught my breath and looked up at John in confusion.

"Keisha stole your laptop and sold it," John said.

His eyes were on me, but I couldn't see them clearly because my vision was blurry. *Keisha? She stole my laptop? Why? How? Did that also mean she'd used my credit card information to buy those gift cards?* Even as my mind spun with the shocking information, I knew exactly how. And I could probably guess why.

"I want you to press charges," John said, his voice taking on a steely resolve. "That's the original receipt there. I've made a copy for myself, and I'll support you 100 percent."

I breathed out. *Press charges against Keisha?* But she was family. She was . . . John's daughter. Poor Shannon. She was such a great stepmother, but Keisha was an adult now, and it was just too bad she was prone to making poor choices. Disbelief gave way to anger. How could Keisha do this to me? I'd treated her like gold, like one of my own.

My eyes burned hot with tears as John spoke. "Ruby, I am so sorry. With Keisha . . . you know she's been through a tough time, but if she doesn't pay the consequences for this, I don't know what else will be in store for her."

I nodded. He was right, but I was still wrapping my mind around it all, replaying the evening I had returned from Greece and first called Shannon. My breath caught. Had Shannon suspected then? How horrible for her . . . wait. How horrible for *me*. I slumped in my chair and brought a hand to my trembling mouth. "How long has Shannon known?"

The hesitation on John's part told me everything. I felt sick. My own niece had covered up for her stepdaughter.

"Shannon's devastated. I think she suspected from the beginning but didn't want to face the reality of it. You can imagine what it's like to have hope—at last—then be faced with this. Especially when it involves *you*. She didn't know for sure until Monday; I asked her to tell you, but she hasn't. She's . . . struggling with all of this and is determined to help Keisha in any way she can, but in my opinion, she's making it worse."

It seemed like Shannon and I were a little too similar—both going to great lengths to protect the ones we loved.

John continued. "We had an argument. Shannon wants to find Keisha a rehabilitation center. But she's an adult now, not some juvenile delinquent." He looked hard at me, his own voice trembling. "I know it will be difficult, but if you have any compassion in your heart for Keisha at all, you need to press charges. I already filed charges against her for having drugs in my house. She needs to be accountable, Ruby. I think it's the only thing we can do to help her now."

"Tough love," I choked out, then shook my head. I was still reeling over the fact that Shannon hadn't told me, had possibly figured it all out early on but had kept it from me. That hurt more than what Keisha had done. I took a deep breath. "How do I go about pressing charges?"

* * *

The phone call had to happen. I didn't trust myself facing Shannon, and I couldn't wait any longer. John had left about twenty minutes ago, after he'd stood by my side as I'd called in the information to the police station. They said a warrant would be issued for her arrest within twenty-four hours. With all of Keisha's information, she'd probably be arrested pretty soon.

With John gone and the charges filed, I knew I had to tell Shannon. Dialing her number, my eyes started to water. I'd probably botch up what I wanted to say, but I knew I couldn't continue through the day without saying it.

It went into her voice mail, and I left a brief message. My heart ached, but I knew I'd done the right thing. I just hoped that Shannon would see it that way.

As the hours passed and Shannon didn't return my call, I realized she probably knew from John by now. I'd just have to wait until she was ready to talk to me. Really, the only thing that made the day even a little bit decent was a call from Tori. I'd left her a couple of messages just to check in on her. She sounded much better over the phone, although she still didn't reveal who the mystery man was that she was so smitten over. She told me some funny stories about her job, and we had a nice chat. I even told her a thing or two about Gabriel. We set up a lunch date for the following week. After such a crummy morning, I was relieved that at least something was going right for someone.

* * *

I woke early on the day of Debbie's wedding. I was still tired from decorating the lunch room at the senior center the day before. I didn't want to get out of bed, although I had a lot to do. Turning over, I saw the *Zen* book, as if it was just waiting for me to read it. I fluffed my pillows and settled against them. The book started out with the author out on a motorcycle ride with his son. Robert described the countryside and compared all types of roads, from country roads to busy freeways. I immediately liked his tone and voice and how he seemed to lay out the truth without holding back.

He picked on city living by saying that people think "the real action was metropolitan." And perhaps he was right. I'd always lived in crowded California, so maybe that's why the beach was such a draw for everyone. On the beach, you felt separate from the busyness of life. You felt less rushed and more willing to relax and look around, soak in the beauty of nature.

I paused at the phrase, "We're in such a hurry most of the time we never get much chance to talk." Although I'd slowed down considerably since Phillip's death, I did keep myself quite busy. And the women of the book club seemed even busier. It was hard for them to schedule a simple lunch with a friend.

An hour of reading flew by, and I realized I had to start getting ready. I set the book down reluctantly, looking forward to reading a little more tonight after the wedding festivities. Preferably with a long bubble bath.

Three hours later, the wedding was over, and I found myself in the restroom at the senior center with Debbie. It was like I blinked and the time flew by.

Debbie turned around, showing off her dress.

"You look beautiful, Debbie," I said, clapping my hands. I leaned forward and gave her a light hug so as to not disturb her impeccable appearance. She wore a pale-blue dress that had a bit of swing in the skirt. "Will you be able to dance in those?" I teased, pointing to her strappy heels.

"Slow dance," Debbie said, then laughed.

"I'm so happy for you." I grabbed her hand, my heart feeling like it might burst. I'd never have with a man what Debbie had with Lark, but I was truly pleased for her, as though it were me wearing her strappy shoes. "You've got to get out there. Everyone is waiting."

"I just didn't want to eat in that white dress suit."

I agreed. She'd worn a lovely linen suit for the nuptial ceremony in the church. Now she looked like Debbie, and the blue dress set off her eyes. But before I could tug her down the hall, she said, "I saw you with Maria; what did she say?"

"Oh, she was very nice and gave me a huge hug. It was almost like she forgot about ever yelling at me." I'd told Debbie about the whole Maria exchange in Greece. "In Gabriel's latest e-mail, he said she'd stopped pestering him—well, at least about us."

Debbie smiled. "Today would be even more perfect if—"

"The only people you have to think about today are you and Lark," I said. I didn't want Debbie to feel a bit sorry for me.

I was completely and totally fine. I'd only shed a few tears at the wedding, and it wasn't because I was missing Gabriel or anything like that. It was because it was so wonderful to see my friends so happy together.

I pulled on Debbie's hand and led her down the hall. Once we stepped into the main hall, everyone cheered. Lark came forward, looking debonair in his tuxedo, and took Debbie's hand in his, giving it a gallant kiss.

"Let's go in," he said, and they walked in front of me, followed by several of the guests, into the decorated garden room.

I'd spent the last two days decorating the place with a group of ladies, and I was pleased with how it had turned out. Debbie's chosen colors, blue and pale-green, made the place look like an atrium. I'd even rented a portable waterfall that we used as the backdrop for the gift table. One of Debbie's granddaughters sat at the table, adorable in her pale-green chiffon dress.

I handed the young blonde girl a card. Debbie would protest when she discovered I'd given her yet another gift, but I couldn't resist the Santa Monica getaway deal I'd found on the Internet. Three days and two nights at a luxury resort, and the gift certificate was good for the next twelve months.

It made me happier to spend part of my little nest egg on others.

We settled down for lunch—delicious croissant sandwiches and hot crab cakes. Dessert was Greek baklava, which everyone enjoyed. Neither of them had wanted wedding cake. Lark stood and made a sweet toast to Debbie, then she stood as well and made another toast right back. When all eyes turned on me, and Debbie and Lark smiled at me encouragingly, I decided to make a toast as well.

I held up my wine glass and said, "To our wonderful friends, Debbie and Lark." They grinned up at me, making my throat tighten with emotion. "We've been blessed to have friends who bring sunshine into our lives with their love. I'd like to toast to second love and many years of happiness."

Everyone cheered, and the clinking of glasses filled the room. Debbie stood and embraced me. Lark hurried from the table and dimmed the lights, then turned on a projector he'd set up. The laptop he had connected to it played music to a picture slideshow. It started out as pictures of both of their families in various shots. Then pictures of Lark and Debbie when they were younger—in elementary school up to high school. Everyone chuckled at those.

There were a few pictures of Lark and his family, then Debbie and her family. The slideshow switched to pictures around the senior center, and people laughed when they recognized themselves. The room grew quiet when the next pictures were of Greece. Everyone knew that's where Lark had proposed, and they were anticipating some pictures surrounding that event.

I stared unblinking at the screen, grateful that everyone's attention was diverted. It was like Gabriel was in the room. He was in several shots, and his smile seemed to reach into my heart. I'd looked through my album many times, but seeing Gabriel on the large screen was somehow different and more real. The music transported me back to intimate dinners at Greek cafés.

My heart hammered as the pictures changed from one to another. I was in several of them too. When a picture appeared of Gabriel and me sitting with Debbie and Lark at one of the cafés, my breath caught. I looked like a different Ruby. I was smiling at the camera, and Gabriel was looking at me, humor and tenderness in his eyes.

I brought my hand to my heart. It hurt. I had tried to forget as much as possible, tried to see him as a good friend, someone I could look on with fondness but not feel anything other than friendship. I had been very wrong.

I said something to Debbie, although I wasn't sure quite what. I slipped past the tables, staying at the edge of the room. Once in the hall, I rushed outside to my car. I felt as if I was literally drowning, and the weight against my chest was making it impossible to breathe. I sat in the car for several minutes, trying to talk myself into going back inside. I was being ridiculous. Surely people had noticed my exit and were now making speculations.

I couldn't bring myself to open the car door and go back into the senior center. Besides, my makeup had smeared with the tears that wouldn't stop. I turned the key in the ignition, offering a silent apology to Debbie and Lark and begging for their understanding. I hoped they'd be too caught up in each other to mind that I was missing.

We weren't scheduled to clean up the decorations until the next morning, so at least I didn't have to feel bad about that. Surely by the morning I could return. It wasn't like the slideshow would still be showing on that large screen.

* * *

If it was possible for a house to mock a person with silence, that's what my home did when I returned. I'd left a perfectly lovely and joyous party to come home and stare at my meticulously painted walls. I kicked off my shoes, leaving them in the middle of the floor, and curled up on the couch. *Zen and the Art of Motorcycle Maintenance* sat on the coffee table where I'd left it.

I read the inscription from Gabriel, then a second time, and a third. With a sigh that traveled through my whole body, I turned to the page I'd bookmarked and started to read. I knew I was indulging in self-pity, but I couldn't face anything else. Not my empty bedroom, not my cheerful kitchen, not even my flowers that I hadn't watered today. Shannon was still avoiding me, and I couldn't call any of the book-club ladies, at least not while I was on the verge of tears. They'd think a stranger was calling them to blubber about some Greek vacation that involved a tour guide.

I spent several minutes reading before realizing I hadn't comprehended a single word. The sentences swam before my eyes, and finally, I closed my eyes, letting the exhaustion of the past few days overtake me.

I was startled out of my doze by the door bell ringing. I wondered who'd be stopping in on a weekend at this time of day. Jehovah's Witnesses had been patrolling my neighborhood for a couple of days, but I'd already politely turned them down once. I noticed that the light coming through the windows was now orange with the setting sun. My skirt was crumpled, and I thought about changing when the doorbell rang again.

Jehovah's Witnesses weren't usually so persistent. Maybe it was a neighbor looking for an escaped dog or something.

I shuffled to the door, thinking I needed to put my shoes away and change. My face probably needed some attention as well. My phone hadn't rung, making it seem like no one at the reception had worried about my flight.

Pulling open the door, I looked up at the man standing there. I was about to say, "I'm not interested," when I realized the last time I'd seen the man was thousands of miles away. "Gabriel?"

Chapter 21

THE WARMTH OF HIS EYES made my skin feel like it was going to ignite.

"Ruby," Gabriel said.

He didn't move, and I didn't either. I just stared at him and his white button-down shirt and dark-blue checked tie that was loosened at his collar.

"My plane was delayed, and I missed the wedding."

I nodded, not sure what he was saying.

"I wanted it to be a surprise—but it didn't quite work out that way. When I got to the reception, Maria said I missed you by about ten minutes."

"Maria?"

His mouth turned up. "My sister. She was at the reception."

The blood rushed back into my face. "Why . . . you came for Debbie's *wedding?*"

His face reddened, actually reddened.

"I'm sorry. How rude of me. Come in," I said. "You must come in."

Since I wasn't moving, Gabriel stepped past me into the entryway. I almost reached out to touch him, to see if he was real or part of a dream that was some strange extension of the slideshow.

"The living room is straight ahead," I croaked out, feeling mortified.

He's here! I was bawling my eyes out an hour ago because I missed him, and now he's in my house! I could just imagine the sensation he'd caused walking into the senior center. Half of the ladies probably fainted at the sight of him, and the other half still conscious probably mobbed him.

I followed him down the hall, unable to take my eyes off of his shoulders. Had he been this tall in Greece? Somehow, I didn't remember him being so tall. Maybe because I hadn't seen him in proportion to my house.

As he entered the living room, I said, "Watch out for the shoes." I moved around him, bent down to get them, and stood up so fast that tiny points of light edged my vision.

Gabriel looked around at the room, and I tried to see it through his eyes, but my heart was pounding so loud I couldn't concentrate on anything.

"Debbie invited me to the wedding, probably just to be polite, but I thought I'd come over for it," he said, turning to face me.

I hadn't moved much since I'd scooped up my shoes, so he was only a couple of feet from me. Much too close for me to breathe normally.

"Really?"

He chuckled, and the sound poured through me, reaching my toes. "Not really. That was probably just a very small catalyst."

My hands were sweaty, and I pointed to the couch. "Well, have a seat and tell me about your trip over."

Gabriel raised an eyebrow but sat down. I sat across from him, conscious of my rumpled clothing once again. What would he think if he knew I'd just been napping on the couch after crying my eyes out?

"I came to settle some things."

"With Rhea?" I blurted out.

He didn't seem to mind my boldness. "That's one of them."

I had so many questions, but instead, I sighed.

"Are you that happy to see me?" Gabriel teased.

I felt like crying, to tell the truth. "I can't believe you're here. I thought you said you couldn't ever come back with all the . . . well, you know."

"My sister threatened that if I didn't see a therapist, she'd never knit me another sweater again," Gabriel said. "I was tempted to take her up on it."

His voice resonated throughout my entire body, filling each curve. I smiled. I still couldn't believe Gabriel was in my living room, just as I remembered him. Tanned, brown eyes . . .

He was studying me as well, and I had to force myself not to smooth my hair. My cheeks were surely too pink as it was, not to mention the state of my mascara. I wanted to throw my arms around him, but I stayed seated and subtly folded my hands together and pinched my fingers.

"So you chose the therapist to keep the sweaters coming?" I said. One side of his mouth rose. I had missed his expressions so much it hurt. "Did the therapist have any . . . interesting insights?"

"That's a mild way of putting it," Gabriel said. His eyes scanned the room, then moved back to me. "He told me to stop moping and to face my demons."

"Demons, huh? Is that why you're here?"

"Not *here* in your house, but yes, that's one of the reasons I'm back in California."

"You must have quite a list of reasons, then," I said, trying to sound lighthearted.

He didn't look amused. In fact, his eyes were very serious, focused on me. "Ruby . . ."

He left my name in the air, and it floated between us. Before I knew it, he was standing, holding his hand out to me. I placed my hand in his, and he pulled me to my feet.

I knew what he was going to do before he did it, so it was like I was watching a slow-motion movie. He raised my hand to his lips and kissed it softly. It seemed everything around us paused, including time. For a moment, I could believe we were back in Greece with a brilliant blue sky above us and the surf crashing a dozen steps away.

But we were in my house, the one I had shared with Phillip, the one where I had a lifetime of memories that were *not* Gabriel.

"Will you come on a drive with me?" he asked.

What else could I say but yes? I didn't know all the reasons he had come here, but the main one was clear. He'd decided to take on guardianship of his ex-wife. No wonder Maria had been so happy at the reception. I wondered how long she'd known about Gabriel coming over, and I wondered why he hadn't told me.

I guessed that was the difference between a casual friend and a close sister.

"Let me change first. I'll be down in a minute."

Gabriel released my hand, which was a very good thing. His properness as a gentleman was hurting me at very deep levels. Levels that hadn't been felt since the discovery of Phillip's affairs. Gabriel was as good as gold, but he had his own complications that didn't include someone like me in the mix of them.

In my bedroom, I slipped out of my dress and vacillated over what to wear. I settled on a pair of slacks and my Greek tunic—Gabriel would get a kick out of it. Then I changed my mind. I needed to leave the Greek memories behind in order to maintain a level head on our drive.

I buttoned up a white blouse with blue edging at the sleeves and collar. In the bathroom, I tackled my face as best and as fast as I could. I didn't want Gabriel to think I was doing a complete makeover.

Gabriel.

The name spun in my mind, and I had to close my eyes for a second to get my balance. I couldn't believe he was here, all the way from Greece. I had stalled long enough, and I walked down the steps to where he was waiting. He stood in front of a Monet replica I had hanging over the fireplace in the living room.

It was a painting I'd always loved of a woman sitting beneath a row of trees in full blossom. I had put it up after Phillip's death when I'd redecorated. He would have never cared for something so simple and serene since he liked the more bold strokes of cubist painters, like Picasso. But I could never stand those disjointed bodies.

Monet was soothing and peaceful.

"I love this one," Gabriel said, hearing me come in.

"Me too, and it matched the couches."

I stopped in the entryway and watched him look at the painting. Now that I was over the shock of him showing up, the zings were back in full force.

He turned and said, "Ready?"

His gaze met mine, and I saw appreciation there. The kind of appreciation a man shows a woman when he thinks she looks nice.

The days and hours spent with Gabriel in Greece came flooding back.

"I'm ready," I said, my voice feeling off.

"Mind if we take my car?"

"Of course not." I had to remember that Gabriel lived in California. He probably still had a car here, and it would be natural for him to drive it around. He wasn't a visitor. Was this a car he'd shared with Rhea? I didn't know what kind of car I was expecting him to drive, but it was a regular Honda Accord. Clean and nice but nothing that stood out. It was a slate gray with a gray interior.

He opened the door for me, and I tried not to inhale as I passed so close to him. But I did, and my eyes watered when I smelled his familiar scent. It was going to be a long drive, which I was hoping for but didn't know if my heart could handle it.

There was no traffic on the street, and he pulled out without having to wait. I didn't say anything, determined to let him steer the conversation. I paid more attention to the roads we drove on and the people we passed, thinking of the *Zen* book and the author's observations as he compared the types of people who lived in certain areas.

When it became apparent we were heading south on the PCH, I asked, "Are you staying at Maria's?"

He glanced over at me. "I have a hotel for now."

"There's plenty of room at my place. I could stay with my niece . . . if you need a place to stay."

He smiled as he slowed for a traffic light. "I wouldn't put you out, Ruby. And my sister's place isn't exactly conducive to my agenda."

My eyebrows shot up, but I didn't want to pry. Did it have something to do with Rhea? Did the therapist convince him to give his marriage another chance? Or was he only here for a few days—to sign guardian papers?

"Have you talked to Rhea, then?"

"Not yet. I have a court date Friday and other business to attend to first."

I had questions, but I clamped my mouth shut. He must have been planning this trip longer than I'd thought. Really, though, it wasn't my business.

"It's mostly just paperwork."

I breathed out. The last time we'd talked about the situation, he'd been so upset. Now he practically sounded like a robot, as if the whole Rhea thing didn't faze him at all.

"My niece has a court date coming up," I said in a quiet voice. "I was the one who had to press charges."

"What happened?" Gabriel asked, throwing me a concerned glance.

I explained the stolen laptop and gift cards Keisha had purchased under my name. And how it was Shannon's husband who had told me the truth—not Shannon herself. "The worst thing is not that Keisha betrayed my trust but that Shannon hasn't returned any of my calls."

Saying it out loud to Gabriel made it feel even more devastating. I blinked against the burning in my eyes. "I love Shannon, I love Keisha, but this has been so hard. I just want Shannon to know I'm here for her. Her silence tells me she's really hurt."

Gabriel was quiet for a moment. "She's probably feeling horribly guilty, and she's afraid she's hurt you now."

I nodded, swallowing against the tightness in my throat.

"You'll probably just have to show up at her house." He glanced at me with a half smile. "Knowing you, I'm surprised you haven't done it already."

Despite the ache in my chest, I laughed. "You're right. I just need to get up the courage."

Gabriel pulled off the PCH and parked at Laguna Beach. It seemed our drive would be extended somewhat.

"Care for a walk along the beach?" he asked, looking over at me.

Of course, I couldn't say no. He opened the door for me, holding out his hand to help me out. He released it right away.

We walked together toward the shore as the sun sank lower, its orange cast now purple against the horizon.

If I closed my eyes I might have been able to imagine we were back in Greece, but we weren't, and I didn't close my eyes.

Gabriel kicked off his shoes and left them under a bench. I did the same, and we walked together toward the surf. Right before we reached the moist sand, Gabriel stopped.

I came to a stop next to him.

"Do you want to know the main reason I came back here?"

I swallowed against the sudden lump in my throat. "Of course," I said.

"I wanted to see if the California Ruby was anything like the Greece Ruby."

Zings hit my body, but I wasn't exactly sure how to take what he said. "And what's your verdict?" I asked, keeping my eyes out on the ocean even though I felt him looking at me.

"That she's just as lovely as ever."

I had to look at him. "I looked a little nicer at the wedding."

His brows drew together. "I'm not talking about what you look like, Ruby. I'm talking about who you are. I wondered if I had been bewitched—Greece can be a very romantic place, you know."

"Yes," I said, but it was a whisper.

"My reality is rooted here, and frankly, I wanted to see how you measured up."

My face went hot. I didn't know whether to be insulted or flattered. I turned back to gaze over the ocean.

"I'm ashamed that I even questioned our relationship, especially when you told me I should do the right thing by my ex-wife." He moved closer to me.

Even though he wasn't touching me, it was like I could feel the warmth of his skin.

His fingers brushed my hair, and I still couldn't look at him.

"As soon as you opened the door," he said, "I knew nothing had changed."

I closed my eyes as his fingers trailed down my neck, then rested on my shoulder. His voice was a whisper against my ear. "Ruby, I'm in love with you."

I couldn't move. His words washed over me like the surf that had reached our feet. This made things much more complicated. He moved behind me, and his other hand rested on my other shoulder, and I leaned back against him. I had no words, no reply. Just questions, but I was tired of the questions.

He was here, in California, and my heart felt full for the first time since I could remember. My eyes burned with awe and gratitude, although I didn't know if I could truly believe this was happening to me. His hands slid down my arms and wrapped around my waist so he was holding me against him.

I never wanted this moment to end. I never wanted to move again as the night took over the sky and the stars multiplied against the vastness.

"What are you thinking about?" he whispered.

I swallowed, wondering if I could speak at all. "You," I managed.

He chuckled, his chest vibrating against my back. "Good or bad?"

"Mostly good."

His arms tightened around me. "What's the bad?"

"You're making it really hard for me to swear off ever having a relationship with another man."

"Ah yes, your resolve never to marry."

There. He'd said the *M* word.

"I'm just trying to get used to the idea that you're in California," I said.

He pressed his lips against my neck, then said, "Now's a good time to get used to it."

I turned around and wrapped my arms about his neck, burying my head against his chest. I breathed him in, remembering how I'd thought I'd never do so again. He was real, tangible, and telling me things I thought I'd never hear from a man—nor ever want to hear.

The best part about it all was that man was Gabriel.

We stood holding each other for a few moments, then I raised my face. The streetlights at the top of the beach combined with the moonlight made it just bright enough to see the warmth in his eyes.

"We've really only known each other two weeks."

"I'm counting the e-mails."

"Okay, then six weeks."

"What are you saying, Ruby?" his voice teased.

"Just that it seems fast that you're already declaring such . . . deep feelings for me."

"You mean when I said I love you?"

His words pushed straight into my heart.

"All right," he said, his hand moving to my face. He ran his thumb along my cheek, leaning down so close his breath touched my face. "Come with me tomorrow to the psych ward. I want Rhea to meet you so she'll know who is a part of my new life."

My heart thudded—mostly in fear. Gabriel wanted me to meet his ex-wife. This was getting serious. There was no way I could tell him no. I was too curious, and if there was ever going to be a future between Gabriel and me, I had to take this step. Better earlier than not at all.

I marveled that I was thinking about a future—when had that happened? Maybe it was when he told me he loved me, but I knew it was more than that. Nothing had ever felt more perfect than being wrapped in his arms.

Chapter 22

I STARED AT MYSELF IN the mirror. I'd taken extra care with my makeup this evening to match my newer peach blouse, but now my hands were sweating. I applied another layer of deodorant. Things had been different this week with Gabriel here. He'd spent his days at the agency, helping his sister, and we'd gone to dinner each night.

Tomorrow, I'd meet his ex-wife. But now, the confidence I'd felt the past few days with Gabriel had turned into cold, stark fear.

What was I doing? How could I let another man lead me down this blind path again? Phillip had once been my everything, even when I'd had so many doubts.

Those doubts weren't the same with Gabriel; all of the doubts I had were because of how things had turned out with Phillip.

What was to guarantee that things wouldn't end terribly with Gabriel?

"He says he loves me," I whispered to myself. "How can he know? How can anyone know?"

I looked at my carefully lined eyes in the mirror. "Do I love him?" I stared so long at my image without blinking that my eyes started to water. I couldn't answer that for myself because then I would lose the fragile control I had over the darkness that lurked in the corners of my soul.

He was making me stretch, wanting me to meet Rhea and talk to Shannon. I'd promised him I would visit Shannon. Since I promised him, I felt like I couldn't put it off any longer. I didn't know what made me more jittery—meeting Rhea or confronting Shannon.

It was nearly 7:00 p.m., and I knew I had to go to Shannon's now in order to catch her—John had just called me a few minutes ago to tell me she was home.

Fifteen minutes later, I stood in front of Shannon's door, my heart pounding. I had to act now or continue to worry about my niece. I rang the doorbell. I'd done it.

Shannon opened the door, looking like she'd had a busy day at work. She still wore her scrubs, which looked wrinkled and dingy. Thankfully, she didn't shut the door in my face but smiled—although it disappeared almost as soon as it appeared.

I smiled back but held mine. Shannon's gaze quickly dropped. Oh boy. I decided to start with the nitty-gritty. "Full disclosure," I said. "John called and told me you were home. I didn't ask him to do it, but, well, you chose a good man, and he doesn't want this to continue to hang between us."

Had I said too much? She looked at me—so that was a good sign. "I didn't know what to say."

Relief shot through me. The door was still open, so I rushed on. "I don't know what to say either, except that I don't want this to ruin our relationship. You're the closest family I have, geographically and friendship-wise, and I don't want to lose that."

"I don't either," Shannon said.

Good. Another shot of relief. "Then you're going to need to forgive me for filing that report." I wasn't sure if turning it that way was best, so I added, "*And* I need to forgive you for not telling me the truth. It should have been you, not John, who talked to me about it."

"I know," Shannon said with a nod. "And I'm sorry about that, but—"

"You can't amend an apology," I burst in. "As soon as you say 'but,' you're not really sorry." I smiled, feeling a bit bad that I'd jumped on her. I softened my tone. "Can we just talk about this? Lay it on the table so we can put it away?"

"Yes," she said, taking a step back. "Will you come in?"

A sigh escaped. *Thank goodness this is going somewhere.* "I thought you'd never ask." I moved past her and found a place on the couch. Shannon sat across from me on the love seat.

"I am sorry," Shannon said. "It wasn't that I wasn't going to tell you; I was just trying to figure out the right way."

It was so good to finally talk about this. "And I can understand that, but we're family, Shannon, and I love you. You could have told me any way it came out. I wouldn't have been angry."

"You pressed charges," she said.

I tried not to let it hit me like an accusation. "John asked me to," I said quickly, then paused and lifted my hand. "But I'm not blaming him for it. I agree it was the right thing to do. Keisha's troubles run deeper than I thought; I hope this will help her get better."

"Going to jail isn't going to help her," Shannon said, her tone defiant. "She'll be locked up with the very worst people out there, and she'll have a criminal record for the rest of her life. John's wrong to think this is the right solution."

I didn't want to start a full argument, but Shannon couldn't really be serious. I assumed it was emotions talking. "Are you sure about that, dear?" I asked, tilting my head. Shannon had to understand that Keisha was considered a criminal now. "She *did* steal from me. That's a crime I hope she never repeats. Getting away with it would only make it more likely that she'll do it again."

Shannon went into stubborn mode and proceeded to say that Keisha needed help with her depression, as if that would stop her from stealing, and everyone should just love her and not condemn her. I felt my face grow warm. Everyone did love her, and she'd been given so much, yet she continued to defy her parents, and that was an insult. She folded her arms and looked away. "I'm frustrated that no one seems to see the effort I'm putting into helping her. Maybe if I'd had some support, things would have turned out differently, but it feels like everyone's against her now, like she can just be written off."

This was getting way out of hand. "Shannon, honey, I'm sorry you feel that I'm working against you. That wasn't my intent. But I'm also just recently coming to terms with some hard truths in my life and realizing that pretending things are different doesn't change them." She looked at me then. I took it as a good sign. "It's admirable that you want so much good for Keisha, but pretending she isn't responsible for her choices doesn't change the fact that she is. I don't hate her, and I don't love you less for what's happened and that you didn't tell me sooner. But I think John is right—you aren't seeing this correctly, and sparing Keisha from the consequences will help no one."

Shannon seemed to be thinking about it. I smiled, hoping to diffuse the tension of a moment earlier, and said, "I've done so much soul searching these last weeks that my soul feels in need of new stitching around the edges, but the other night I had a thought that's made me very uncomfortable ever since." I hesitated, wondering if I should say more. But here I was, trying to give Shannon advice, so I decided to be brutally honest about a few things.

I fingered the straps of my purse, feeling suddenly fidgety. "I wonder what would have happened if I'd confronted Phillip when I found out about the first affair." I met Shannon's surprised gaze. "Instead, I waited until after number two—Lisa—when I was beyond reconciliation in my heart. I'd held so much anger and hurt inside all through his first affair. And because I waited to confront him, waited until he'd gone even deeper down the path, I think it made our relationship impossible to reconcile. A woman might be able to forgive her husband one indiscretion, but two?" I exhaled. "I have to wonder what would have happened if, right after discovering those long-distance phone bills, I'd served him his dinner, looked him right in the eye, and said 'Are you being unfaithful to me?'"

I took a deep breath. Had I gone too far? Shannon was still watching me, but I couldn't exactly read her expression, so I continued. "Perhaps he'd have lied to me, I'd have believed it, and we'd have carried on like we did. But maybe he would have realized it hurt me and stopped. And there wouldn't have been all of those women who followed. Or maybe he'd have made a choice between her and me. It would have been difficult for me if he chose her, but maybe I'd have found a different partner. If he'd stayed, then maybe we would have been better. Maybe I'd have ended up with a happy marriage, or at least a comfortable life as a divorcee."

I shrugged and fiddled with my purse again. Shannon still didn't say anything, so I said, "As it was, when I did blow up at him after affair number two, we were both too far down the path. I chose to suffer in silence and slowly grew to hate him because he was getting away with something so horrible, and I was essentially allowing it so that I could keep the family together and both parents in the home for Tony. I was so afraid of Tony having to live in a broken home, being shuttled between parents, seeing his dad date other women . . . Despite everything I had to put up with, staying with Phillip was security. I was afraid of what our friends would say, what our neighbors would think, what my life would be like as a single mom. I didn't want to lose the security that Phillip provided." I held Shannon's gaze. "Keisha isn't Phillip, and I know the situation is very different, but I hope you're not doing all this protecting because you're simply afraid of losing whatever security she gives to you. Fear is no way to live."

Shannon was quiet for several moments, and finally things took a turn for the better. She promised to consider what I'd said, and I knew that with John feeling the same way I did, Shannon would come around eventually. Her heart was just so invested, as were all of ours, but she was letting her emotions cloud her judgment, which I didn't blame her for one bit.

We ended by talking about book club, and Shannon promised to start reading *Zen and the Art of Motorcycle Maintenance*. At the doorstep, I gave her a long hug and told her I loved her. She said she loved me too, which made everything seem right again, even though I was sure there were still more bumps in the road ahead of us. But we were family and would get through it together.

* * *

On Friday morning, Gabriel was a full twenty minutes late, just enough to make me start to question everything and anything. He'd texted me several times the day before, each text sweet and happy. But I still worried that overnight maybe he'd changed his mind about me. Maybe he wasn't coming. Maybe he'd decided it wasn't a good idea after all.

When he pulled up to the curb, I had to restrain myself from flying out the door. Instead, I watched from the side window to see if I could gauge what mood he was in or if he was still the same man from last night.

When I opened the door, he pulled me into a tight hug. All my worries dissipated.

"I thought you weren't coming."

"Sorry I'm late," he said, pulling back, his eyes searching mine.

"Are you usually late? Is this something I need to know?" I tried to keep my tone light, but I had been more rattled than I'd thought.

"Rarely late—must be all that tour guide practice—but I underestimated Orange County's traffic." Before I could say anything else, he leaned down and kissed me full on the lips. A morning kiss. So . . . married-like. But then again, so unmarried-like because it was Gabriel standing on my porch.

"All right," I said when he pulled back. "I think I'm ready now."

He laughed, but I could tell that both of our nerves were in high gear. I didn't know what he expected out of the meeting between Rhea and me, but I guessed we'd find out soon enough.

Gabriel held my hand on the drive to the hospital unit, although he didn't say very much. It was quite a surreal moment to walk into such a public building as a psychiatric clinic hand-in-hand with Gabriel. It was like we were a true, official couple.

I took strength in his grip as we entered the lockdown unit and had to be buzzed in through the door. We were led to a community room, where we were told to sit and wait for Rhea.

I didn't exactly expect to go to her private room, but I had hoped for a little more privacy. Several residents, along with a couple of nurses, occupied the room, working on various activities. There was no television on, and the noise level was a low hum. The decorations looked pleasant yet simple. House plants were suspended from the corners of the ceiling, and one of the walls was painted with a mural of trees.

We sat at a round table anchored to the floor. The chairs were anchored as well. Along with everything else, I didn't know what I'd expected when I saw Rhea, but when she entered the room, she looked quite different from her desperate photograph I'd seen in the album she'd created.

Her formerly untamed hair was cut short so it fell in soft waves around her face. Her skin looked healthy, although she was still very thin. Her smile was what shocked me the most. It was all for Gabriel, and her eyes were bright, not the haunted, confused look I'd thought might be there.

Gabriel slowly stood as she walked toward him, her arms wide. I hesitated, not knowing if I should stand or stay seated. I stood while Rhea threw her arms around Gabriel's neck. It was hard to watch this beautiful woman cling to Gabriel, knowing they'd been husband and wife for two decades. There was a lot of history in that embrace.

I tried not to stare, but there was really no other place for me to look.

There was no emotion on Gabriel's face, and finally, she pulled away, then grasped both of his hands. "I knew you'd come for me. Didn't I tell you? I knew you'd get me out of here." She smiled at him, a fierce adoration in her eyes. "I haven't packed anything because I never want to remember this place."

Gabriel glanced toward me, and I sensed the concern there. Was this typical of Rhea?

He guided her into a chair, then released his hands from hers. Instead of telling her he wasn't taking her home, he simply said, "I'm to be your legal guardian, Rhea."

Her finely arched brows came together. "You're my husband. We can be each other's guardians."

I'd rarely seen Gabriel flush, but this was one of those times. But again, instead of contradicting her, he said, "I brought a friend to meet you. Her name is Ruby."

"A friend for me?" Rhea looked at me for the first time. Her gaze was open, curious. She even smiled. "Are you Maria's friend too?"

Gabriel nodded slightly in my direction.

"I am." I tried to say it in the same soothing tone Gabriel was using. I realized the less I said, the better.

Rhea started complaining about the meetings she had in the unit and how she didn't like any of the other patients. Her hands fidgeted on the tabletop as she talked.

Gabriel listened quietly, and I said nothing as well, although Rhea kept glancing at me, a look of concern growing on her face.

She stopped her complaints, and said, "Why are you here?"

My throat felt tight, but I said, "I'm a friend of Gabriel's."

Her voice raised a notch. "I thought you said you were a friend of Maria's."

"Of Maria's too," I said, glancing at Gabriel, wondering how I should handle this.

"Why are you looking at my husband?" she asked. Then she turned her focus to Gabriel. "Why are you looking at that *woman?*"

Gabriel reached for her hand, which drummed on the table. "Ruby is my friend. I brought her to meet you."

Rhea seemed to relax, but her eyes flitted back and forth between us. "I'm ready to go right now. Tell the nurse I'm ready to go."

Gabriel's jaw tightened, and I was very curious about his response. "I'm signing court documents today to become your legal guardian."

I breathed out. I could tell he was trying not to correct her in any way.

"He's my husband," Rhea said, her gaze on me now. Her hands trembled, and all calmness in her eyes fled. "You need to leave!"

I drew back, shaken on the inside, but taking my cues from Gabriel, I remained calm. I was floundering for an answer when Gabriel stood. "I'll come back to visit soon, Rhea," he said. His eyes went to me as if assessing me to see if I was all right.

"Why do you keep looking at her?" Rhea said, her voice rising so everyone in the room was now watching us.

My heart pounded. I couldn't see any good way out of this situation. The only comfort I had was that perhaps Gabriel was well versed in handling this woman.

"Let me know if you need anything," he said and moved around her, leaving her huddled on her chair. "The nurses have my contact information."

Rhea jumped up and grabbed his arm. "You can't take that woman with you," she screamed. "You're supposed to take *me!*"

The others in the room had stopped what they were doing to stare at Rhea. Gabriel didn't move, even though her nails looked like they were digging into his arm. "I'll come back soon."

Just tell her she's not coming with us, I wanted to yell back.

A nurse crossed the room and took ahold of Rhea's arm. "Come with me, honey," she said.

Rhea wrenched out of the nurse's grasp and reached for Gabriel again, this time shrieking, "Don't leave me! You *promised* not to leave me."

My heart twisted, both for the fear and panic in Rhea's voice and the abject look on Gabriel's face.

Rhea turned on the nurse, yelling, "Don't touch me!"

The nurse held on tightly while calling out above Rhea, "Security!"

Gabriel tried to pry Rhea off of him, but she lashed out, scratching at his face and drawing blood.

Two men in scrubs hurried into the room and grabbed Rhea. They practically carried her out of the room, with the nurse rushing after them. A couple of other nurses who had come into the room during the commotion checked on Gabriel. One cleaned up the scratches, and he answered their questions quietly while I stood there feeling helpless. My hands shook, and my mind could hardly comprehend all that I'd witnessed.

Then my thoughts zeroed in on Gabriel, and my heart felt like it would break as I thought of what he'd just gone through and all the other episodes he must have endured. When the nurse finished applying antibiotic to the scratches, Gabriel's eyes met mine. *Let's get out of here*, he seemed to be saying.

I crossed to him as the nurse stepped back. "We'll need you to sign an incident report," the nurse said.

Gabriel pulled out his business card from his wallet. I noticed his hands trembled slightly as he handed the card to the nurse. "You can fax it to this number."

I sensed he didn't want to stick around one more minute in order to sign anything. I followed him out of the room. When we arrived at the main lobby, he slowed and reached for my hand. At least he wasn't shutting me out of the turmoil he was going through.

Neither of us spoke as we settled into his car. He put the key in the ignition but didn't start the car, just stared ahead, his face like stone.

I had to say something. "I probably shouldn't have come. I didn't mean to make her upset. I'm so sorry."

Gabriel exhaled. "I needed you to come."

I fell quiet, not sure what I could say that would comfort him. What could anyone say?

"I hoped her delusions had eased, but she hasn't changed at all." There was pain in his voice, and I wished I could find a way to help him.

"Whatever you decide to do, Gabriel, I'll support you."

He looked over at me then, his eyes showing a depth of sorrow I didn't wish on anyone. "I'm not changing my mind again. I need to do what I came here for."

I nodded in agreement, although I had just caught a glimpse of what he was committing to, and I was tempted to tell him to find another solution.

His eyes were still on me. "I don't want you to apologize for coming. Somewhere in her subconscious mind, she needs to start absorbing the information that our marriage is over and that I'm in a relationship with you."

We're in a relationship moved through my mind.

"But I am sorry you had to see that," his voice lowered. "I hoped she'd be better behaved."

It was my turn to exhale. My mothering instincts wanted to take Gabriel far away from this place and tell him he never had to come back and face that woman again. But I knew he didn't want a mother right now. "You were so careful with what you said to her; you did nothing to provoke her."

The sorrow in his eyes lessened, and his mouth turned up. "If I wasn't trying to provoke her, I wouldn't have brought you."

I stared at him. "You knew this would happen."

He pulled my hand toward him and encased it in both of his. "Not to that extreme. I knew she had to start learning about you though—and the best way was to see you."

"Gabriel . . ." I said but didn't finish because he leaned over and kissed me softly.

"I'm serious about us, Ruby," he said. I could only nod because I was starting to internalize how serious he really was. "I want you to know all the parts of me, whether they are good or bad."

I was grateful to be sitting down; I didn't think my knees would have held me up at this point. "There's *nothing* bad about you, Gabriel."

He brought his hand up to stroke my jaw. "You're amazing."

I let his words infiltrate, really settle into my soul. Of course I'd seem amazing compared to Rhea, but even with knowing his rollercoaster relationship with her, what would he think of my cruelty to my husband in his dying days? I was nothing like Gabriel—who'd seemed to forgive his ex-wife moments after she'd assaulted him. I had refused a dying man's last wish.

I drew back, my thoughts becoming too large for the confined space of the car.

"Are you all right?" Gabriel asked. Of course he'd notice my shift in feelings.

"I'm . . . I just wish I could help you with all of this. It's hard to stand by and do nothing."

"You're already helping me." He squeezed my hand. "Do you still want to come with me to sign papers?"

Right then, I knew I'd do practically anything to help Gabriel. I never wanted to see him in that situation with his ex-wife again, and this next step was necessary. I wouldn't abandon him now. "Sure, I'd love to."

The depth of gratitude in his eyes was profound, and more importantly, his smile was back.

* * *

I stared at the closed door after Gabriel brought me home. Signing the papers to become Rhea's guardian had gone smoothly. On the drive back to my place, Gabriel had held my hand, making his devotion plain.

The question was whether I could give him the same commitment and whether I could open up with the truth. I left the closed door and walked into the living room, where Gabriel had spent time. The room seemed different somehow, brighter and more alive. I looked around with new eyes, seeing the Monet painting with appreciation and noticing the tidiness of the room. What had been going through Gabriel's mind when he'd walked through my house?

Then I thought of the closed-up master bedroom upstairs and the memory box locked inside the closet. It was as if I was living two different lives. Down here, things were bright and cheerful. Upstairs, the memories were dark and oppressive.

I walked into the kitchen, suddenly feeling exhausted. I'd made some tea and read more of *Zen*. I recognized that I was avoiding making the decision I needed to, but avoiding it was easier than calling Gabriel back and telling him the truth about my marriage.

Out of habit, I checked the house phone, and there was a message from Debbie. They hadn't made any real honeymoon plans, so they'd used the gift certificate I'd given them to go to Santa Monica.

"Ruby, sorry I didn't say good-bye to you at the reception. No one seemed to know where you'd gone. We're loving Santa Monica. It's so romantic." Debbie laughed. "Thank you. Thank you! We'll be back Thursday. I'll call you then."

I listened to the message a second time with a smile on my face, reminding myself that there was happiness out there—even in our flawed world.

The doorbell rang. Had Gabriel returned? I hurried to the door but was surprised to see Tori standing on my porch. She'd had to cancel our lunch date the other week, and we hadn't talked since.

The look on her face told me not to make too big a deal about her visit. I could tell she'd been crying; her beautiful eyes were red and a bit puffy. "Come in," I insisted, and without asking for any explanation, I pulled her into a hug. I was so happy she'd come over, but the knot in my stomach foretold bad news. What could have possibly driven her over here? "What brings you to my neighborhood?"

"I had to make a stop at the shoe repair place up the street that I love. And I still feel bad about cancelling our lunch date, so I thought I'd stop in and say hi."

"Wonderful," I said.

Her eyes studied me. "Who was the man I saw leaving here?"

I looked toward the road before shutting the door. "Gabriel." At her smile, I added, "Yes, he's back from Greece. Although, I'm not sure for how long." I tried to keep a smile off my own face.

"He is seriously good looking, Ruby!" Tori said, her voice bright.

I could tell her cheerfulness was false. I led her toward the kitchen; it would feel less formal that way, and a couple of brownies and a glass of milk never hurt anyone.

"It's so great to see you," I said without prying for more information, then quickly added, "Do you like brownies?"

"Do they have chocolate in them?" Tori laughed, but it was hollow.

I wondered how long she'd dance around the reason for showing up at my house unexpectedly. She fell quiet, staring down at her twisting hands as I poured two glasses of milk and placed brownies on a small plate.

When I set everything on the table, Tori said, "Really? You just happened to have homemade brownies on hand?"

"I woke up extra early this morning," I said, thinking of the worrying I had done about meeting Rhea. And worry usually led to baking, just so I could smell the goodness in the air. "And maybe I sensed I'd have such a lovely visitor."

"Oh, Ruby," Tori said, her smile tentative. "You always say the sweetest things. I wonder what it would be like to see the world from your perspective for just one day." Her voice started to tremble, and I braced myself . . . Here it came. "I am not a good person. Not good at all."

I shook my head. That was absolutely not true, unless she was a serial killer, which I was pretty sure I could rule out. I reached out and patted her hand, then asked *the* question. "What's wrong, honey?"

Large tears filled her eyes and dripped onto her cheeks. With lovely tears like that, she could be in the movies—ironic that she worked on the other side of the camera.

"It's Christopher."

"Christopher Cain?" The lead of the reality show she was producing? Had he gone AWOL and ruined the whole show?

"He's the one I'm in love with."

My hand stilled over hers. Tori was an assistant director, not one of the contestants who was throwing herself at Christopher each week on national television.

"Oh my goodness," I whispered.

"Yeah." Tori laughed, which then turned to crying. "*Oh my goodness.*"

"When . . . did this happen?" I said because I couldn't quite believe it.

"I don't know when it happened, but it did, and I'm a complete mess," she said.

Tori was a beautiful woman and about a hundred times more intelligent than any of those half-fake women on the show. But there had to be all kinds of legal disclaimers for this sort of thing. From what I knew, Christopher had to propose to his final choice. It was part of the contract.

So where did that leave Tori? This could ruin the whole show—lead to lawsuits and everything. "Oh my goodness!" I said louder.

Tori slumped over the table, her head in her hands.

"What are you going to do?" I said in a gentler voice.

She shook her head against her hands, then lifted her tearstained face. "That's why I'm here. I need your advice."

My advice? I couldn't quite believe it myself.

"You had a good marriage," Tori continued, using one of the napkins I'd set on the table to wipe her eyes. "You know what it takes and the sacrifices required to make a good life." She brushed at another tear. "That's why I'm here. To know how you made it all work. To know if it's possible to make things work if love is the central ingredient. Because . . ." She hiccupped back a sob. "If I tell him how I feel, it could ruin everything—the show, my career, his reputation . . . my reputation."

My heart twisted, and I had to do my own steady breathing. I could sit here and let Tori think I was the one to give her counsel because I knew what made a strong relationship centered on love, but I was a floundering fish. I was no better at giving her advice about her love life than I was at opening a restaurant.

"My husband, Phillip, was the worst person I could have chosen to marry."

Tori froze, staring at me. "What?" she whispered.

"It was never right, not even in the beginning. The chemistry wasn't there. I was always trying to force it or to justify why I didn't feel it. And when I realized what was truly wrong, it was too late. I had a son by then who needed his mommy."

"What do you mean, Ruby?" she asked. "I thought you had a wonderful marriage."

"Everyone thinks that," I said, then thought, *Except for Shannon and Gabriel . . . and you now*. Although nobody knew the whole truth. "But it wasn't just the lack of chemistry. It was a lack of something more important. Trust. Respect. And the idea of another person making you want to be better, to love deeper, and to cherish more."

Tori stared at me for a moment, the shock plain on her face.

"Just the fact that you're sitting here in my kitchen, your heart breaking into a million pieces because Christopher is dating other women, tells me you're deeply in love with him." I paused, not wanting to hurt her, but she needed to know the truth. "The only way it will work is if *both* of you are willing to sacrifice for each other. If it's one-sided, like it was in my case, you'll be miserable."

"How will I know?" Tori said, her voice just above a whisper.

"You might not know until you tell him how you feel," I said. "But it's a risk you need to take . . . to find out his feelings. If he's not willing to risk everything he's committed to in order to be with you, then you'll know, and you'll know it won't last."

Tori nodded. "I'm just so scared."

I knew scared, and lonely, and my scars of rejection ran deep. I squeezed her hand. "If you don't tell him, you'll regret it."

"Is that how it's been with Gabriel?" Tori asked.

"Gabriel? What do you mean?"

Her expression softened. "You know what I mean. You can't deny it. It's so obvious on your face when you talk about him."

I stood from the table and took my full glass of milk to the sink. I couldn't let Tori see me blush—I was a sixty-two-year-old woman, for heaven's sake. "He's a very nice man, and I really care for him. But I have no plans to remarry, if that's what you're thinking."

Tori laughed—at least there were no tears mixed with it this time. "Look at you. Telling me to sacrifice my career to go after a guy who's completely unavailable, and you are avoiding the real thing standing right in front of you."

I kept my back to her. "You don't know anything about Gabriel. He's a friend to everyone." Although, telling me he loved me on the beach the other night had certainly blown that theory apart.

Tori's voice sounded right behind me. She had crossed the room. "Ruby," she said, placing her hands on my shoulders. "I saw the pictures from Greece. He was smiling at you in every single one. He didn't even care that someone was taking pictures. And . . . you were smiling back."

"Maybe the pictures were doctored," I said, but I was melting. I turned to face Tori. Her eyes were dry, though evidence of her distress still lingered.

She folded her arms, waiting me out.

"All right. I like him," I said. "I can't even describe why, but I feel like my whole self when I'm with him. And he only knows the basics of the . . . problems . . . I had with my husband. He doesn't know the whole story."

"So tell him!"

I barked out a laugh. "Listen to *yourself*."

Tori covered her mouth, her eyes wide, and started giggling.

And then I joined in. We were like the old saying—the blind leading the blind. When we both stopped laughing, Tori said, "Let's make a deal, Ruby."

I frowned, not liking the sound of this.

"You tell Gabriel about your marriage, and I'll tell Christopher my true feelings."

Staring at her, I said, "Are you serious?"

"Unless you want to back out," she said. "It will be really tough to tell Christopher I—" Tears pooled at the corners of her eyes, and she took a shaky breath.

I grasped her hand and took my own shaky breath. "Deal."

Tori pulled me into a fierce hug, as if she could take courage from it. "Thank you so much. You have no idea how much you've helped me."

I could only nod. Telling Gabriel the truth was sure to be the end of our relationship. Of course, it could be the same for Tori and Christopher.

After Tori left, taking a plate of brownies with her, I dialed Gabriel's number.

Chapter 23

It seemed that Gabriel was at my house in five minutes, though I knew it was really over thirty. I'd planned all sorts of ways to back out, even just leaving the house and hiding on the backyard patio until he gave up knocking.

My heart thumped as his car pulled up, and I gripped my hands together and forced myself to stand still. I couldn't chicken out now. But it took all of my resolve not to scurry through that house and hide behind something. Maybe I could tell him I'd been mistaken. That I couldn't give him what he wanted in a relationship. That it wasn't going to work between us after all.

He didn't ring the doorbell but knocked softly. I inhaled, wanting to scream or cry or both, but I took the remaining steps to the door and opened it.

My eyes started to burn.

I was never going to make it through. I couldn't even speak.

Gabriel stepped inside and closed the door behind him.

My hand covered my mouth to stop the trembling, and I turned away, worried that I was about to collapse in his presence. His arms wrapped around me, which only made the tears fall faster.

Gabriel didn't say anything for a couple of minutes. This was going to be harder than I'd thought. I prepared my mind for Gabriel leaving when he found out the truth. He wouldn't be trying to comfort me then. He'd probably tell me he needed some time to think about my confession, then our communication would dwindle.

And it would hurt. The pain had already started.

"Hey," he whispered in my ear. "You don't need to tell me anything. I'm fine with you keeping your secrets. It won't change how I feel about you."

I choked out, "I need to tell you. Then you can make the best decision for yourself."

He pulled away and gazed at me. I could literally feel how much he loved me, which made the pain even worse.

But the time had come. I stepped out of his embrace and said, "Follow me upstairs." I was going to have him wait in the living room, but I didn't trust myself not to climb out a window and scale down the side of my house, breaking my ankle in the process.

It was strange having Gabriel follow me up the stairs, then into the bedroom I'd shared with my husband. I wondered what Gabriel was thinking. I flipped the light switch on the wall in the dark and sterile room and unlocked the closet door, opening it wide to reveal its dark hole. I turned on the closet light and forced my feet forward. One step, then another until I'd retrieved the memory box.

Gabriel took it from my hands without a word, as if he knew, which, of course, was impossible. He turned off the light and drew me out of the closet and then the bedroom as if he could sense the painful memories of the room.

A thought flashed through my mind—maybe he had a sealed bedroom as well.

I wasn't sure what Gabriel's intention was, but I was surprised he'd taken the box. He started down the stairs, and I followed, trusting in his agenda.

He set the box on the coffee table in the living room and turned to look at me, his eyes questioning.

I had envisioned laying out the items in the bedroom like I had with Shannon and tearfully telling him about each woman. But now that we were standing in the living room, with that ugly box in my beautiful space, I suddenly felt anger. It didn't belong there. Phillip's mistresses didn't belong in my redecorated room.

I wanted the thing out of the house.

Then I realized Gabriel was speaking to me. "What's in the box?"

"Memories . . ." I couldn't finish. Staring at the box, I sat on the couch. It was like a black hole on the table and in my heart.

Gabriel sat across from me, sensing that I needed my space. He waited, saying nothing, just waited.

I opened the box and pulled everything out. I told him about all of the women. About the first one I'd discovered upon returning home from Greece—Janelle—and the other ladies, ending with Pamela and the dried rose.

Gabriel was quiet, and I couldn't read what he was thinking. He didn't touch any of the objects, just kept his gaze on the collection.

And then came the hard part.

"This is all in the past," I said in a slow voice. "I've told you about some of it—not this much detail—but I don't want you to feel sorry for me." My breath felt shallow, like I couldn't get a full breath in. "I guess I wanted you to understand why I did what I did." A tear dripped down my cheek, and I brushed it away. "But I know it was still wrong of me. I know I didn't have the right to deny my husband forgiveness." My voice started to tremble, and I stopped talking, wondering if I'd be able to continue.

Gabriel waited, then said, "Your husband asked you to forgive him?"

He had figured out what I was trying to say, and it was like a huge weight was lifted from my soul. "Yes," I breathed out. Then the tears came faster. "I wouldn't give it to him. I told him *no*." I wiped furiously at my cheeks, feeling like my heart was going to pound out of my chest. I'd done it—I'd told Gabriel. Now I just had to wait for the verdict.

Even with Gabriel sitting across from me, I pictured Phillip's pale eyes pleading with me. The image of his sorrow was etched forever in my mind. I didn't even realize Gabriel had stood and walked across the room. He was staring at the Monet, not saying anything. I had stunned him, disappointed him. And now he'd have to tell me what he thought of my declaration.

I laid the rest of it out. "He told me he'd always loved me, that after he messed up the first time, he didn't know how to take it all back. He figured he'd already ruined everything." I clutched my trembling hands together. "It was all too late, much, *much* too late."

Gabriel turned around, and I couldn't meet his eyes. He must have wondered why I'd stayed with Phillip if I didn't love him too in some way and why I wouldn't allow that closure to come in our marriage.

"He asked me to forgive him, but I refused. Even when . . ." My voice cracked. "Even when his lungs were collapsing and he struggled to speak, let alone breathe. I still refused." It was like I couldn't breathe now, like my lungs were being slowly paralyzed with ALS like my husband's had been. I was a horrible person. Phillip's last days had not only been filled with tremendous physical pain and fear but also the worst kind of loneliness.

"Ruby," Gabriel said, his tone gentle.

I gripped my hands together, preparing for the inevitable. Then I felt Gabriel prying them apart. He knelt beside me and threaded his fingers through mine. "You can't change what you did or did not say to Phillip. He's gone and has found his own peace—whatever that might be. But you, Ruby, you need to forgive yourself."

"Myself?" I gasped, meeting his eyes.

"Yes." His grip tightened. "You've felt guilty for years, first because you couldn't make your marriage be what you wanted, then because you took a stance at the end of Phillip's life that you regret."

He was right about the guilty part, but I had never thought I needed to forgive myself. I didn't even know if it was possible.

"Ocean or fire?" Gabriel asked.

"What?"

"Do you want to toss the box into the ocean or burn it?"

Staring at him, I shook my head. "I . . . I don't know."

Gabriel rubbed my arm. "Let me help you. Please."

I nodded, my brain numb. "You're not leaving?"

"No." He stood and held out his hand. "Come on, Ruby."

I looked at his outstretched hand, relief and exhaustion flooding through me at once. He wasn't leaving, and he didn't seem upset. I didn't know what he had in mind, but I did know that once I put my hand in his, it would be like putting trust in him as well. Taking a deep breath, I placed my hand in his, and he pulled me to my feet.

We stood facing each other, near enough to touch yet not touching, except that he still held my hand.

"Where do you want the box?" he asked.

"I—I don't want it in my house anymore."

He released my hand and picked the box up. "Let's go." He turned and walked out of the room, giving me no chance to question or argue.

I followed him out the front door. I didn't know where he was going, but it felt both strange and good to have the memory box out of the house.

Gabriel opened the car door for me, and I sat down, my heart drumming. He set the box in the backseat, and for some reason, I was glad he hadn't put it in the trunk. Then he climbed in the car and started the engine.

He drove north this time, and soon we were in the heart of Newport, heading in the direction of the beach. He pulled up to a private parking garage, where he apparently had a pass to get us in.

"Did you used to live here?" I asked. I hadn't even thought in all of this time to find out where he used to live.

"No, I have a boat in the harbor." He squeezed my hand. "I thought we could take your box out on the boat, then you can decide what to do with it from there."

A lump formed in my throat. Was I ready to cast away the things in my memory box?

We climbed out of the car, Gabriel carrying the box as we walked to the wharf hand in hand. I should have known Gabriel's skin was tanner than just his heritage would allow. I had chalked it up to being a tour director, but owning a boat made a lot more sense.

Phillip and I had been on friends' boats, but he'd never had the desire to purchase one. I hadn't much liked the idea of being in a small, confined area with him—for any length of time.

I slowed when we reached a row of boat slips. "Sailboats? You have a sailboat?"

"It was my dad's, but it's still in great shape."

We stopped at a covered sailboat. Gabriel set the box down and pulled off the tarp.

The sailboat was a deep green on the outside and a beautiful honey-colored wood on the inside. The collapsed mainsail was tan. "It's gorgeous," I said.

Gabriel smiled, and I could see the pride in his eyes. "She's been around a lot of years, but she's still running smooth."

He helped me onto the boat, then grabbed the box and set it on one of the seats. He started the engine, and we jetted out of the slip. I leaned back, the wind pushing through my hair, and looked around at the other boats we were passing.

It was a beautiful evening, the sun low in the sky. Gabriel steered out of the harbor and past various incoming fishing boats and charters filled with tourists. Once we hit the open sea, he handed me a jacket from the small cabin. It wasn't a cold day, but the wind made it seem so.

Despite the surroundings, I couldn't take my eyes off of the box across from me. It looked so black against the tan seat.

Gabriel left the cockpit and came over to sit by me. He put his arm around my shoulders. "Are you ready?"

I leaned against him. Was I ready? I didn't know about the whole forgiving myself thing, but having the memory box gone from my home was feeling better and better. Gabriel's hand squeezed my shoulder.

"All right, I'm ready." I reached for the box. Gabriel stayed next to me as I opened it and took out the starfish and rolled-up telephone bills.

"Janelle, right?" Gabriel said.

I marveled that he remembered. I held the items in my hand, looking into the dark blue waves slapping against the side of the boat. Taking a deep breath, I tossed them over the side.

Gabriel pulled me close and kissed me. "Well done."

My heart hammered in my throat and tears threatened, but I reached for the glass-bead necklace. This I handed to Gabriel. He smiled at me, then chucked it in an arc over the water. The beads caught the light of the orange sun, sparkling for a few seconds before plunging into the waves.

I did the honors with the ace bandage, then handed the postcards to Gabriel. He tossed them overboard one by one, where they caught the wind like Frisbees and sailed a couple of seconds before making contact with the water and sinking beneath the surface.

I picked up the dried rose Pam had given back to me. This memento represented Phillip perhaps more than any of the others. I stared at it for a few seconds as tears escaped.

Gabriel's hand closed around my other hand, and I concentrated on his warmth and strength. I held the dried rose out over the water, then simply let go.

The rose bobbed on the lulling waves, moving farther and farther away.

Gabriel's arms went around me as we both watched until it was hard to tell what was the rose and what was the sun glinting off the water.

"Ready for the box?" Gabriel's breath warmed my ear.

"You throw it in," I said, my voice hoarse.

He released me, and the wind rushed around me. I turned to watch him pick up the box and lift it over the side. Then it was gone. I stared at the floating darkness for a few seconds, then wrapped my arms around Gabriel's waist and buried my face against his chest. He held me tightly, and all I could hear for a long time was his heartbeat and the wind.

When I looked out over the water again, the box was nowhere to be seen. Maybe it had already sunk or it was too far away to spot. Gabriel smoothed my hair back, but the wind just stirred it up again.

"How do you feel, Ruby?" Gabriel asked, his brown eyes on me.

"Different." Could throwing away the mementos have really helped? Or was it just being on Gabriel's boat, standing in his arms? I was suddenly exhausted. "I'm ready to go home."

Gabriel kissed my forehead, then released me. I sat back down while he guided the boat back toward the harbor. As the wind pushed against me, I burrowed farther into the jacket, taking comfort in the warmth and the lingering smell of Gabriel.

As we neared the harbor, leaving the sunken mementos farther and farther behind, I closed my eyes and realized why I felt different. For the first time in more than thirty years, I felt hope.

* * *

It was dark by the time we reached my house, which worked out perfectly because Gabriel pulled me into quite the breathless kiss right on the front porch. If the porch light had been on, a passing neighbor would have received an eyeful.

In just the past few days, I'd learned so much more about Gabriel— about his father's sailboat, his heartbreaking situation with Rhea, his determination to face his demons, and how he truly felt about me.

His kiss left no doubt.

When I finally pulled away, if only to breathe, he cradled my face in his hands. "You are so brave," he whispered.

"I couldn't have done it without you," I whispered back. "Thank you for taking me out on your boat."

"Anytime, Ruby," he said, leaning down again and kissing my neck. "I mean that. *Anytime.*"

And I knew he meant it. I felt it deep in my heart, where some of the darkness had been crowded out, replaced by sweet hope.

I pulled him closer to me, and his arms tightened their hold.

"You're amazing and beautiful," he said, his voice caressing my ear. The darkness served another purpose as it concealed my blush. "But that's not why I love you," he said. "I love you because you make me a better man."

I couldn't imagine anyone better than Gabriel. There was no one more patient, more kind, and more devoted. "I wouldn't change a thing about you, Gabriel," I said.

He exhaled like he was relieved. I realized he'd told me he loved me, more than once, and I hadn't returned the sentiment . . . My feelings were pretty plain, even to my stubborn heart, but it was still so new that my heart needed adjustment time.

"Are you busy tomorrow?" Gabriel asked.

"I'm always busy," I said with a smile. "But I'm sure I can squeeze you in."

"I'll be the one calling you over and over."

"I'll try to remember that." The moonlight was starting to bewitch me, and I was tempted to invite Gabriel inside, to ask him to stay as long as he wanted. Instead, I let go of him and stepped toward the door.

"Good night, Ruby," he said.

"Good night." I slipped inside the house and shut the door between us. Leaning against the closed door, I exhaled. The box was gone.

I walked through my darkened house, not turning on any lights, but the moonlight coming through the high windows was enough for me to make my way up the stairs.

I paused in front of the master bedroom door, then opened it. I crossed to the covered windows, pulled aside the drapes, and lifted the room-darkening shade. Then I opened the window—for the first time in over two years—and let in the night air. I breathed in the fresh air as it moved around me, finding its way into the stale corners of the room.

Then, still leaving the lights off, I pulled the bedding from the bed and rolled it up all together. I took the bundle downstairs and into the garage, where I stuffed it into the large garbage can. Tomorrow was garbage pick-up, so I opened the garage door and rolled the container out to the curb.

When I entered the house again, it already felt different. I decided that tomorrow I'd start the process of turning the master bedroom into a library. I'd bring all of the books I'd stored over the years and put them on new bookshelves.

Maybe Gabriel could help me.

I smiled at the thought as I walked into my bedroom and turned on the light. There, on the side table, was *Zen and the Art of Motorcycle Maintenance.* After changing for bed, I slipped under the covers and picked up the book. Out of habit, I turned to the cover page, where Gabriel had written a note to me. My eyes started to water as I looked at his handwriting. Even in Greece, he was taking care of me and thinking of my future.

Today I'd told him everything about the horrible things I'd withheld from my husband and the feelings of hatred I had toward certain women. But instead of being disgusted and leaving, he'd taken me out on his father's boat. He'd helped me move forward. He'd given me hope. And then he'd told me I made *him* a better person and that he loved me.

I pressed the book against my heart, realizing I had a phone call to make.

He picked up on the second ring. "Ruby? Is everything all right?"

"I just wanted to hear your voice."

His chuckle was warm and caressing. "So you're saying you miss me already?"

"Maybe," I said, feeling breathless as my pulse thundered beneath my skin. "I called to tell you I love you."

If there was ever a time I could feel someone smiling through the phone, this was it.

Ruby's Red Velvet Cake

2 C. sugar
½ lb. (2 sticks) butter, room temperature
2 eggs
2 T. cocoa powder
2 oz. red food coloring
2 ½ C. cake flour
1 tsp. salt
1 C. buttermilk
1 tsp. vanilla extract
½ tsp. baking soda
1 T. vinegar

Bread Pudding Mix:
3 C. half-and-half
3 large eggs
1 large egg yolk
Pinch salt
1 tsp. vanilla extract
8 oz. cream cheese, room temperature
¾ C. confectioners' sugar
Vanilla ice cream, for serving

Preheat the oven to 350. Grease a 9 x 13 x 2-inch sheet pan.

In a mixing bowl, cream the sugar and butter, beating until light and fluffy. Add the eggs one at a time and mix well after each addition. Mix cocoa and food coloring together and add to sugar mixture; mix well. Sift together flour and salt. Add flour mixture to the creamed mixture alternately with buttermilk. Blend in vanilla.

In a small bowl, combine baking soda and vinegar and add to mixture. Pour batter into a greased sheet pan. Bake for 20–25 minutes or until a toothpick inserted into the center comes out clean. Remove from heat and cool completely. When the cake is cooled, cut into 1-inch cubes.

Place cubes on 11 x 17 cookie sheet. Place in oven for 10 minutes.

Bread Pudding Mix

Combine the half-and-half, eggs, egg yolk, salt, and vanilla in a medium bowl. In a large bowl, beat the cream cheese and sugar with an electric hand mixer until smooth. Mix in the half-and-half mixture.

Place the red velvet cubes in a large baking dish or 8 individual ramekins. Add the pudding mixture to the dish, making sure the cake cubes are completely covered. Bake for about 30 minutes or until the pudding is set. Serve with ice cream.

PRAISE FOR THE NEWPORT LADIES BOOK CLUB SERIES

OLIVIA

"I love to find a new series and the Newport Ladies Book Club doesn't disappoint. I enjoyed . . . the personal connection I felt with the main character, and subsequently for her family members, book-club buddies, and even her husband. It was extremely tender and so well-written."

—Jenny Moore, *The Write Stuff* blog

"I really loved following Olivia through the process of self-awareness. She has become so wrapped up in making her home and family the ideal that she has forgotten that her own soul is equally important in that whole 'ideal' scenario. The book seemed to be made of very real-life-type stuff. It was easy to relate to and it was easy to find a bit of myself in there too."

—Aimee Brown, *Getting Your Read On* blog

DAISY

"I really enjoyed . . . the character growth in Daisy. It was so subtle and well-crafted and really makes you take a look at your own inner child and what it means to grow up. The characters are so real and flawed, it added that sense of realism to the story in that it felt like we were peeking into these people's lives. Really well done."

—Julie Coulter Bellon, author of *All's Fair*

"I loved this book. I enjoyed getting to know the characters of the Newport Ladies Book Club through Daisy's eyes. I enjoyed the book-club meetings, and it was as if reading them for the first time. I loved Daisy's character; she is a very strong, smart gal. I enjoyed her journey, and the lessons she learned about herself, her family, and also the joys of close friendships. Most of all, how she needed to ask others for help."

—Mindy Holt, *Min Reads* blog

PAIGE

"This book is intriguing—the details and influences in Paige's life paint a deeper and more textured picture of her personality. Lyon has created characters that are both endearing and infuriating and woven them tightly with the characters previously introduced in the series. The book drips with emotional uncertainty and doubt, but it also engages readers in tender moments that pull at the heartstrings."

—Melissa Demoux, *Deseret News*

"The premise—looking at the same four months in the book club from four different points of view—is increasingly intriguing to me. Author Annette Lyon, a much published writer and editor, treats her subject with her usual clarity and thoroughness. Lyon's writing itself is delightful. Her cleverness with language sometimes makes me laugh out loud. Paige's experiences at book club again make me pull the first two books from the shelf to remember how Olivia and Daisy learned from the discussions."

—Kaye Hanson, author & reviewer

ATHENA

"The Newport Ladies Book Club series is such an interesting, unique concept in publishing: a series of novels, each written by a different author and telling the story of one of the women in a book club. Heather B. Moore's writing is by turns funny, sad, and poignant. I had tears in my eyes reading about Athena's ailing father: 'What did my father dream about? Did he know my name when he slept?' And Grey: handsome and kind, handyman, cook, and owner of a bookstore—swoon!"

—Laura Madsen, *Laura's Books* blog

"*Athena* is a beautifully written and emotionally touching story that had me giggling and crying. This book is the only of the four in the Newport Ladies Book Club series that has a romantic ending, but that didn't take away from the reality of the story and the feeling. Heather B. Moore artfully uses true emotion to reach down inside her readers and leave them always wanting more. This book was a fantastic read for anyone that has ever been—or wanted to be—in love as well as for anyone who has experienced a hardship."

—Nashelle Jackson, *Just a Little Glimpse* blog

VICTORIA'S PROMISE
COMING JANUARY 2014

Julie Wright

A NEWPORT LADIES BOOK CLUB NOVEL

Victoria's Promise

Preview

Chapter 1

A MAN SHOULD NEVER PROPOSE to a woman in a public place. Not unless he'd already talked to her about marriage and he'd caught her flipping through bridal magazines while doodling hearts around his name.

And even then . . . there were no guarantees.

I worked on a reality TV show called *Vows*, where a marriage proposal was a matter of contract—something the bachelor had to do whether he wanted to or not, and even then—with a few million dollars on the line and several nations watching—there were still no guarantees. Relationships were unpredictable, wretched things.

I opened my mailbox and rubbed at my eyes, which burned from staying up late the night before then getting up early and spending nearly the whole day studying flash mob marriage proposals. I wanted a few new ideas that might be useful and fresh for the next season of *Vows*. It was good to be well informed on the job—especially since I was now the second assistant director.

What I'd learned from watching guy after guy get down on one knee in front of basketball fans, circus patrons, and live studio audiences was that you'd better hope your mom wasn't watching as the would-be girl of your dreams widened her eyes in horror, shook her head no, and ran like someone had called in a bomb threat.

I rubbed my eyes again, wished I'd been smart enough to have caught a small nap during the afternoon, and tugged the envelope out of my mail box.

My heart went into some strange sort of arrhythmia after I caught sight of the return address on the envelope. It was from Ballad Studios. News about my screenplay. Ballad was one of the few studios that still wanted screenplay submissions in paper. Most were happy to work via e-mail, but not Ballad.

And I now held an envelope from them in my hands with a decision waiting for me on the inside.

I almost threw up on my own feet.

The sound of a car horn blaring behind me startled me enough that I almost dropped the envelope.

I tossed a quick smile to Lawrence, which would hopefully keep him from laying on the horn again. I had neighbors, and some of them worked graveyards. Some had children. None of them would approve of Lawrence and his car horn.

I wanted to turn around and go back into my house to read my letter in private, but Lawrence was taking me to the Walt Disney Concert Hall to see Holst's The Planets. Hiding out in my apartment and reading this letter by myself wouldn't exactly be the show of support my best friend from since forever ago had wanted when she asked me to the event. Janette had organized the concert and really wanted me there for opening night. Lawrence wasn't all that impressed with me wanting to go to see the Los Angeles Philharmonic do a musical rendition of our solar system, but I hadn't really cared when I told him I didn't want to do anything else for our four-month anniversary.

I had to go.

Besides, Lawrence would be insanely ticked if I missed our anniversary, which totally baffled me. Four months of casual dating was not a milestone to be celebrated. It was something to be commented on, shrugged over, not thought of again until you hit five months—if you hit five months.

Lawrence's hand went to the horn again, but I waved, smiled, and headed his direction before he actually made contact with it. We probably wouldn't hit five months. My dad wasn't all that fond of Lawrence. When I asked Dad why, he said something about Lawrence being the poster child for an entitled white guy and left it at that.

Dad never made racial slurs, for obvious reasons. He was also a white guy, and he was married to my Barbadian black mom. Between the two of them, one of my brothers looked like a pasty European, and one looked like a dark-chocolate candy bar. I was caught between the two, which was nice because my naturally darker skin and my black eyelashes and brows meant my monthly makeup expense consisted of a tube of dollar store lip gloss— any flavor but cherry.

Thank you, Mom and Dad, for good genetics.

I stuffed the letter in my purse and sent up a prayer that whatever the envelope contained wouldn't make me cry anything but happy tears. Sad tears were simply not allowed.

Lawrence was out of the car and opening my door before I had time to properly paste on a smile. "What's wrong, babe?" He brushed a quick kiss over my lips and motioned for me to get in so we wouldn't be late.

"Nothing."

Nothing. Nothing. Nothing. Please don't let me be a liar.

He reached over and took my hand as soon as he was back in the car and turning off my road. Our hands were a contrast and not just in color. He had baby soft hands because he had a manicure-and-pedicure habit he couldn't seem to kick. It was almost embarrassing that his hands were soft, pink things—something you'd see on a newborn—while my hands were calloused and one sported a bandage from moving camera and light equipment on my job.

"You look amazing, you know," he said, which was always nice to hear.

I smiled and thanked him for the compliment. My mother taught me that pretty girls who never said thank you when they were complimented were ugly inside. She said she didn't care how pretty I was outside if my insides hid a repulsive monster. She never let my looks go to my head, but sometimes it was nice to be told I looked amazing.

"How was your day?" Lawrence asked.

"Great. Max said they were down to the final bachelor pick, so we'll start filming in the next month."

His smile turned down for a moment. "Oh. That's too bad. That means we'll never see each other."

We'd had this argument before. He'd been complaining about my job more and more as time ticked down to when I'd have to start keeping erratic working hours.

His hand hit the horn as someone cut him off.

I imagined my father raising an eyebrow at Lawrence's behavior and winced inwardly.

I know, Dad. Not what you want for me.

I met Lawrence at a bookstore. It was part of why I liked him. I did a lot of reading on set because I wasn't allowed to make any noise during a take, yet I was required to be present for every one of them. A handsome guy in a bookstore, holding a copy of *To Kill a Mockingbird* in his hands, seemed like a miraculous discovery. When he asked for my number, I nearly girl-screamed. And I never girl-scream. I leave that silliness to the bachelorettes mugging for reality TV.

It turned out the book had been a gift for his sister. But I hadn't known that when we'd gone on our first date, though I'd suspected by the end of the second date. By then, we'd already become semicomfortable with each other. He was easy enough to talk to—which was weird, considering how little we'd known of each other. But he was safe and polite, to me anyway. He wasn't always nice to everyone else. But to me . . . he really tried hard to be a gentleman.

And I wanted a gentleman for myself. I wanted a man like my father.

Lawrence *was* a gentleman, but he *wasn't* anything like my father. He had a way of making other people feel uncomfortable. He snapped at waitresses, belittled cashiers, and treated the world with disdain in general.

And he didn't read books.

He actually laughed at me when I told him I was in a book club in Newport with a bunch of other women. At least, he laughed until he realized I wasn't laughing. Then he was all kinds of supportive. But I'd seen the scorn, and I couldn't unsee what I had already seen.

The time apart would likely be good for us. Lawrence might decide to move on to someone who didn't work sixteen-hour days for three straight months. I shot him a sideways glance as he continued to whine about me going back to work. He talked pretty much nonstop the rest of the way to the concert hall. I let him. He liked talking more than I did.

"Told you we needed to hurry," Lawrence said as he finally found parking and opened my door for me.

I laughed. "We're fine. Don't panic. Janette wants me to support her, but she didn't say we needed to be an hour early. Relax."

"I'm relaxed." He smiled and rolled his shoulders, but he didn't fool me. He was as relaxed as a hurricane hitting land.

We entered the concert hall and found our seats right up front.

Janette looked beautiful with her brown hair twisted up in an elegant knot at the side of her head. Her form-fitting black gown accentuated her vampire pale skin. I caught her eye and waved. She waved back but returned to talking quietly with someone in a tuxedo. Knowing she was busy, I went back to chat with Lawrence.

At least, I *tried* to chat. His right leg jiggled in an almost spastic rhythm as he scanned the concert hall. I put my hand on his leg to calm him down. "Are you okay?"

But he ignored that question too. He moved to his feet and mumbled, "I'll be right back."

He speed walked toward the aisle, where he passed Janette with barely a glance. Janette raised an eyebrow at his lack of cordiality but shook it off and moved in my direction.

"You guys having issues?" she asked.

"Maybe he has to use the restroom. He's been kind of weird all night." I stood and hugged her. "Soooo, are you nervous?"

She laughed and kissed my cheek before she let me release her. "I thought I would be, but I'm really not. Super weird, but I'm just excited to be here. We've received permission to use dozens of NASA pictures for the visual display."

"It's great you get to do what you love for a living."

I apparently didn't hide the envy in my tone because she gave me a half smile. "You'll be there. Just give it some time."

"Time . . . right." I leaned over and pulled the envelope out of my purse. "I got a letter today from Ballad Studios."

She ripped the envelope out of my hands. "No way! What does it say?" she asked. I snatched it back at the same time she frowned. "You haven't even opened it yet."

"I'm waiting for the right moment. I want to have a nice evening, you know, enjoying your music and science. If I open it and it's bad news . . ."

"Why are you putting that kind of talk out into the universe? Why can't you assume this letter holds your every dream come true?"

I leaned back a little on the arm rest and sighed. "Because I've received so many letters like this before—well, e-mails anyway. I don't think this is any different just because it's on paper."

She gave me a hmph and swatted my shoulder. "There you go again, putting out all that negativity. Have some hope."

"Janette . . ." The whine had overtaken my voice, but she was too good a friend to swat me for that too. "I'm just so tired of failing."

"You aren't failing. You're working your way through the sludge. Everybody has to pay their dues, love. You aren't the exception. But paying dues doesn't give you the right to give up. Every day, you're closer to being a full-fledged screenwriter. Soon, people will be buying tickets and eating too much popcorn at a blockbuster movie you wrote."

"I hope so."

She hugged me again. "I know so." She looked around when she released me. "Is that boyfriend of yours lost or something?"

I glanced around as well, picking through the dresses and suits to try to find a clue as to where he might have gone. "No idea. Like I said. He's been acting weird all night."

Her pale blue eyes fixed on me. "And things are going . . . okay for you two?"

I gave a wimped-out-one-armed shrug rather than an answer.

"Hmm."

"What are you hmm-ing about?"

She gave me *the look*—the one she'd been giving me since we were kids with crooked pigtails and badly painted fingernails. "You just don't seem like yourself with him. You guys don't do things you like to do when you're together."

I let that statement settle before pointing out the obvious. "We're here tonight. That's something I want to be doing."

"Well, sure, but I bet this wasn't his first choice, and I bet he tried to talk you out of it."

I didn't confirm her suspicions. It was bad enough that she was right, but I didn't need her to give me *the other look*—the one that gloated while remaining compassionate.

"We're fine," I assured her. "But don't worry about me losing myself to the ego of some guy. We're down to the final bachelor pick on *Vows*. We're a little behind on production schedule, but I have to go in for the final auditions. It's back to work for me, which means no dating life."

Janette scowled. "That's not any better. You lose yourself to a guy or you lose yourself to work. Either way *you* lose. You should open that letter. It might have a million-dollar contract in it."

"I'm okay! I'll open it when I get home. Stop worrying, *Mom*." I smiled wide for her, and then I frowned. "Wait a minute. Did my mother put you up to this conversation?"

Janette at least had the good sense to blush over getting caught. It was hard to be mad at her when her cheeks pinked up like that. Some people passed us to get to their seats, which distracted me just long enough that Janette was able to slip away with a wave and a, "I gotta get back to check on the orchestra. We'll talk later."

"Yes, we will." I shot her a look of my own—the one that said I meant business—but she just smiled and waved as though we had nothing left to discuss.

I hated that my mom and my best friend were such good friends. It was tough keeping secrets when the two women I was closest to compared notes.

Lawrence returned, looking flushed and winded.

"You okay?" I asked again as we took our seats. Was he sick? I edged a little farther from him, just in case. With the new season of filming about to start, getting sick was not an option for me.

"Fine, why?" He took my hand in his, which I reluctantly let him do, figuring I would wash my hands later if he really did have the flu or something.

Would he notice if I dug out the bottle of Purell from my purse?

As that thought crossed my mind, the lights went down and the bows fluttered over the string instruments. I loved the warm-up noises of an orchestra, so I pushed aside my misgivings about possibly ill boyfriends and studio contracts and settled into my seat to watch the performance.

Janette had chosen well. I loved Holst's work and The Planets was my favorite. When the lights for intermission came up, I sighed deeply. *This* was what I needed, something relaxing. It was putting me in the frame of mind I needed to go home and have the courage to open my letter from Ballad Studios.

The conductor called our attention to the front before patrons could make the dash to the restrooms. He made a point of giving a special thanks to Janette Rallison for coordinating the event and to the patrons who supported the arts—naming several large benefactors—and then he said something *odd.*

He called up Lawrence Reynolds to make a special announcement.

Lawrence let go of my hand after flashing me a brief smile. He made his way to the front as my heart rate stopped altogether before skyrocketing into something that had to have resembled a heart attack. *No. Please no.* He couldn't be doing what I thought he was doing. My mind flashed back to all of the marriage proposals gone wrong that I'd watched on YouTube the night before and all morning and afternoon. I sank lower into my seat. My face heated up; my hands gripped the armrests of my chair. My head shook *no* while my mind raced for an exit strategy.

Lawrence stood too close to the microphone, so his voice boomed out.

And then he said the words I *didn't* want to hear.

"Victoria Winters, will you marry me?"

The word *no* stuck in my throat until it felt like I'd choke on it. I didn't think my eyes could open any wider.

There was only one thing to do.

I ran like someone had called in a bomb threat. And hoped his mother wasn't watching.

About the Author

HEATHER B. MOORE IS THE two-time Best of State and Whitney Award–winning author of several novels. She lives at the base of the Rocky Mountains with her husband, four children, and one black cat. Her favorite holiday is Halloween because she gets to tell fortunes to all of the unfortunate children who dare to visit. For updates, visit Heather's website, www.hbmoore.com, or blog, http://mywriterslair.blogspot.com. Visit the Newport Ladies Book Club blog for recipes, sample chapters, and ideas on hosting your own book club: http://thenewportladiesbookclub.blogspot.com.